NEVER CAN SAY GOOD-BYE

A NOVEL BY

Robert Farrell Smith

DESERET
BOOK

SALT LAKE CITY, UTAH

Library of Congress Cataloging-in-Publication Data

Smith, Robert F., 1970-
  Never can say good-bye / Robert Farrell Smith.
     p.   cm.
  ISBN 1-57008-991-4 (pbk.)
  1. Eccentrics and eccentricities–Fiction.   2. Mountain life–Fiction.   3. Young adults–Fiction.   4. Montana–Fiction.   5. Trees–Fiction.   I. Title.
  PS3569.M537928N49   2003
  813'.54–dc21   2003004733

Printed in the United States of America   54459-7106
Malloy Lithographing Incorporated, Ann Arbor, MI

10   9   8   7   6   5   4   3   2   1

To my wonderful sister LeeAnne
I miss you

Acknowledgments

If you have ever seen that one movie where that ship sinks, then you know how important the ocean is to that story. I mean without the ocean, that boat would have never moved, much less sank. In my case I don't want to thank the ocean; I would like to thank the "Sky" that has helped me lift off instead of drown.

Unfortunately, it would take way too much paper to thank each and every one who has helped me, what with the concern for trees and all. There are, however, a few people who deserve to be pointed at and talked about. Emily Watts, what you see in me goes beyond charity. Thank you so much for continually believing. Richard Peterson, you are a giant among editors. Your ability to throw out the bath water while holding onto the baby is amazing. Richard Erickson, the only thing that surpasses your talent as a designer is your friendship. I would also like to thank the fabulous group of Deseret Book store managers for their patience and support. You all are a big chunk of that sky.

Second to lastly, I would like to thank my wife, Krista. I can't imagine a happy moment of my life without you. (Except for maybe that one time when I was eight, and Kevin Hartman and I found those fireworks.)

Lastly I would like to tell my parents that I love them and that all the joy and sadness and wonderment this world has given our family would have been unfulfilling and impossible to manage without you two. Thank you, Mom and Dad.

PART ONE

BREATHING SLOWLY

August's eyes burned. He could feel his chest constricting, and he was having trouble breathing. "Don't go," he whispered. "Please don't leave me."

Rachel smiled weakly behind the plastic respirator that covered her mouth and nose. She was struggling to breathe, and her chest moved rapidly up and down, in rhythm with the beating of her fading heart. Propped up in the hospital bed, she looked fake, plastic, and if August had not been sitting by her for the past three days straight, he would have sworn that someone had slipped in and replaced his sister with an old, worn-out woman. Her once-shiny, blonde hair was thin and as lifeless as the impersonal gray machines that surrounded her bed.

The machines were keeping Rachel alive, but they cared

nothing for the person she had been or the thirty years she had spent on earth, doing the things that people do. They dutifully hummed, beeped, and whirred, but were indifferent to the remarkable life that was now being stolen from her.

She pulled the respirator away from her face. "Tell our family I love them," she breathed, no longer even attempting to smile.

"You tell them," August replied defiantly, hoping to break the solemn feel of what they were talking about. Besides, he honestly did not want to ever have to explain anything to his parents again. In fact, he didn't want to ever talk to his parents again.

"They love you," Rachel insisted.

"That's not important or even true," August said, taking his sister's hand and realizing that this was it. He could feel her literally slipping away. The light in the room seemed to grow brighter in spots. It was as though her life was sliding out from under her and curling upward at the edges. She arched her back slightly, as though her soul were gently bucking to escape the body that had done this to her. She squeezed his hand and closed her eyes.

"You're leaving, aren't you!" he cried, trying as hard as he could to maintain his composure. Sure, there was no one here to notice him breaking down, but he still felt like he needed to maintain his front.

Rachel opened her brown eyes one last time.

"August," she whispered weakly, "you're a mess. You've always been way too good-looking for your own good."

"That's better," he whispered back. "Now you're making sense."

Rachel's eyes expanded the slightest bit. "Of course, when you cry, you look awful. Like a fish trying to smile."

August had no idea what she was talking about. He tried to imagine a fish trying to smile but stopped when he realized that it was probably just the medicine making her say these things. He couldn't look that bad.

4

Rachel and August had always been close. Their family, he and Rachel had agreed, was thoroughly dysfunctional, and they had been the first of their parents' children to escape their weird home and attempt to make a go of it out in the world on their own. Rachel had left home first, about eight years before. August had finally managed to get out a couple of years after her. Since then, they had been the only family either of them claimed. Rachel had helped him adjust to life outside their family. She had been there for him, through jobs and girlfriends and trials. She had helped him with his schooling, even paying for his first year of college with money from her own teaching job.

The two of them had purposely not talked much about what they had left behind. In the last few months, however, Rachel had begun to mention and wonder more and more about the family they had left in Michigan and the need she and August had to make it right. Of course, by "them," she clearly meant August, seeing how she had known for over a year that she was dying, but only sharing that bit of information with her brother a couple of months back.

"I wouldn't be crying if you weren't dying," August managed to say.

"Don't worry, August. I'll get heaven warmed up for you," she said, so softly that he almost couldn't hear her.

"Where I'm going is already warm enough," he lamely joked. He had absolutely no idea what else to say, having never been through something like this before. "I don't want to say good—"

Rachel closed her eyes, and August watched in amazement as her spirit seemed to rise up and shoot off in a tremendous flash of white light. His jaw dropped as the reality of what had happened soaked into his consciousness. He looked at her as she lay there. He then looked to the ceiling.

"Rachel," he whispered. He held her hand to his face and cried, not caring if he looked like a fish trying to smile or a distraught sibling, or a grieving monkey for that manner.

A nurse came in and touched Rachel's arm and checked the machines as if it were all rather routine and boring. She frowned and then hurried out.

August cried harder. His sister was gone, and he was alone. And to make matters worse, his last words to her had been stupid. He saw his distorted reflection in the metal railing on the bed. Rachel was right. He did resemble a fish trying to smile. His brown eyes looked wide-spread, and his messy brown hair was a fin.

He thought of his family and of all that he no longer belonged to. He didn't think he could bear the ache inside him, and he leaned forward, begging Rachel to come back.

"Rachel," he pleaded.

There was nothing there. He laid his head on the edge of the bed, grief sucking the oxygen out of the room. He tried to breathe in deep. He felt lost, full of panic, full of grief and fear. It was as if his insides were churning, and there was an ache in his throat. Rachel was all the family he had. She had been the only person who honestly knew and believed in him.

Not any longer.

Rachel was gone, and August was alone. Adding to his hurt was the realization that he had not even been able to finish saying good-bye.

CHAPTER ONE

SALLY

Sally tried not to look. It was actually quite easy; she had never been the kind of person to gaze at an accident or enjoy seeing anything awful. She looked away when people were walking too fast with scissors, or lighting a campfire. She had no stomach for potential horror, no matter how minuscule the potential might be. Which made the question of why she was here so perplexing.

She closed her blue eyes and prayed that when she opened them she would be gazing upon something far more serene—something a lot less life-threatening and fearsome. She clenched her eyelids tightly, knowing no amount of effort would ever be able to block out what was about to happen. It was just like life to do this to her. How could she have helped fate maneuver her into this spot? Why on earth had she ever agreed to parachute out of a plane?

The roar of the engine engulfed her, wrapping her in an annoying reminder of things best forgotten. Sally's legs trembled and her ears pounded as she tried to calm herself. She pictured her apartment: the white bed, the organized cupboards, and the shiny hardwood floors.

She should be there.

She had worked hard to create a life for herself that was normally humdrum and in order. But today that calm, carefully structured reality was experiencing a temporary spike. Sally breathed in deep and then counted to ten as she let the air escape her lungs. It didn't help.

"I can't do this!" she finally shouted over the noise of the engine. "I can't do it!" she yelled again, suddenly feeling one hundred percent committed to backing out of the task at hand.

"Of course you can do it!" Mark hollered. "You would never forgive me if I let you out of this."

"I would!" Sally screamed. "I promise!"

Mark laughed as if Sally had said something hilarious. Being male he had a hard time figuring out when a woman was being serious or when she was trying to be funny—and being Mark, he interpreted the moment completely wrong.

It was just like him to think that this was all one big fun game—a challenge. Being able to say "I've done that" was a driving force and wonderful thing to Mark. Sally, however, had no such compulsion. For her, "I've done that" was a bumper sticker that all dolts should be forced to adhere to their behinds.

Sally realized now that she didn't care if she had "been there and done that." Her entire childhood had been painful and littered with things that she wished she had never experienced. One of the nice things about being an adult was being able to choose what she wanted to do and to avoid things she didn't. Now, here she was, sitting in a plane, in front of an open door, with a parachute strapped to her body. It was insane! She had set aside all she valued about having a settled life.

"It will be over before you know it," Mark tried to comfort. "Think of how you'll feel tonight."

Sally didn't care about tonight, just as she didn't care about two weeks from Friday, or a month beyond that. She cared only about the upcoming moments and the abject fear she was experiencing.

She looked at Mark with her blue eyes. He was cute and all, but not necessarily cute enough to jump for. He raised his right eyebrow and smiled. She knew that he thought he was good-looking when he did that. She was also well aware that he saved that move for the more important moments in life.

Well, in Sally's mind he had just wasted it. She twisted her pink lips into a sneer and fixed her blue eyes on him.

"I hate you!" Sally hollered, not willing to let his looks sway her.

"I know you do," he smiled, still thinking his looks would.

Mark took Sally's hand. "Come on," he wheedled, "it'll be fine. You wanted to do this, remember?"

Sally reluctantly let him pull her toward the open door. Mark then pushed her toward a thin man with a long, skinny head. During ground school, Carlton (she didn't know if that was his first name or his last) had taught Sally all he said she would need to know about parachuting. He'd also promised her that the experience would be "easy, fun, and safe." Sally kept thinking that if he could lie about the easy and fun aspects, what's to say that the safe portion wasn't all a part of an elaborate hoax as well? Now this dishonest man, whom she had only casually known for no more than a couple of weeks, was crouched by the open door of a flying plane and enticing her to come closer.

"I can't do this, Carlton," Sally begged. "I'm going to throw up."

Carlton smiled as if he had been through this kind of situation a thousand times before. His long, skinny head wobbled in the wind of the open door.

"There's nothing to fear!" he yelled. "You've practiced, and you're ready. Mark will be jumping right behind you."

The last thing Sally felt at that moment was ready. She was not a big risk taker. She was not even a *little* risk taker. Trying out a new restaurant was about as far out of her comfort zone as she liked to venture. She even had a difficult time driving an alternate route to work or switching to a different local newscast, even though she could no longer stand the people who delivered it on Channel 2. She lived life by the seat of her pants, but only if the pants were a conservative print that had been sprayed with ScotchGard.

Carlton helped her out onto the strut under the wing of the plane and checked her zip line. Clinging there, the wind tearing at her, threatening to sweep her away, Sally couldn't believe she was doing this. Her stomach rolled as she realized that the ground was such a long way down. She could see the white in her knuckles as she clung desperately to the wing's extension. She looked into the plane at Mark.

"You're beautiful!" he screamed out.

Sally wanted to protest, but that seemed silly, seeing how it was true. She had been beautiful her entire life. Her childhood had been hard, and her self-esteem had taken a bushel full of blows when she was in grade school, but the one thing she had always been told, except by her adopted parents, was what a beautiful little girl she was. And she had grown into a gorgeous, tall, thin, blonde woman, with amazing blue eyes that most people thought were fake due to their brilliance.

"I still hate you!" she yelled back.

Carlton shifted his stance and moved Sally into the ready position.

"Ready?" he hollered. "On the count of three. One . . ."

"No!" Sally hollered back.

"On the count of three," he insisted, shaking his head.

"Really," Sally tried to reason, "I can't do this." But even as she protested she readied herself on the wing and positioned her hand to push off as she had been taught to. Sally knew perfectly well that there was no way she was getting out of this. She had signed up, practiced, and now all she had to do was simply fall.

"One . . ." Carlton began again.

Sally closed her eyes and tried unsuccessfully to squelch the panic that was choking her. This had seemed like a good idea on paper. Sally's whole life had been spent hiding in the proverbial corner. She had lived and experienced things from the sidelines, always a good hundred feet from where the action was. She seemed to fear or worry about almost everything. And it had been her wish that she would someday overcome at least one of her phobias.

It was during one of these fits of self-improvement that she had seen the ad for skydiving. It had read:

LEARN TO SKYDIVE!
Fun, Safe, and Easy.
Call Carlton at 888-2694

It had seemed like such an innocent ad. Posted between an offer to provide biology tutoring and a coupon for a discount haircut, it had seemed to speak to her. It would be a perfect way to prove to herself that she was fearless and ready to take on the world. It would also provide a speedy end to her fear of heights. In retrospect, however, she now wished she had ignored that ad and gone with one of the others. That way she would now be on the ground with either slightly shorter hair or a better understanding of photosynthesis.

She had gone with the wrong ad.

It had been Mark who had convinced her to actually pick up the phone and call Carlton. He had assured her that there was no better time to show the world that she was unstoppable than right after she graduated from college—as she stood on the threshold of beginning a new phase. She had then picked up the phone and dialed. At that point Carlton had been so cruel as to answer the phone, and the rest was history.

So here she was, a few days following her graduation from college, a thousand feet above the earth, unboldly facing her fear of heights.

Sally began thinking of all the ways she could have more safely addressed her phobia. She could have taken an elevator ride to the top of a tall building and looked down through the chain-link fence. There she could have spent a couple of quarters and looked through one of those viewfinders at all the little people and traffic below. She could have taken a long plane ride, or driven to the top of a mountain and eaten dinner in one of those mountain-top cafés. That would have cured her. Instead, she had foolishly decided to put an end to one fear in a way that could put an end to everything.

Mark smiled at her from inside the plane, giving her the old thumbs up, reminding her that he had been there, pushing her from the start, cheering her on. He had told her that this would be great. Now as she stood outside the plane below the wing, staring at the earth far below with the wind tearing at her, listening to Carlton count, she was confident of only one thing:

Sally hated Mark and she would never forgive him.

" . . . two . . ." Carlton continued.

This was an awful idea. Sally twisted her left foot so it faced forward. She looked at the horizon, which contained nothing but blue and empty and space. The wing of the plane tilted just a bit, and

Carlton placed his hand at the small of her back. She was going to throw up.

" . . . three," he nudged her.

She could feel the strut rip away from her hands as the force of the wind pushed her down. She screamed as the airplane seemed to move up and away from her, almost instantly leaving her all alone in the sky. Air rushed through her nose and threatened to explode out through her open blue eyes. She could feel the wide sky pushing her in places and holding her up in others.

She was flying.

The ground was blurry, but the air whipping around her was exhilarating. She stopped screaming long enough to realize that this was amazing. The air seemed to be holding her up nicely. She couldn't believe the feeling inside of her. It was as if she were being baptized by sky. She was alive in a way she had never experienced. She opened her mouth and bit down to taste the moment.

"I'm flying!" she screamed, amazed at what she was doing, and wishing that everyone she had ever hidden from could be here at this moment to witness her courage and daring.

The ends of her blonde hair worked loose in the wind and snapped against her face like tiny rubber bands. Her arms, thrown wide like wings, seemed to press down against solid air. There was no sensation of queasiness or sickness. She had expected to feel as though she were racing down a mile-high roller coaster. Instead, it was just quiet, despite the wind, and calming, despite the height.

The blue in the sky seemed richer, and the emptiness she had seen moments earlier vanished as she was completely absorbed in the moment. The sensation was so amazing to Sally that she couldn't believe that she had ever feared anything. She even almost loved Mark again.

This was what her life had needed, a push.

She could see a single gray bird off to the north of her. It looked huge and misshapen and although not one to boast, Sally felt certain that her form in the air was far better than the bird's.

She laughed. It came out of nowhere, and she could feel her whole body moving as she laughed harder. Everyone needed to do this. She couldn't believe that she had sat still or sat back for so much of her existence. This was *living*.

Just as she began to wonder when the zip line would deploy her chute, she felt a sudden tug that jerked at, then released, her body. She had been expecting to be pulled back as the chute unfolded, but for some reason she was still hanging in the air, falling as before.

Her parachute had not opened.

She glanced up over her shoulder at the empty sky above her, then ahead. Sally could see that the plane was now too far away for her to still be attached.

Her insides began to surge.

The panic she had felt moments earlier attacked her again, with a vengeance. She had no idea what could have happened, only that she was still falling through the air with no open parachute. Her throat constricted as her entire being began to convulse with fear. She screamed, knowing full well that it wouldn't help the situation. She tried to remember what she had been taught to do, but all she really wanted was to see an open parachute above her head. She began clawing at herself, searching for something to pull.

With the return of fear, it seemed as if her body had turned from sponge to stone, and she was hurtling toward the ground even faster. Groping, her right hand found the emergency cord, and she pulled it as hard as she could. Almost immediately she was wrenched up and back. The emergency parachute was out.

Sally wanted to feel relieved, but something was still wrong. Her body was spinning wildly underneath the chute. She glanced up. The emergency chute was only partially open, and even though it had slowed her some, the ground was rushing up at far too fast a pace.

Frantically, she began pulling on the twisted strings, screaming, and forgetting everything she had been taught about what to do in the case of such an emergency. She closed her blue eyes tightly and prayed that this was all just a horrible dream, then opened them, hoping that she would be home in bed, staring at nothing but the ceiling. She had been wrong in doing this. She had let Mark talk her into something she should have never done.

The ground grew ever closer.

"Please, God," she prayed as she plummeted, "don't let me die."

Sally pulled violently on the strings, having no idea what she was doing, but not knowing what else to do. Tears filled her eyes, blinding her, and her fingers were tangled in the ropes of her auxiliary parachute. Frantically, she pulled at them, trying to free herself.

As her hands came free, her chute opened further. She looked up at it, then back at the ground.

It was only inches away.

Her body went limp as she lost all consciousness.

CHAPTER TWO

RYAN

The landscape rolled past, draped in water and green—trees and foliage erupting from the ground in lush explosions. Ryan watched thick streams turning into rivers—those rivers then plunging over cliffs and spilling into deep lakes and clear pools that were veiled in white steam from the unusually cool morning.

"Unbelievable," he whispered. "Unbelievable."

"Looks a lot different than Arizona, doesn't it?" Todd said.

There was no need to reply. The lush landscape of this part of Wyoming was so different from the dry desert around Tempe that to point it out seemed almost absurd. It was as if green were a whole different color here—a richer, deeper, and more vivid shade.

"It's like heaven," Todd added. "People have to be happier here than they are in Arizona."

Ryan smiled. He completely agreed, and talk of heaven made him very happy. He was, after all, about to embark on a two-year mission as one of God's full-time missionaries. Serving would be the fulfillment of a desire he had had since he was a boy in Primary. In fact, he couldn't recall a time when he had not wanted to be a missionary. To him it made no sense for any Mormon boy not to serve. Those who didn't were either scared, or they had no idea what a mission really was.

To Ryan, a mission was a chance to finally get going in life, grow up spiritually, and take a real part in God's work on earth. The desire to get started far exceeded any fear or doubt he might have had.

He couldn't wait to serve.

Now, his chance to prove himself was only weeks away, and this trip to Wyoming was to be his last big fling. But in the tradition of Mormonism, this fling contained few, if any, of the traditional worldly trappings of a final celebration. There would be no temptations or vices or forbidden pleasures. Nope, this last hurrah would consist of no more than his best friend, a couple of fishing permits, and enough gas money from his father to get Todd and him to Wyoming and back.

Ryan had had no problem talking Todd into coming with him. The two of them had been inseparable since they were grade schoolers. Todd was still waiting for his mission call, but in a way this was to be his final fling as well. He was almost as excited about being a missionary as Ryan was. They saw it as a great perk that the two of them would be serving simultaneously for most of their missions.

Todd had always found great strength in knowing and being friends with Ryan. He had thought often about how different things would probably be for him if he had not had Ryan as an example. Everyone liked to be around Ryan. He was the good guy—

the tall, blond kid with the nice looks and a fun personality. He was also a rarity: a popular kid who had not yet figured out that it was his right to be exclusionary. Todd had always felt it was his good fortune to have ended up as Ryan's best friend.

They drove onto a rock bridge and stopped, looking down at the water running beneath it. In the clear stream they could easily see the huge trout swimming in thick patches—the smooth water swirling in lazy circles.

"Unbelievable," Ryan whispered again. "Do people know this is here?" he joked.

"Only the few million that come through every year," Todd said, glancing at the clock on the dash. "I hope we're early enough to be the only ones on the lake."

Ryan gunned the pickup, and the truck rolled across the rest of the bridge. He smiled. "We have plenty of time. In fact . . ."

Suddenly, Ryan turned right, pulling off the main highway and onto a one-way side road.

"Where are you going?" Todd questioned.

"I just want to take this loop," Ryan smiled. "That tall woman with those huge boots at the hotel said it was, 'the perdiest part of the park.'"

"I don't care about 'perdy' at the moment. I'm in this for the fish."

"All right then, I'll hurry."

Ryan pushed on the gas, and the truck shot ahead. Patches of white morning fog hung in the low spots, making the scenery appear like a spectacular paint-by-number canvas that still had a few clean spots that needed to be tipped in.

"Slow down," Todd said, bracing his hand against the glove box but keeping his voice light. "I want to live to see the lake."

"It's a one-way road," Ryan rationalized, "and we're the only ones awake and out here. Besides, like you said, there's fish awaitin'."

Ryan pushed down harder on the gas. A tight curve with a deep drop-off on the passenger side suddenly loomed up out of the fog. Ryan braked, hugging the road where it met the canyon walls. The tires screeched as he successfully rounded the bend. The road then straightened out and began to slope downward. Ryan turned to Todd and looked at him as if to say, "See, no problem." Todd smiled tightly, and Ryan pushed on the gas again, sending the truck flying down the narrow road. The forest hurtled past, as here and there bits of morning sun flashed through the gaps between the trees and illuminated the fog that lay in patches along the road.

"Seriously, Ryan," Todd insisted, "slow down!"

"You worry too much. It's not like something is going to happen. We've got missions to serve." Ryan pushed on the pedal even harder.

He turned his green eyes and full attention to the road in front of him and grinned while gripping the steering wheel. He looked down at his speed and glanced back up. The view was beautiful, but an obstacle suddenly materialized out of the mist—a monstrous, black moose stood in the road, directly in their path!

Ryan barely had time to brake before the front of the truck slammed into the huge beast, sending it into the air and onto the hood of the truck. It crashed through the windshield, its antlers thrashing against them and the airbags that had immediately deployed, then collapsed. The truck bucked and swerved as it struggled to stay on four wheels. The heavy rack of antlers ripped through Todd's shoulder, and Ryan could feel heat as it clipped him in the leg. As the truck careened from side to side, the huge animal tore free and rolled off the hood onto the road, and the truck went into a long, slow spin. Wild with panic and his heart in his throat, Ryan fought the steering wheel. He didn't know if he was screaming or if it was Todd, or both of them, as the truck skidded onto the shoulder of the road, plowed through a road sign, and shot over the edge and down toward the water below.

The truck plunged front-first into the river, and a wave of cold water rushed through the shattered windshield, filling the cab almost immediately. Choking, Ryan reached frantically for anything that would give or set him free. Through the dark water, he could see Todd struggling and knew that the only hope either of them had was to get out of the sinking truck. Ryan pushed against the already fractured driver's side window, and it popped out of the door, which allowed him to try for the surface. He came up, sputtering, and thrashed frantically, wanting nothing more than something solid to hold onto. His hands caught the bank, and he pulled himself into the long grass that was wet from the morning dew. He looked up at the place they had just flown off and spotted a man running down the roadside and toward them. Behind him Ryan could see the huge moose that had been standing in the road.

The big beast stood, shook its mighty head, and staggered away.

Ryan turned to go back for Todd, but blackness encompassed him. He collapsed where he lay.

CHAPTER THREE

AUGUST

Death did not become August's sister. He couldn't stand the way his world now seemed, without any family. All of his friends seemed one-dimensional and shallow. Even the scenery seemed flat to him. It was as if he could reach out his hand and wave it all away. Every conversation anyone brought up or question anyone would ask seemed ridiculous.

"Do you want to get something to eat, August?"

"How are you doing, August?"

"Are you glad you're done with college, August?"

August felt completely misunderstood and alone. Of course he had nobody to blame but himself for his being alone. He could have at least still had a girlfriend if he hadn't been so stubborn.

August had been dating a girl named Claire for a few months, but he had broken it off during the final weeks of his sister's life. It was just too much for him. He had tried to maintain a balanced life, but Claire had a way of demanding that even in times of his personal crisis, she was the most important person alive.

She had been determined to have August all to herself. It was a sweet thought, in a possessive, manipulative, codependent kind of way. But any dolt could tell that surrendering to Claire would have been like putting yourself under a really big, vinyl beanbag and asking your heaviest acquaintance to sit on you.

Suffocating.

Claire liked August because of his looks—his brown eyes and exceptional height being two of the many features she enjoyed. She had made no secret about this. He had met her in an elective art class where she had begged him to pose for her. Her first line was, "You'd be beautiful in oil."

She then explained how she had been looking for someone like him forever, and how she had awoken that very morning to see a double rainbow over the men's dorms, and doesn't that beat all, seeing how he lived there and everything?

It did beat all for a while. They had had a nice couple of weeks where she was content to simply walk arm in arm around campus with him, waving and calling loudly to anyone she remotely knew.

He had been her trophy boyfriend.

Then came the news that August's sister was dying, and Claire suddenly found herself living in a universe that was too small to accommodate anyone other than herself. August kept trying to convince himself that he was lucky to have Claire during this difficult time in his life, but it was hard to feel grateful when she had no real thought or concern for anybody's feelings besides her own.

"How's your sister?" she would ask.

"She's not doing well," August would reply.

"That's awful. So do you like my new shoes?"

So, August broke it off. It wasn't easy. Claire felt abandoned and cast aside, or at least that is what her best friend had told him over the phone. Still, August had a really difficult time working up much sympathy for her. It wasn't that he was uncaring, he was just having a hard time even seeing straight at that point in his life, and Claire's lack of concern for anyone but herself dulled any feeling he might have had for her.

Strangely, however, despite the abandonment, Claire felt that he was worth fighting for. She called him every fifteen minutes. She tried acting like he hadn't actually broken up with her. She sent him cards and pictures of her to put around his apartment—he tossed most of them in the trash can, thinking how nicely they accentuated his garbage.

August had never really loved Claire. He had just been too complacent to stop her from telling others that they were an item. Luckily, she stopped bothering August as soon as she found another guy, who was a couple inches shorter than August, but who drove a much nicer car.

August now watched that very car, with Claire and her new boyfriend in it, pull up to the mortuary where his sister's funeral was about to take place. August stood inside the double doors, looking out into the gray and wishing that God would see fit to smear a little light over the area in tribute to Rachel.

There was no light—only the radiant Claire climbing out of the car with the help of her new beau. She took his arm and smiled alluringly at him. August thought about slipping away from the entrance, but he figured it would be easier to get it over with than to dodge her all morning.

He pulled open the door and greeted the two of them as they stepped up.

"Hello, Claire."

"August," she said sadly. "I'm so sorry."

August nodded.

"This is Richard," she brightened. "You might recognize him from the TV car commercial."

There was never even an instant when August thought that Claire had come to the funeral to honor his sister or to support him. From the moment Richard helped her out of his expensive car, August knew that Claire had come for only two reasons. One: to show off her new, completely inappropriate-for-a-funeral red dress. And two: to demonstrate that her new boyfriend was superior to August. Her remark about the commercial was intended to reinforce that second reason.

"I'm surprised you're on time," she smiled at August.

He couldn't take offense at the remark. It really was quite the miracle that he was early, seeing how he was late to almost everything.

The truth is, August was *perpetually* tardy. He had been born three weeks late, and from that point on things had not gotten any better. There had not been a point, or an event, in his life where he had shown up with time to spare. If the invitation said seven, he would be lucky to arrive by seven-thirty. If the movie began at nine, he had better hope and pray that the first fifteen minutes were not crucial to the plot.

It wasn't as if he planned to be or wanted to be late, it was just that no matter what was happening, he somehow could never pull off being on time. It wasn't in his makeup to be counted on.

It also wasn't as if he were slow or dimwitted, he was just constantly absorbed with whatever he was doing. He couldn't briskly walk through a park where there were people and places to look at and study. When he had taken up jogging a few months before, it was a mystery to others why it took him three hours to run two miles. But the thing was, he just couldn't jog in a straight line. He would see alleys and fields that called to him to be explored.

24

Everything was intriguing to August—a mystery to be solved. He rarely went from point A to point B without getting sidetracked by something he saw along the way.

His girlfriend before Claire had broken up with him because she was sick of his "pathetic sleuthing." It frustrated her to no end to ask him to do something simple, such as run and get a newspaper. He would always show up an hour later, with no paper, but with detailed descriptions of every garden and mailbox between here and there.

August liked the details.

The small things of life were like tinsel to him—strings of magical silver that made the view interesting and gave him a lot to think about and discover. He had barely gotten through college. He would never have made it if it had not been for his sister and a professor by the name of Jonathan Still. Professor Still recognized August's brilliance and helped get him into the right classes. He lined him up with patient teachers who could appreciate the genius in August and who were willing to give him room to be himself.

While getting through college, August had briefly held twenty-three different jobs, all of them, except one, lost due to either being late or being too distracted to perform the work they required. The one job he hadn't lost for those reasons was at the Record Shop. He had lost that job because the owner's only daughter, Skye, had fallen in love with August and had done just about everything she could think of to make him like her.

It probably needs to be mentioned that August was way too good-looking.

Women were just naturally attracted to him. His dark brown hair, deep brown eyes, and killer smile sat well on his six-foot-two, well-proportioned frame. From a distance or from up close he looked a lot like the man of most women's dreams. Unfortunately he made his moves so slowly that most women would eventually grow tired of waiting for him to make any kind of move on them and give up trying to hold his attention. Skye had not given up as easily as the rest, but when August never advanced, she told her daddy that he needed to fire him because she needed him to hire someone she'd have a shot at.

Shortly after Claire had come along, August received the news of his sister's illness, and he had become even more distracted than usual. Nothing seemed right to him anymore. Now, here he was at a funeral for a person who God had refused to rescue, wondering why he had not gotten his wish. One miracle, that was all August had asked for. Apparently his request was unreasonable because the life he had wanted to save had been snuffed out.

The strange feelings of selfishness and invincibility that August had felt briefly right after his sister's passing began to build again within him. Focusing on himself seemed to help bury the ache. If no one else mattered too much, he couldn't be hurt.

"Are you okay?" Claire asked, staring at him as if he were crazy as he held open the door.

"Fine," August lied, realizing that he might never be able to honestly say that again.

Claire flounced her red dress and her smiling, car salesman-boyfriend into the funeral home and found a seat.

The funeral went a lot better than August had anticipated. He had thought that he would cry and lose all composure, but oddly he had never felt so sure of himself. The reverend gave a nice talk, August remained composed during his remarks, and two beautiful songs were sung by a woman with huge white hair. But in the end, his sister was still gone forever.

While the coffin was being lowered into the ground was the first time in years that August felt guilty for not letting his parents know what was happening in his life. He knew that he owed them more than he felt they deserved, but he also couldn't find it in himself to want them around at something as personal as their daughter's funeral.

August was the last person to leave the grave site. As he was driving toward the gate of the cemetery, he passed two old men with shovels over their shoulders. One of them was whistling, and the other was singing. August knew that they were going to close the grave, and he wanted to stop and shout at them to quit being so happy. Didn't they know that his sister was gone for good?

Instead of stopping, August pulled out onto the highway and drove down into the city and toward the school where his sister had taught. He wanted to see and touch things that reminded him of her. He was not prepared to let her life slip completely away.

Summer Side Elementary School was locked up thanks to it being Saturday. The day was fading, and an appropriate dusk was settling in. After trying the front door, August walked around to the back of the school and found the window that opened into the classroom where Rachel had taught. He didn't even feel guilty as he picked up a rock and broke open the small pane of glass above the window's latch. He reached through the broken glass and unlatched the window, then pulled it open and crawled into the room. He stood up and dusted himself off, amazed that he hadn't received a single scratch or wound from the broken glass.

He didn't recognize anything in the classroom besides Rachel's old desk and the green door that led out into the hallway. Rachel hadn't taught here for months, and it was obvious. Some other, less creative person had taken over. Gone were his sister's drawings and letters and posters. Gone was the fish tank with the little goldfish and green plastic weeds. It now just looked like a room where people might gather to talk about the act of learning instead of coming together to discover the thrill of things you might not have known before.

There were two candles near the art center, and August felt as if the moment called for them. He took the fattest one and lit it with some matches that he discovered in one of the desk drawers. The warm light from the small flame was perfect. August carried the candle to the other side of the room and sat down on the floor in front of the green door that Rachel had painted when she first got her job there. She had been so adamant about her classroom looking different from all the rest. She had thought about and stewed over the exact color of green to paint it. The color she finally went with was "Blushing Sage." August thought it looked a lot like "Light Green." He stared at the dancing flame for a time and thought about Rachel's insistence that he get in touch with their parents.

He set the candle down on the floor next to him. "I'm not going to visit them," August said aloud to the darkened, empty room. "You tried to and it only made things worse, remember?"

The small flame wiggled, making the shadows dance.

"Dad said he wouldn't talk to me anyway. I am no longer an official part of the family. As far as I'm concerned my only relative is lying in that coffin up on that hill. That's you," he added, feeling like he needed to clarify things in case Rachel was confused.

August couldn't understand why losing Rachel was so hard on him. He had never been the kind of person to dwell on things until they drove him crazy. Now, here he was feeling as if things would never be good for him again—as if things had *never* really been good for him. It wasn't even as though his sister and he had always gotten along. For the first ten years of his life, she had teased him mercilessly. And for the last six she had simply been there for him when the rest of his family had vanished.

It felt good to August to downplay her importance in his life.

August leaned his back against the green door and stared at the flame next to him, letting its movement make him drowsy. He could feel the anxiety of the last week and of his loss weighing him down. Sleep, stronger and heavier than any he had known before, was settling over him. He stretched his legs out in front of him and leaned his head back as his mind gave out and sleep took over.

While he slept, the candle gradually burned down, spilling a puddle of hot wax on the floor and sending flames licking at the green paint on the door.

It took only a moment for the flames to shoot up the door like bionic spiders, quickly spreading out and across the wall and ceiling of the classroom. August opened his eyes with fire encircling him and beginning to pick at the empty desks.

Coughing because of the smoke, he leaped to his feet and frantically looked around him at the fire that now engulfed nearly every item in the room. If it had not been for the intense heat he would have thought he was dreaming. The fire was completely out of control. He ran to the window he had previously crawled through as flames were going at every wall and fixture. Ignoring the broken glass on the sill, he dove headfirst through the open window and landed hard, banging his head on a concrete curb.

August realized nothing more until he awoke hours later in the tri-county hospital, covered in ash, strapped to a gurney, and staring into the face of one extremely irritated-looking police officer.

CHAPTER FOUR

BITTEN ALIVE

Sally Moore's life had been a challenge from the beginning. Before her mother had even become pregnant with Sally, the doctor had warned her parents that it would be dangerous—"very risky," had been his exact words—for them to try to have a baby. He had informed them that due to a hereditary problem, giving birth could kill Sally's mother.

Tina and Ron Moore had not listened.

They had been the kind of people who usually responded well to instruction or warning, but not that time. Tina had had a miscarriage a year before she had become pregnant with Sally. For both Tina and Ron the miscarriage seemed to make them even more determined to have a living baby of their own.

Any fear they might have had was not as strong as their desire to have a family.

Besides, they were people of means who had always found a way to get what they wanted, and they trusted that Tina would somehow give birth successfully. Once labor began for them, however, all those confident feelings flew out the window.

"Focus on something and breathe," Ron had told Tina. "Breathe."

"I can't," she had replied, her face red with strain.

At that moment, the machines in the background began to beep and hum in an alarming way. And for the first time in his life, Ron could clearly see the future—something was not right, and his wife was in trouble.

The doctor had been in just minutes before and had told them that everything looked fine. But no sooner had he left the room than things had turned drastically for the worse.

"You have to breathe, sweetheart," Ron had begged. "Please breathe."

Tina's eyes had opened wide as she choked and struggled for air. Ron had yelled out for the doctor.

"Breathe, Tina," he had pleaded.

Doctor Adams had come quickly into the room, followed by two nurses and another doctor who was wearing a surgical mask. They had circled and touched Tina, looking for some signal or sensation that would let them know more. The man in the mask finally motioned for one of the nurses with a wave of his hand. He signaled for her to remove the husband. The nurse had turned immediately toward Ron.

"Mr. Moore, we're going to have to have you wait outside," she said. "We'll take it from here."

There was no "Everything's going to be fine," or "This is normal, no need to worry."

Nothing but a, "We'll take it from here." Ron had found no comfort or hope in those words, or in the tone of voice the nurse had used.

"I'm not leaving my wife," he had insisted, holding tightly to Tina's hand.

The masked doctor nodded, and the second nurse had come up beside Ron and pulled his hand from Tina's. Together she and the other nurse pulled him away.

"Come with us," she had said softly. "They'll take care of her."

The beeping became wilder and louder.

"I'm not—"

"Out!" Doctor Adams ordered, never taking his eyes off of Tina.

Sally's father had let the nurses push him toward the door and into the hall. He could hear the door shut behind them. He had tried to listen to the nurses dragging him away, but he wasn't able to make sense out what either of them was saying. They seemed to be babbling.

"Why don't . . . I'm sure . . . fine . . . worry . . ." they rambled.

Ron stared at them pleadingly as they guided him into a purple chair that was next to a pile of magazines and a TV that was airing a Spanish soap opera at that moment.

"Can I get you anything?" the short nurse asked.

"My wife," Sally's father had answered sadly.

Ron could see from the hurt in the nurse's eyes that the situation was not good. He could tell that there was a very real reason why nobody had promised him that everything would be okay.

Tina was in trouble.

"I'm sorry," the red-headed nurse apologized. "We can't do that right now. Doctor Adams will be with you as soon as he possibly can."

They turned and walked off quickly, down the pink tiled walkway and back into the darkness of the room the three of them had just left. As the door closed behind them, any trace of hope dissipated from within Ron.

It had already seemed so final.

Ron began praying. He had not talked to God for so many years that he struggled to recall exactly how to go about it. He was surprised at himself for even remembering that heaven was there. He felt guilty that it had taken a crisis to open up the lines of communication again—guilty, but not guilty enough to cease.

"Please don't let her die," he had begged.

Sally's parents had not always wanted children, but as they had grown older they had discovered that their relationship needed it. Once the idea of having one had settled over them, they had become so excited that there was very little else they could think about. After Tina's first miscarriage they felt an even greater resolve to make it happen.

Now, as Ron sat in the waiting room worrying, he couldn't remember a single one of those previous feelings. A child would be wonderful, but they had so much already. Their lives had been full and successful. Why had they let their desire to have lineage outweigh the fact that giving birth for Tina was dangerous?

He promised the heavens that if everything turned out all right, he would return to the faith of his childhood, and he would be the kind of human that he knew God wanted him to be.

"Please, help us," he had whispered.

The TV flickered as the shows changed. Ron stared at the screen, watching a short man in a bumblebee costume chase a beautiful woman around a table. The dialogue was in Spanish, but that had made no difference. Had the show been in English it would have sounded similar, thanks to the confusion and mess in his head.

"Please help her," he had pleaded, praying for his wife. "I don't care what happens, just keep her alive."

Ron was emotionally and physically exhausted but still surprised to feel sleep weighing in on him. He struggled for a few minutes to stay awake, but shortly after the big bumblebee caught the beautiful woman, Ron slipped into a fitful sleep. He kept jerking in his chair as his body tried to rest. His hands were shaking, and he kept whispering Tina's name, until the family sitting near him got up and moved away.

An hour later, the now unmasked doctor shook him awake with both good and bad news.

"Mr. Moore," he said solemnly. "Ron, is it?"

"Yes," Ron said, pulling himself from sleep. The panic that sleeping had temporarily squelched was back immediately. "How is she?" he demanded.

"Your child's fine," he smiled weakly. "A beautiful girl."

"How's my wife?" he had trembled, not interested in anything but her well-being at the moment.

"I'm sorry, Mr. Moore," the doctor said, shaking his head. "Your wife didn't make it. She . . ."

Ron stared at the wall. His eyes focused on the poster of the food triangle pinned to the big bulletin board. There was a big stalk of wheat waving at him and telling him he should eat more grains. He could not believe what was happening. He opened and closed his eyes as if waking himself again. The unmasked man was still there.

"I am so sorry," the doctor said. "She had a . . ."

Ron had not wanted to hear any more words. He could feel the reality of his wife's death crushing down on him and seeping through his entire body. A feeling of despair like he had never known left him feeling weak and lost. The doctor went on trying to console him, but Sally's father paid no attention.

A moment later he began to cry, weeping until the two nurses returned and helped him into a private room.

🌲 🌲 🌲

Now, all these years later, Sally had once again escaped her own death. With her auxiliary chute only partially open, she had hit the ground with the force of someone jumping from an eight-story building. She would have most likely died there if it had not been for the ill-fitted cushion fate had placed beneath her. Normally the presence of ants is unwelcome, but the huge fire-ant hill that she landed on quite possibly saved her life. Angry at being disturbed, the ants bit Sally over a hundred times. The shock to her system kept her heart pumping until those on the ground could reach her and rush her off to the hospital, where she lay in a coma for over two weeks.

At first the doctors gave her little chance of coming out okay, but almost instantly she began to miraculously heal. The fragile, next-to-death girl that the hospital had wheeled in a couple weeks earlier had become an obvious miracle who everyone liked to look in on and talk about.

When she finally awoke, she was told that she was lucky to be alive, that she had broken seven bones, that she had already had two surgeries, that she would still need more, and that her so-called boyfriend, Mark, was nowhere to be found.

Sally did not feel lucky to be alive.

She watched as a nurse named Deni moved around, looking at charts like an investor checking her portfolio. Apparently, the economy was soft at the moment.

"Not good?" Sally weakly whispered.

Deni stopped and smiled. Her teeth showed white against her dark skin, and the uniform she wore was old and wearing thin in spots. She patted Sally gently on the hand. "Good mornin', Sally."

"Good morning," she managed, feeling that her reply lacked an awful lot of honesty.

"It's always a treat to see you awake," Deni smiled. "You're about the luckiest person I know. Imagine, fallin' out of a plane and livin' to talk about it. God must be happy with somethin' you've done."

"If this is what he does when he's happy," Sally said, raising her arms an inch, "then we're all in big trouble."

Deni put her dark hands on her big hips and frowned. "Don't you go decidin' you know better than God. Sometimes he lets us get banged up so we can remember that we're blessed even to be livin'."

Sally liked Deni. She was like a preacher who administered prescription drugs and wore a white uniform. And even though she was at least forty years older than Sally, she seemed young in her eyes and in her smile. Her dark skin made her look exotic and as if she might have stories to tell, despite the fact that she had probably grown up right here and had lived no more an interesting life than any other.

"Sorry," Sally said, knowing full well that Deni wasn't really mad at her.

"Makin' jokes at a time like this," Deni continued to chastise, "after your life has been spared. Somethin' kept you alive, child."

"Ants," Sally said sarcastically.

"Who knew they were good for anythin'?" Deni said, smiling. "I've worked here over twenty-three years, and I don't recall ever having anyone been rescued by ants."

"I'm a lucky person, remember?" Sally joked.

"That's better," Deni smiled, missing the sarcasm completely. "Now let me see if I can't find someone to bring you some lunch."

As Deni stepped from the room, Sally looked at the phone. It had been weeks now, and Mark hadn't even called. The hospital staff had told her that he had stayed by her as she was brought in, and that he had spent the first two nights by her side. But on the third day he had told the doctor that he was going to go home to clean up and that he would be back.

That was four weeks ago, and he had never returned.

As soon as Sally had become conscious and she had the strength, she had tried to call him, but his roommate kept answering the phone and insisting that Mark was not there, or that he was unavailable. After about the fiftieth call Sally hung up for good, writing him off forever. She was mad, but she almost couldn't blame him. She had been beautiful before, now she was broken and bruised. They had had possibilities before, she had had a job, a future—now she had nothing but the promise of physical therapy and pity.

Lucky to be alive?

The only visitors she had seen aside from staff and doctors were a couple of Mormon missionaries who had told her that they were assigned to the hospital and had asked if she would mind if they spoke with her occasionally. They were nice enough, but how could she ever think they were sincerely interested in her well-being when they were simply carrying out an assignment?

She had known some Mormons before, and even though they seemed like nice people, she had never felt easy around them. A couple of years before she had taken a trip out to Pennsylvania to see the Amish country. She had been surprised at how weird she felt being in their houses and learning about them. She couldn't make the world she knew fit into it. For some reason Mormons had a similar effect on her. How could she work the culture and ways of something she didn't understand into her life?

Before her accident, she had worshipped at a small church on the corner of Spain and Ridgecreek near her apartment. And she was planning to stay in her comfort zone, making sure that outside influences and habits didn't complicate her life. Mormonism was something she could go her whole life without and be fine. But she let the missionaries come by, wanting nothing more than some-body other than Deni to talk to. They always left her something to read or a spiritual challenge to perform.

"Will you read the Book of Mormon?"

"Will you pray?"

"Will you ask your Heavenly Father if this is true?"

"Heavenly father?" she had asked them, the two words sound-ing wrong together.

"Your Father in—" the youngest one had begun to explain. But Deni had stepped in and enthusiastically shooed them out. She didn't like Mormons, she had said, and the young ones in ties espe-cially made her stomach uneasy. The missionaries had laughed politely, but Sally knew Deni was not joking.

"Stay away from those two," she would say. "I've heard lots of stories about Mormons, and it seems to me a person would have to be dumb as a post to believe what they say."

Sally didn't listen to Deni, and the missionaries had continued to drop by and visit her. She had never addressed the issue of a heavenly father again. It had come up a number of times as they talked to her, but she would always just let it go. The concept of a heavenly father made her nervous. She had never had a good father here on earth. In fact, she had experienced just the opposite. She didn't know if a heavenly father would be a good thing, or just another thing for her to feel uneasy about. She had thought about it often but had never asked the question again.

Sally looked at the casts on her arms and legs. Nothing mat-tered. For the time being she was here and she was hurt. She wanted to cry, but she was so sick of doing so that she stopped her-self and closed her eyes, trying to remember her life before all of this.

There was nothing, just this—this bed, these broken bones, and the prospect of nothing. She would have given up completely if it weren't for the fact that despite her condition, or the bleak horizon out in front of her, she couldn't deny that something had kept her alive. For some reason falling from a plane and being bitten over a hundred times by fire-ants, and having her heart broken and her body banged up, was not the end that fate had intended for her.

She wondered if she would ever discover why she had been spared.

CHAPTER FIVE

I'VE FALLEN, AND I CAN'T GET UP

Ryan was born on a hot August day during his state's worst drought in ten years. His father, Darrell, had gotten the news of his wife's labor and had dropped everything. He had told his secretary to take care of things and then jumped in his old Ford and sped down the dirt road that connected his shop to the main highway. He hit the switch on his CB and waited for a familiar voice to answer.

"Susan's in labor," he said with excitement to the voice on the other end. "Rudy just drove her to the hospital. I'm on my way now."

"Everything okay?" the voice asked back.

"I think so. I'll have my boy by this afternoon."

The truck flew over the dirt road and whined as it got up to speed on the highway. It was almost noon, and the sun was high in the sky, making the day brilliant. Darrell had seen good in everything that day. Suddenly the small town they lived in was wonderful. The old roads and vacant storefronts along Main Street were quaint. The people in their ordinary clothes doing ordinary things seemed spectacular.

His baby was on its way!

He had known since the moment he first set eyes on Susan that the greatest day of his life would be the day the two of them had children. Right after recognizing how gorgeous her eyes were, he knew that Susan would be a spectacular mother. His friends had always teased him about how dumb that was, but he couldn't help it. He wanted kids, and this woman was the one he wanted to be the mother of those kids.

The hospital was a ten-minute drive from his shop, but Darrell made it there in six—making every light except the two he ran. He raced inside and over to labor and delivery. He had practiced all this with Susan, but at the moment it all felt new.

"I'm Darrell Mite," he said, as if the woman at the reception desk should already have known. "My wife—"

The woman pointed. "Second door to the left." She tried to smile, but it was obvious that the job she performed had grown far too routine for her to recognize miracles anymore.

Darrell entered the delivery room just as his wife was pushing hard. He took Susan's hand and smiled. He said something about loving her, and she breathed heavily and screamed something in return.

"Try to relax," he lamely offered.

"Excuse me?" she breathed. "How could I possibly relax?"

"Maybe I should go get you some ice or something," he tried.

"I wouldn't go anywhere," the doctor said kindly. "This baby's almost here."

Darrell didn't dare smile. He was afraid if he did that he would never be able to stop. His feet were fidgety, his hands were numb, and his wife was having a baby.

"Push," the doctor ordered.

"Push," Darrell echoed, thinking that maybe she would take it better coming from him.

Susan tried to smile, but the pain was too intense.

"It's coming," the doctor declared.

Darrell looked at his wife and then began to sway. He tipped a little to the left and then righted himself. It was hot, it was cold, it was turning black. The next time he swayed to the left, he couldn't save himself. He passed out, falling to the floor with a loud slap.

"We've got a father down!" the doctor hollered to the nurses.

A couple of nurses rushed to Darrell as he lay on the floor.

"Is he okay?" Susan screamed in between pushes. The irony that she, while giving birth, had to worry about her husband did not escape her.

"He's smiling," one of the nurses said as she helped Darrell stand and get into a chair behind him.

"Push," the doctor ordered Susan again.

Darrell regained his sight and mental awareness just as his wife was executing her final push. The baby arrived. The doctor shielded what he was doing when he cut the cord, so as to not have Darrell passing out again, and put the baby into Susan's arms.

"A beautiful, healthy boy," the doctor smiled. "Does he have a name?"

"Ryan Tyler Mite," Darrell said weakly as he stepped up to his wife and child. "Ryan Mite."

Everyone acted as though that was the perfect name, going on like they had never heard it before and acting as if it actually possessed originality. This despite the fact that four of the people there in the delivery room had someone in their immediate family named Ryan as well.

"Our boy," Darrell said proudly, reaching out to touch him.

Susan smiled, but held Ryan close to her, not yet willing to have her husband and his weak knees take him. "Wait until your face isn't quite so pale," she laughed.

Darrell kissed his wife on her damp forehead and smiled at the doctor.

"Well, he's lucky to have landed in such a nice family," one of the nurses commented. "You going to be okay?" she then asked Darrell.

"Better than that," Darrell answered. He leaned over and kissed his boy.

🌲 🌲 🌲

Ryan couldn't stand the way Todd's mom was looking at him. It was so painful. He couldn't believe that his parents had asked her to speak to him. He didn't need any additional people telling him what to do or feel. An anger he hadn't known before the accident percolated in his chest like a toxic fizz. The fact that he hated anything bothered him almost as much as the way she was looking at him.

What was done was done.

There was nothing he could change now. If he could go back, he would go back in a second and slow down so as to avoid the moose. He would go back even further and never take the turn-off. Or further still, he would have skipped the trip to Wyoming altogether and instead stayed home and fished at Fenton Reservoir. But he couldn't go back. He couldn't change a thing. And he certainly couldn't fix what he had done.

Ryan thought he had known guilt previously. There were a few minor things he had done in his life that had needed correcting before. Those things had made him feel uneasy and sorry, but that guilt was nothing compared to what he now felt.

Todd's mom was still looking at him.

"I am so sorry for you," she cried. "I can only imagine how you feel." She hugged him and sobbed quietly. "It was an accident."

Ryan wanted to scream. He wanted her to lash out and blame him. He wanted her to tell him how awful he was and how if he had driven responsibly her son would not be in a coma with little chance of ever recovering.

Ryan began to cry. There were a million reasons why the tears came easily. He couldn't walk yet; the accident had fractured both his legs. He could also cry for the fact that no matter how long he lived, he would never be able to forget Todd's terrified expression as they had been trapped in the submerged truck cab.

He could cry for the poor family that found them—the father and mother and three little kids who had come up behind the accident and witnessed enough to forever change their lives. He could cry over the memories of finally coming to, days later, to learn that he wouldn't walk for a while and that Todd might never regain consciousness.

He could cry for the mission he could no longer serve—the people in Africa who would never be able to hear his testimony or receive his help. His whole life he had desired to be a missionary. Now, because of one wrong turn, he would have to postpone the opportunity. What made it even worse was the feeling that he might never feel worthy or right about ever going at all.

He could cry for his parents and the pain they had experienced over their only child having almost killed his best friend and ruining his own future, all with one reckless act.

There was no shortage of things to cry for.

"He wouldn't want you to hate yourself," Todd's mother reasoned. "You have to try to forgive yourself."

"I can't," Ryan whispered.

Todd's mother drew back, her expression similar to the one her son had worn when he and Ryan had been trapped in the truck.

"I will never forgive myself for what I have done," Ryan whispered vehemently. "Never."

"He's going to be okay," she insisted. "We have to believe that."

Believe? The word didn't even sound right any longer. It was a word that conjured up magic and illusion. He had *believed* that he would be going on a mission. He had *believed* that he would be looked after and protected. He had *believed* that he was watched over by heaven. He had *believed* that his life was blessed and mapped out.

He thought back to when he had gotten his patriarchal blessing. He had been promised so many amazing things. He could still remember opening his eyes after saying amen and seeing his mother and father sitting there with their mouths open, as if they had just witnessed something amazing. Nowhere in that blessing was there mention of making the kind of mistake he had just made. There wasn't a word of it that indicated that he would one day drive his friend into a moose and over a cliff to their near deaths.

"Todd will be okay," she insisted. "You have got to know that he wouldn't want you to be beating yourself up like this. He loves you."

"I wonder if he'll feel the same if he ever wakes up," Ryan said coldly.

"Of course he will. You know Todd as well as I do."

"I don't know anything anymore."

She looked at him with tears in her eyes. She moved to hug him again, but he held her away.

He could not understand why he had been kept alive.

CHAPTER SIX

MISTS OF GRAYNESS

In the summer of 1978, Buttercrest, Michigan, felt like it was on fire. There were no flames, but if a person were to remove their glasses they would be wise to worry about where they held them for fear of the intense sun catching the lenses and setting the entire place ablaze. A woman had gotten heatstroke after gardening for ten minutes in the shade. A man had left the windows closed in his house and had almost suffocated. The temperatures had reached heights that no forecaster had seen before in that part of the country.

And whereas fire had been a major concern, had there actually been any open flames that summer, the suffocating humidity might easily have smothered them.

It had been one hot, humid, miserable summer.

Buttercrest was not a well-known town, and its residents liked it that way. It was a town whose citizens prayed daily that they might be left in peace. It had been established not long after the founding of America, by a religious gentleman named Garrett Feathers. Feathers had settled the area so that he could have a place to practice polygamy. His father had been a preacher who had married his wife's sister, after her husband had died. Finding such an arrangement to his liking, he then also married two of his wives' cousins. Garrett was a child from the taller of the two cousins.

Having been a product of polygamy and feeling that it was his righteous duty to continue the tradition, Feathers settled Buttercrest, and a few followers joined him. The followers of those first inhabitants were from that time on always referred to as The Settlers.

It was in this town that 200 years later, August Thatch was born. His father, Grover Thatch, was a devout Settler and was married to three woman simultaneously, all of whom were due to give birth that July.

Well, July came and went and not a one of them delivered.

No sooner had the second day of August arrived than the whole populace grew ill. A fever that no medicine could break swept through the town. Entire families became infected, and some parents, who were themselves sick, lost all their children to the mysterious ailment.

It was during this fearsome epidemic that all three of Grover's wives gave birth. First Sarah, then Ester, and then Edith—all within a twenty-four hour period, each of the three having a boy. No sooner had they given birth than each of them came down with the illness. Grover became sick, too, as well as almost all of his progeny who lived under his roof.

The rest of the month was a fog. Sarah, who had prided herself on keeping a journal every day of her life, now had twenty-three blank pages.

It was as if the month had never happened.

It was September before any real healing or relief reached the isolated town. Upon rubbing their collective eyes, the locals were shocked at the loss. Most families had suffered the loss of a child or an elderly loved one. Some had lost two, but only one family had lost three—the Thatch family.

Ninety-year-old Aunt Merta had passed away in her fevered sleep as well as two of the three recently born children. There was some mention of how fortunate they were to not have lost more, but that fortune felt thin in the absence of those missing. To add to the general confusion and hurt, nobody knew whose child had actually survived. There had been three, and now there was only one. All had been boys, all had been born at home, all had had a small amount of dark hair, and all had been babies.

Those three women poked and prodded the surviving infant, searching for some sign or freckle that would help them determine the rightful owner. Sarah swore that if you squinted and viewed the child's feet underwater they were identical to hers. Ester said that he had her heavy arms, and Edith considered the child's odd manner to be proof enough of her claim.

So there were inclinations and maybes, but no solid proof of ownership. Extensive tests could have been performed, but that would have required outside help and outside questions and outside headaches. So the decision was made: the child belonged to all of three of them.

One child, three official mothers.

There was some discussion about which name they should go with. Each had had a name picked out for hers, but no one was willing to concede.

Until an accord could be reached, they agreed to call him

August, due to the month he had arrived. Eventually, with no consensus likely in the foreseeable future, they gave up their personal preferences for a name and stuck with August.

Because of the uncertainty about whose child he was, August spent most of his childhood feeling as though he didn't belong to anyone.

🌲 🌲 🌲

August stared out through the bars of his cell, wondering how he had gotten himself into what he was now into. He was not supposed to be here. He had been honoring his sister, not looking to torch an elementary school that was also an historical landmark. Apparently the first governor of the state's grandchild had built the thing, and it turned out that the old school meant a lot to a lot of important people, not to mention the few hundred displaced children who had attended there.

The whole thing had become an amazingly painful, drawn-out nightmare for August. His future was history, his car was history (thanks to leaping flames), and for the next ten months his freedom as he had known it was also history.

The school he had broken into and then accidentally lit on fire, being so special to so many, turned August's case into a political and social cause celebre. The local paper covered the story closely, enjoying the fact that August claimed to have started it in his sleep and yet magically had walked out of the fire without a scratch or burn. Plus, August's name lent itself to particularly clever headlines:

"August Is a Scorcher."

"August Sleeps while Summer Side Elementary Burns."

"August Is A-guilty"

An additional perk for the community was that August looked so good in the newspapers. Write-in campaigns were started up by a number of women's groups—organized by females who found him too attractive not to save. People even began sporting "Free August" T-shirts and bumper stickers. And a small diner down by the college named one of its sandwiches "The August Bump." It had double meat, no lettuce, and red peppers. When asked why that sandwich, the female manager explained: "Because August is hunky, poor, and hot."

None of this helped August in the end. The judge, who was a great-nephew, three times removed, of the said grandchild who had built the school, couldn't let August off without any jail time. So he gave August ten months—to appease the community, his heritage, and maybe justice.

August sighed, looking out of his cell and into the depressing corridor that crossed over to more bars and more inmates. He needed something to be hopeful about.

Anything.

He tried to feel good about his cellmate, but truth be told, his cellmate made him feel more uneasy than good. It wasn't only that Douglas was physically threatening; it was more like the guy reminded August of one of his meaner grandfathers, but with a criminal record and murderous tendencies.

The night before, August had fallen asleep to the sound of Douglas vocally listing all the people he would pay back as soon as he got out of the pen.

"Do you mind listing your victims a little more quietly?" August had politely asked.

Douglas had stopped for a moment and then continued on with his list. " . . . August Thatch, Johnny Chapman, Thomas Percy . . ."

August decided to keep his thoughts to himself from that moment on. For the next ten months he would do more listening than speaking. There was no need for him to make his surroundings any more uncomfortable than they already were. And there was no way his mouth could ever be trusted to say the right thing, here in an environment so completely foreign to that which he had always known.

So he drew into himself, making sure that the only conversations he had with anyone were completely benign. He would spend his time in thought—thinking and listening. Listening to those around him and thinking of those things that he missed and longed for. August still couldn't put into words or accurately describe what his sister's passing had done to him. Whenever he tried to explain his feelings, the agony was more than he could bear. So he decided to keep his pain to himself, thinking that as long as he thought of no one beside himself, he could never be torn apart like this again.

He also began to occasionally think of his parents. This surprised him. He had not seen them for years. He had left Michigan and moved to Texas at eighteen and had never looked back, wanting nothing more to do with their weird ways. He had been raised in Buttercrest, but he didn't have to like or agree with the bizarre tradition his father had been too foolish to give up.

When he had left at eighteen, he was determined to become something completely opposite of his father and family. They were misguided and stubborn. They were uneducated and unlawful.

Of course, here August sat, in jail. But his crime somehow seemed different than those of his family, more benign. He had accidentally started a school on fire while not paying attention. His family, however, had made the mistake of purposefully looking the other way when there were signs everywhere that what they were doing was not right.

August also thought often about Rachel. She had been the one who had given him the guts to leave Michigan. She had left two years before August turned eighteen, begging him to get out with her. August had let her down, deciding instead to stay and toe the line. She had written him a number of times, but her letters had never gotten through. Their father had destroyed every one of them before August ever got a chance to see any. Rachel had come back once, to visit and to find something to celebrate in their family relationship, but the family had turned its back on her.

August couldn't believe it.

He had done nothing but miss his sister, and as she had made an attempt to show that she still cared for them, they had cast her away. Showing little or no remorse at the loss, recommitting themselves to the unlawful and foolish tradition of The Settlers.

Two weeks after Rachel's visit, August packed up and left Buttercrest for good. He walked for the first six miles of his journey, until a trucker named Bear picked him up and drove him a number of states away, far from everything he had ever known.

CHAPTER SEVEN

PICKING A NAME

Following the death of his wife, Tina, Ron found comfort in nothing. He spent days and nights in the hospital, looking at his tiny daughter, Sally, willing himself not to be angry at her. Yes, he and Tina had wanted a baby, but he had wanted a wife more. And now his wife was gone. People weren't supposed to die giving birth anymore he had thought. This was a time of enlightenment and technology.

Mothers didn't die giving birth.

Wives didn't die giving birth.

But Ron's wife had died, and every time he looked at Sally he saw nothing but misery and loss. It was within this grieving that he had begun to listen to the twisted logic in his head—logic that allowed him to think about abandoning Sally. It had seemed to make sense to him.

He couldn't stay around.

He couldn't bear looking at Sally.

Every step she would ever take or word that she would speak would remind him that if it had not been for her, his wife would still be here. He knew that he couldn't get up tomorrow and pretend to be grateful that he had Sally. He couldn't go to work and show people pictures or tell them cute stories about her growth and antics.

He couldn't be a father to her.

So Sally's father packed up and left. He quit his job, gathered his things, and slipped out of town during a dark August night—leaving no forwarding address, no contact numbers, and no desire to ever be found again. If the fates had taken the one person he loved from him, then he would pay them back by leaving the one person who now needed him.

Six months later, Sally was adopted by a couple who promised the state that they would love her as if she were their own.

Promises, unfortunately, are way too easy to break.

🌲 🌲 🌲

The mornings were hardest for Sally. The sun would shine through the window and send the long shadows of the hospital equipment and all its trappings up against the wall. It was a giant reminder of where she still was. Her life had changed so greatly in the last few months that even if her body hadn't been dinged up, she still wouldn't have recognized herself in the mirror. She felt as if she had something before. Now she had nothing. She had spent her whole life feeling and being alone, and just when things looked to be changing for the better she had done something stupid like jumping out of a plane.

What was I thinking? she thought to herself.

Her body was healing; her soul, however, was a different story. The doctors and Deni kept telling her how well she looked and how spectacular she was doing. But, they would always add, "We have got to get you stronger before we can let you go."

This greatly depressed Sally. She didn't know if she could last another week there. She was discouraged and depressed.

Sally hated hospitals.

She had been told over and over by her adoptive parents that her father had left her in a hospital because she had killed her mother. As a little girl, whenever she messed up or acted out, they used to warn her that if she didn't watch it they would send her back to the hospital where she came from. Sally never doubted them. She didn't realize that people could lie about such huge things until she left home and began to see the real world.

She now loathed her adoptive parents.

They had been fairly kind to her the first few years of her life, but then the father had lost his job and begun drinking and fighting with the family. He became abusive to his wife, who in turn took it out on the kids. She was much harder on Sally than she was on her others. She would make Sally do everything around the house and then scream at her like a speaker throwing out feedback when she made a mistake or moved too slowly. Sally's only comfort had been school, and her mother would pull her out at least once a year in an effort to punish her. She wanted to teach Sally that she would never be smarter than her mother, and that she had better stop trying to be something she wasn't and focus on what she was—a no-good brat who didn't know Tuesday from Saturday or which month Christmas fell in.

At sixteen Sally had run away from home. She moved in with a friend named Shauna whose parents didn't care what their daughter was doing. They also didn't care if another warm body had taken up residence at their house. They were always traveling or away on business, so having Sally around actually helped them feel less guilty about leaving Shauna home alone with the nanny. At first it wasn't a bad arrangement, but as soon as Sally began to be prettier than Shauna, Shauna wanted her out.

So at sixteen Sally had lied to a man at a movie theater about her age and had gotten a job cleaning the theaters at night. With that money she had lied about her age again and gotten her own apartment. After she had saved enough money and turned nineteen, she got into college where her life finally began to work.

As her existence leveled out, however, she began to draw into herself. Each day as she witnessed more of the world, she began to realize that she really had beaten the odds. Most people had never come out of such a bad situation. But she had, and for some reason that frightened her. She felt as if she now needed to make sure that the good she had found wouldn't get away from her. She went out less, spending her nights studying and with herself. She mapped out her way to the places she had to go and was content only going to those places. Each week of her life became just as the last week had been. At 10:15 on Monday morning you could bet your bank account that she would be passing the Byron Building and going into the library. At 3:27 on any Friday, the doorman of the Willow apartments where she lived would have been worried if Sally didn't walk in carrying one bag of groceries, two rented videos, and a magazine from the stand out front. There was not a moment of her days that was not spelled out or planned. On Tuesday, Wednesday, and Thursday evenings she was studying in the library. On Sunday she went to church and then spent the afternoon doing laundry and making lists. Each day she grew more withdrawn and determined to stick to what was safe.

At age twenty-two, Sally had met Mark. He had been walking out of her building on Friday at exactly 3:27 after visiting a friend of his. They accidentally gently collided, and it only got better from there. He was everything everyone else had never been to her. He was funny, smart, caring, and driven. He thought Sally was brilliant, and that she could be anything she wanted to be.

Six months later Sally graduated with honors and a degree in secondary education. She then secured a job and foolishly signed up for skydiving lessons and a chance to tackle one of her biggest fears—heights. Although she felt that with skydiving, she was really conquering thirteen Goliaths at once.

She had finally been proud of herself. Of course, all of that had changed now. The jump hadn't made her a different person, it had just made her even less confident with life. She thought about how insistent Mark had been that she parachute.

"You'll never forget it."

He had told her the truth. There was no way now that she would *ever* forget the stunt. And chances were she would also never forget Mark. She pulled out his picture, which she still kept hidden in the pages of her journal. He looked so happy compared to the person she saw in the mirror these days. He was smiling, and his deep green eyes looked as though they were camouflaging something funny. She tried to cry, but since the fact that he was gone was no longer a new revelation, the tears wouldn't come. She put the picture back and looked toward the door of her hospital room just as the two Mormon missionaries appeared.

"Hey, Sally," Elder Heybourne said.

Sally shifted in her bed as the two of them came all the way into the room and took a seat on the empty bed next to her. "You guys are nice to stop by, but I'm still not going to join," she joked.

"Could you at least pretend like you might," Elder Heybourne kidded. "I need something good to write home about."

Sally enjoyed it when Elder Heybourne talked about his home. He described having a great relationship with his parents and brothers and sisters and talked fondly about the activities they shared. She couldn't imagine growing up in a home like that. She hadn't really enjoyed all the lessons (he called them "discussions") he had given her, but his references to his home and family fascinated her.

His current companion, Elder Stimpson, had only been there a few weeks and had replaced a tall, dark elder from Samoa. Elder Heybourne had been there the whole time Sally had been in the hospital. Lately, he had begun talking about how he would probably be transferred soon and how she would soon be free of him bothering her. Truth be known, however, she had come to like having him around. She liked the way he talked. She liked the way he smiled. And she loved the way he talked about his hometown, as if it were the very spot where God rested when he had a chance to put his feet up.

Seven Pines, Montana.

"My mom's sick of me telling her about how many doors I've had slammed in my face," Elder Heybourne continued. "It's so normal she doesn't even feel sorry for me any more."

"Neither do I," Sally smiled. "You're out here by your own choice. You could always go home."

Elder Heybourne smiled. "You obviously don't believe yet," he added. "If you did, you would know that all the door slamming in the world isn't going to stop me."

Sally didn't really enjoy it when the elders talked about religion or having conviction. Such talk reminded her of how completely empty her life was. If she believed in something, she didn't know what it was. God was a presence in other's lives, but not in hers. He had left her alone at birth, and as far as she could tell he had not come back to check on her since then. She went to church every Sunday, but it was something she did because she had been told to, once. Religion was a place or an act, not a way of life or a personal discovery.

She didn't mind the missionaries talking about home, or just visiting about what was happening in the world, but when they started to get into their testimonies and pulled out the gospel they were peddling, she became extremely uneasy.

"Tell me some more about your home," she said, changing the subject. Having grown up in a big city her whole life, she loved the descriptions of the little town Elder Heybourne spoke so fondly of. It seemed so secure.

"What can I say without making my companion jealous?" Elder Heybourne joked.

It amazed Sally that these elders even went on missions, what with the way they talked so fondly of the homes they had left.

Elder Heybourne smiled. "Well, for starters it's the most amazing piece of earth that God ever created," he obliged. "Beautiful in winter, spring, summer, and fall."

Sally listened, enjoying the vision of such a place as Seven Pines. But just then, Dr. Scott came in, wearing what Sally thought was way too serious a face to be good. He looked at the missionaries and asked if he could have a moment alone with Sally. They said their good-byes and then left Sally and the doctor alone.

"You don't look happy," Sally tried to smile. "I promise I'll eat my peas next time. It's not easy getting used to this hospital food."

Dr. Scott tried to laugh politely, then turned serious again.

"Sally, there are some complications."

"Complications?" she said, anxiety showing in her eyes. *Complications? Like falling out of a plane? Like being saved by ants only to lose your boyfriend? Like surgery and having to stay in this place? Like bruises and scrapes and breaks and loss and pain and confusion?*

"The test we ran yesterday came back conclusive," he clarified.

Like dying?

Sally knew what the test had been for. They had found some problems while doing blood work on her, and the test had been an effort to confirm if what they thought was actually happening, was happening.

"I'm dying?" she whispered.

"We're not sure, Sally," the doctor said sadly. "There are some more tests we would like to run and a few things we want to try before we'll know exactly what we're looking at. But I have to let you know that it could be very serious. More tests will tell."

Sally didn't know whether to laugh or cry. She had only recently become strong enough to think about leaving the hospital, and now this. This was so out of the blue and so huge that she figured it had to be a miscommunication or something. She had been saved for a purpose. Had she lived only to come up with some mysterious illness? Despite what she was hearing, she knew it couldn't be true. There was no way that she could be destined for death when she had survived what she just had. There was no way.

"I want to go home," she insisted. "I don't want to be here anymore."

"We'll see," Dr. Scott answered. "We'll do whatever we can. I promise. I am so sorry." He squeezed her hand and tried to smile.

Sally didn't try to smile back. She had heard his words, but for some reason she knew he was wrong. Sally wasn't about to die, she was about to live, and she knew it. He could have shown her every chart in the building and pointed out just what was wrong and how there was no way she could ever change anything, and she still wouldn't have accepted his words.

Sally was about to live, and that was that.

CHAPTER EIGHT

PAWNING AWAY

Ryan had no idea he could hit a ball so far. But there it was, soaring over the outfield fence and into the parking lot of the mall next door. He listened for the sound of a windshield shattering, but the deafening cheers of those in the stands would have drowned out a ten-car pile up, much less a single windshield shattering. He was sixteen, and he had hit a home run—his second of the day.

He dropped his bat and ran the bases as coolly as he could. Everywhere there were faces looking at him—pointing, clapping. He couldn't believe he had done it. As he rounded the bases, his team exploded out of the dugout, racing for home plate, where they pounded him with their hands and hoisted him onto their shoulders, chanting his name.

"Ry-un, Ry-un, Ry-un!"

He looked all over trying to spot his father. He loved the attention from his team, but he wanted to see his dad. He knew his father had been wearing an orange hat, but Ryan couldn't see a speck of orange anywhere.

Ryan spotted Todd running toward him. He twisted to reach down and give his best friend a high-five.

"Lucky hit," Todd had yelled, making fun of him and congratulating him simultaneously.

Ryan would have returned the ribbing, but he suddenly saw orange.

His father came running toward him, looking more proud than ever. Ryan slid off his teammates' shoulders and hugged his father.

He felt his father hugging him, and in his happiness Ryan imagined the look on his mother's face when he'd get home—knowing she would be happy for him.

Ryan had never been able to understand why he was so lucky. For as long as he could remember, his life had been blessed. Even at sixteen years old he had known that. If he picked up a stick, he could throw it farther than anyone. If he found a ball, he could kick it harder and straighter than anyone. Good grades came easily, the piano was a breeze, and good friends seemed to seek him out. And always when he stepped into his home, his parents were there to tell him how lucky they were to have him as a son.

He never got tired of hearing that.

Ryan recognized what he had. He told his parents constantly that he felt as if there was something important about his life. Something special he had to do.

"I'm certain there is," his father would say. "You're Darrell Mite's kid."

His mother would always say, "Ryan, after Sears, I would believe anything about you. Anything."

Ryan had been two and a half years old when his mother had

taken him to Sears so that she could look for a new vacuum. It had been a hard year for his father's business and money was tight. Consequently, Ryan's mom couldn't find a vacuum that fit into their budget. After looking for a while she took Ryan's hand, and the two of them walked over to the washers and dryers to gawk. Which is exactly how Ryan's mom phrased it whenever she recounted the story.

Susan had wanted a new washer and dryer so badly. She and Darrell had sat down a number of times trying to figure out how they could get one. Reality always set in, however, reminding them that there just wasn't the money for that right then. Susan couldn't remember how long she had stood looking at the appliances before she noticed Ryan was not by her side. She looked quickly down the aisles, hoping he would be right there. He wasn't. She had run frantically around Sears, calling for him.

"Ryan! Ryan! Ryan!"

There was no answer. A man in an orange vest paged the store, and the security team immediately put people at the doors to stop anyone from leaving. Susan wept as she and hundreds of people combed the store. The panic in her had eventually become so great that she began screaming and begging those around her to look harder.

Ryan was nowhere to be found. Darrell was called, and he came as quickly as he could. He could offer no help, however, except to try to take some of the pain his wife had been feeling by herself. More police had been called in, and news crews arrived to document the unfolding tragedy.

Four hours later the police got a call from a woman who lived almost three miles from the mall. She said she had been sitting on her front porch waiting for the UPS man to deliver her new dress when she had seen a tiny child coming up the street. At first she thought he was older, or that he was with someone. But eventually

Ryan passed her front yard. He stopped at the edge of her property and smiled at her. She smiled back and asked him where his mommy was.

"At Sears."

She told him to have a seat next to her on the porch and that she would call his mom. Fifteen minutes later Ryan had been reunited with his frantic parents. Nobody knew what had happened. Everyone assumed he had been abducted, but no matter how the counselors and police questioned him, he never let on that there had been anybody but himself involved. It seemed that he'd just wandered off. Way off. Through a mall parking lot, across a six-lane main road, through two apartment complexes, over a culvert, and down through the neighborhood where he was eventually found.

Ryan became a momentary celebrity—the handsome little boy who had walked off and been recovered without a single scratch—whose mother had lost track of him while gawking at appliances at Sears.

Susan had been humiliated, but her discomfort had been eased considerably when, in the name of customer relations and good will, Sears had given the Mite family a brand new washer and dryer, a vacuum, a toaster (a model that they were having a hard time selling), and a baby stroller with seat belts. Susan and Darrell had gladly accepted the plunder, all the while marveling over their only child and the luck that seemed to follow him.

🌲 🌲 🌲

"I'm not interested in trophies," the bearded man sniffed. "I'm in this to make money. These have already got a name on them," he said, waggling the stub of a cigar in his mouth. "How'm I gonna sell a trophy with someone's name on it?"

Ryan looked at this man's name tag. "Please, Tony."

"Bigger people than you have begged me for hours with no results."

"Fine," Ryan said, pulling the box of trophies back off the counter. "Will you take the watch and the CDs?"

Tony flipped through the CDs, touching them like they might be carriers of some fatal disease. He picked up the watch and then set it down, sighing.

"There's nothing great here. I'll give you a hundred and twenty for it all."

"There's over fifty CDs," Ryan protested.

"And over a hundred people just like you looking to unload ones just like these. One hundred and twenty dollars."

Ryan pushed the box of CDs toward Tony and held out his hand.

"I've got no choice," Ryan conceded.

Tony counted out six twenties, and then made Ryan sign a pink piece of paper. Ryan turned and left the pawn shop as quickly as he could. With the money he had just gotten he finally had enough to get out of Sharfield. He couldn't stay here any longer. His legs and body were healed, and it was time for him to get out. It seemed as if every person he saw or interacted with was connected to Todd and the accident. There wasn't a single day when someone didn't bring up the subject. Though no one said it directly, the inference was always the same: why was he alive while Todd remained in a coma?

He was constantly being reminded of how blessed he was. How fortunate he was. How good he looked for someone who had been so near to death. What a tragedy that Todd was not doing well. What a miracle that Ryan was.

What a mess.

Ryan couldn't deal with it any longer. The accident had changed him. He had undergone months and months of recovery and physical therapy. And now that he could walk and drive and he looked normal again, he wanted out. He doubted everything about himself and what he was doing. The guilt over what he could have prevented gnawed at him every waking moment and even in his dreams. During the first few months following the accident, he had prayed every second he could for peace. He wanted to know that there was still a place for him in heaven despite what he had done.

But he received no answer.

The law had been lenient, and Todd's parents had forgiven him quicker than Ryan was comfortable with. But Ryan knew that there was only one place he could receive true forgiveness.

So he had prayed and prayed, looking for some sign that he had been forgiven. Nothing came to him. In fact his life seemed to now testify of how out of sorts he was with heaven. His parents had been forced to take out a second mortgage on their house to pay his medical bills. Due to his injuries, his mission had at first been postponed, but now, because of the guilt, he didn't feel worthy to serve.

And he was starting to go bald.

That seemed like such a petty thing compared to everything that he had experienced, but losing his hair was like the final testament that fate had ceased to favor him.

So, on a warm night after his parents had gone to bed, Ryan slipped out of the house and into the family car. With one suitcase and almost no hope that where he was heading would change anything, he left Sharfield for good.

CHAPTER NINE

PEDIGREE OF WEALTH

Let's just say, the Settlers of Buttercrest didn't really know what they believed. Their doctrine and traditions had grown fuzzy and confusing. Some thought it was fine to marry only one wife. Some thought that those who thought that should be stoned or at least severely made fun of. There were issues of education, and what to, and not to, teach their children. There were questions of worship. Doctrine had become so muddled that no one knew for certain what it was they should be espousing. The populace of the town that had been named by fate was confused and out of step.

You see, when Garrett Feathers had settled the place he had named it Buttercrest because of the fact that a few months earlier a herd of cows had gotten out and worked themselves high up into the mountain. Their whereabouts were not discovered for a few days, and when they were finally located they were trapped up on the top crest of a small mountain where the grass was as long and as thick as palm leaves. Unmilked, the cattle had gorged themselves to the point that the udders of two of them had burst, leaving those two cows dead and parts of the crest drenched in milk. It had been a gruesome sight, but it provided the area an intriguing name.

Buttercrest.

The Settlers of Buttercrest were now dwindling. It was a religion with no direction or faithful devotees. One family would be living one way while another was living completely differently. The Smiths were keeping the Sabbath day holy and practicing polygamy while the Joneses struggled with the Sabbath day but had that "thou shall not steal" principle down.

The town of Buttercrest was, and had been, in a very real sense dissolving. Like an Alka-Seltzer tablet, it had been plopped down, caused a brief, small spitting stir, and then fizzled out to nothing. The principles that had been so clear at its founding had become muddled and were being forgotten.

That is, until Darin Tanstone discovered the power of multi-level marketing.

Darin had attended a seminar three towns over and returned to begin selling vitamins and oils. It took only a few sales to discover that polygamy provided perfect down-lines. If a true Settler sold only to the people in his immediate family, he could do pretty darn well for himself.

The entire place went crazy with it.

Families were coming together. The city park was filled with community activities, where there was square dancing and circle drawing. Every day it seemed as if somebody or some family had discovered a new product or way of life to peddle—shoes, magnets, lotions, weight loss, insurance, soap, videos—you name it, they would be throwing parties to tout the latest wonder product and enlist their numerous family members to market it.

Then, as suddenly as it had all begun, everyone simultaneously decided to sit back and let their efforts pay off. The payoff wasn't what they had all expected. Some funds trickled in, but for the first time in their histories, the sprawling families just weren't big enough. Fifty members simply couldn't provide the kind of residual income that would keep everyone eternally comfortable.

So with nobody else to sell to, the pyramids crumbled. Those at the bottom didn't enjoy buying from those at the top while not making a cent for themselves. Those in the middle knew that they were holding the whole thing together and began looking for ways to leapfrog to the top, where an endless income stream seemed more imminent. Then, a few people discovered that most of the products that people were selling could be bought in some form or another at Wal-Mart, for half the price. That did it. The town began coming apart at the schemes.

In the end most people were left with garages full of vitamins and shoes and weaker family relations than they had begun with.

From that point on the town of Buttercrest never really regained any more of its supposed glory. No one knew what he believed, or where he was going. Everyone was so stuck on the foolish traditions of their fathers that they couldn't see that those same traditions were destroying their kids.

🌲 🌲 🌲

August was working outside of the prison cafeteria, sweeping the walkway and trying hard to look as though he wasn't listening. Over the many months he had been in prison, he had learned how to be an excellent silent observer. His ability to go unnoticed and keep his mouth shut had paid off in hundreds of ways. He had been privy to information that he might never have known, simply because everyone knew he would never say anything.

August had thought at first that remaining silent in most situations would be a strain, but it had turned out to be his salvation. He had been able to work through many things in his head, and puzzling parts of his life that he had wrestled with and run from had now come into focus. At least that's what he kept telling himself.

From the moment August was incarcerated he made it his goal to be the model prisoner. The judge had said that with good behavior he could be released in eight months instead of ten. That was August's plan. If there was something he could clean or some way he could help, he did. After a couple of weeks he stood out as a quiet, helpful inmate that didn't cause problems and could be trusted.

It was in this good behavior that August began to feel the presence of a heavenly somebody. He had been taught religion in Buttercrest, but the whole concept had never been very clear, especially because those teaching him would often end up scratching their heads whenever questions were asked. It seemed to August that all they really understood was that Buttercrest had been founded on polygamy. Beyond that, they didn't have many answers to heavenly questions.

Yet in prison, surrounded by ner-do-wells and hoodlums, August was experiencing heavenly intervention at almost every turn. The mere fact that people left him alone was as great a blessing as he had ever received. He began to believe that there had to be more to life than what he now knew.

Now, as August continued to sweep, he couldn't believe what he was hearing. The two men quietly talking on the other side of the partition were a couple of the worst thugs in the prison, and the things they were saying were not only interesting, they were potentially profitable.

August knew that if they discovered he was eavesdropping, he would be in big trouble. But he was too engrossed in what they were whispering to simply walk away. Instead, August stopped sweeping and leaned closer to the wall.

"There's nothing we can do about it now. In case you haven't noticed, we're both stuck in here."

"A little time's not going to change anything," the other one argued. "The boy said—"

The talking suddenly stopped. There was silence for a moment and then there they were, both of them, looking around the corner and staring at August as he pretended to sweep.

"Listening in, Mute?" The bigger one said angrily, calling August by the nickname he had earned.

"Did we say something interesting?" the other one asked.

"I didn't hear anything," August lied. "I was just cleaning this floor. There, that should just about do it." August swirled the broom and then picked it up as if preparing to walk off.

"He really does talk," the bigger one joked, acting surprised. "In that case we better make it so he never says another word." He grabbed August's arm and spun him around.

"Listen," August said with force. "I was just cleaning up."

"Well, we're just going to make sure you know how we feel about eavesdroppers."

August backed against the wall. The smaller inmate ran toward him, fists clenched and arms swinging. August put his hands out and avoided the blows easily, holding the broom handle up between him and his attacker.

The big one stood there watching and laughing at his partner as he flailed at August to no effect.

"That's enough," he finally said, pushing his friend aside and facing August himself. "I think it's my turn."

August knew he should be scared, but the feeling of invincibility that had been growing in him ever since his sister had died, crested, spilling over into every inch of his being. How could these two hurt him more than he had already been hurt? He didn't know where he found the strength, or how he had the ability, but with almost no effort at all he knocked his assailants down a number of pegs, stripped them of all pride, and taught them in a very clear way that they should never have touched him.

A third inmate, seeing the beating that August was administering, jumped in to even the odds. August didn't miss a beat. In the end all three were strewn on the floor with nothing to say.

A number of prisoners who had witnessed the fight stood still and in awe. August glanced down at his own hands and feet, wondering if he had somehow switched places with somebody else. He had never been a wimp, but he wasn't exactly the greatest fighter in the world, either. Once, when he was sixteen, a couple of his older cousins had cornered him and begun giving him a hard time for not believing in the ways of their family. August had become so outraged that he had lashed out at them. It was not much of a fight. They creamed him. He had gone on to defend his point of view a number of times, but never convincing a single soul of the rightness of his opinion, and always ending up with at least one black eye.

Now, however, he had effortlessly handled three people—two of them considerably bigger than he was and one with a criminal record that would make most inmates on death row green with envy.

August breathed deep. He couldn't explain what he felt, but he didn't want the feeling to go away. It wasn't heavenly or calming, but it was powerful.

He didn't speak to anyone for the rest of his stay in prison, and not a single soul ever tried to get him to do otherwise.

CHAPTER TEN

RUN, RUN AS FAST AS YOU CAN

Sally stared out at the sky with her big blue eyes and wondered why it looked so different this morning. The blue was loose and seemed to be more of a front for something bigger and better than what the eye simply saw. It was as if she could see holes in the sky-painted dome. A familiar voice spoke to her.

"You're gawkin' at the sky like it was a good-lookin', available bachelor," Deni quipped. "You been stuck in this hospital for far too long."

"I'm not going to disagree with that." Sally nodded toward the window. "I'd be happy to be out of here."

"People get happy 'bout things like a nice parkin' space or free soda," Deni pointed out. "You'd be thrilled, and that's all there is to that. Life's too short—" Deni stopped herself and began folding a blanket in hopes of changing the subject she had just opened.

Sally smiled. "I suppose I should take it all in while I can."

"Don't think 'bout that right now," Deni scolded. "If God wants you back, then there ain't a thing you or nobody else can do 'bout it. They don't know anythin' for sure yet." The whites of Deni's dark eyes grew larger whenever she felt strongly about something.

"I know that God doesn't want me back yet," Sally insisted. "I can feel it."

Deni tried to smile. She of course knew all too well about how fragile and fleeting life could be. She had seen many people who were sure that they were overcoming their illnesses—right up until their dying day.

"I think heaven will put you where you're bes' suited," Deni tried to comfort without being too unrealistic.

Sally looked at Deni, realizing that she was the one thing she would miss most about this place. Over the months, Sally had spent many hours talking to Deni about her life and where she had come from. Deni in turn had sensed how much Sally needed someone and had taken her under her wing. Sally felt closer to Deni than to anyone she had ever known in her life. The kindly nurse was like a grandmother and a best girlfriend all wrapped up in a really comforting package.

"I don't want to be here anymore," Sally complained. "I am strong enough to leave."

"Now where would you go, honey?" Deni asked.

"My apartment. I feel fine."

"The doctor needs you here for a little while longer," Deni insisted. "We are obliged to make sure that you are in the right state of mind and health when you leave."

"I'm not dying," Sally insisted. "I'm not dying, and I am perfectly able to take care of myself now."

Deni said nothing, not wanting to argue either of those points.

"Just a couple of days at home," Sally begged. "I wouldn't go anywhere. I have no job, no family, and no friends. I guess I could go hang out with the Mormons. But that would be as wild as I'd get."

"Don't sell your soul for a little company," Deni scolded. "If and when you do get out, do somethin' normal—clean your apartment, dust, do some laundry. Then go somewheres you never gone before. Eat an expensive dinner in a fancy restaurant. Buy a bike, or roller skate. Jus' do somethin' different."

"Eat an expensive dinner?' Sally laughed. "Is that your idea of living?"

"There's nothin' like an overpriced meal," Deni smiled. "But that's not important. You're not goin' anywheres."

"I'll miss you when I do," Sally said honestly.

"That's dumb. I'm too fat for someone to miss," Deni said, trying to keep her emotions in check. "'Sides, like I said, you're not goin' anywhere and I'll always be right here. Of course, at the moment I'm goin' home. But I promise I'll keep after the doctors. If we can get you out of here for a while, we'll do it."

"Thanks, Deni," Sally said sincerely. "I don't know what I would have done here without you."

"There been billons and billions of people on this earth that have done jus' fine without me."

"Thank goodness I'm not one of them," Sally smiled.

Deni left the room, and Sally listened for her to check out and then counted to three hundred. Then she crawled out of bed and closed herself in the bathroom. Feeling weak and a little breathless, she changed into her street clothes that had sat folded in the closet for all this time, and then stood near the door listening for anyone in the hall. At just the right moment, Sally slipped into the hall and onto the elevator without anyone noticing.

She rode the elevator down and then stepped out into the bottom floor lobby. The place was alive with nurses and doctors and patients hurrying about. Sally could see Deni standing over near the lobby reception desk, laughing with the receptionist. Sally stood back against the wall, willing Deni to hurry and leave and wanting nothing more than to be out of this place. Sally's nerves almost did her in. She could tell that her strength was not as wonderful as she had hoped. Deni laughed again, the sound bouncing around the entire bottom floor. Sally would have given up if it had not been for the blue sky she could see through the windows. Nothing short of physical restraint was going to stop her from walking out the door.

Deni finished the conversation she was having and walked out. Sally thought about counting to three hundred again, but she only made it to fifty. She then walked quickly across the lobby and into the great outdoors.

She had no idea what to do.

It had not occurred to her to plan anything beyond this point. Luckily fate had bought into her escape. At that moment an empty cab pulled into the circular entrance of the hospital. Sally spotted the cab and waved it over. She climbed into it and shut the door. Her heart was pounding, and she felt as alive as she had while falling from the plane.

"Where to?" the cab driver asked.

"Home," Sally answered.

"That could be any number of places."

Sally gave him her address and then sat back and watched the scenery pass as the cab wandered from the business district of town and into the apartment district she was a little more familiar with. She was surprised at how moved she was simply from seeing people out on the streets and in their yards. She had been in the hospital for way too long. While in captivity, there had been very few minutes where she had not dreamt of being right where she was now.

Free.

The streets became narrower and the buildings shorter as the cab rolled through town toward Sally's apartment. The sky lightened as sprinklers exploded over green lawns and light winds played in the water.

"It's the tall brick building on the right," Sally said to the driver.

He stopped and Sally handed him some money and told him to keep the change. She then stepped out and stood on the sidewalk, staring at the front door of her apartment complex. She hadn't been here since the day of the accident. She had called her apartment manager, Steven, and he had let her know that he would keep an eye on the place for her. She wished now that she had a cat, or a bird—anything to come home to other than her dusty furniture and empty refrigerator.

Just to the east of her building, two large men were breaking up the sidewalk with jackhammers. The noise was deafening and Sally could feel the vibrations running down her body. One of the construction workers looked at Sally and smiled. He then elbowed his companion who looked up, looked at Sally, and smiled also. Sally smiled back.

Sally had always been beautiful. Even when her life was ugly, she had still looked good. During the time she was being pushed around as a child and when she was having difficulty finding her way as an adult, the one thing that she was always told by others was that she was gorgeous. This had both flattered her and bothered her. What bothered her most was that she never felt her life was as attractive as everyone claimed she was. Because her life was in ruins, she felt like a fraud because of her beauty. The two sides of her had never been in balance.

Sally looked at her reflection in the clean glass of the front door to her apartment building. Her blonde hair had not been cut or styled since she had first entered the hospital. She was amazed at how much better it looked at this length. She could see her blue eyes and was shocked by the amount of life they had in them. She was tired, but she was alive.

Sally knew that she would be okay.

Thanks to the jackhammers she could barely hear the taxi drive off. Harvey, the doorman, commented on how well she looked and how surprised he was to see her.

"I had thought . . ." he started to say and then stopped himself. He looked concerned.

"Thought what?" Sally asked curiously.

"It's nothing," he waved. "I must be mistaken."

He opened the front door, and she entered her apartment building. The bulletin board on the wall above the mailboxes was full of ads and inquiries.

"'98 desktop computer, mouse included."

"I lost 20 pounds in 40 days."

"I lost 23 pounds in 35 days."

Sally pushed the button for the elevator and waited. In a moment it was there and the doors were opening. She stepped in and pressed her button. She had thought about taking the stairs, but she was already more tired than she had anticipated.

As she stepped out of the elevator and onto her floor, she realized that the jackhammers outside had stopped and that the air was quiet. It seemed like a more fitting atmosphere for her arrival.

Sally stopped in front of her door and dropped her bag. She stood looking at the number on the door. 408. She glanced at the doorknob and then back at the number, knowing that she was about to reenter her old life. She was almost completely back to normal. Her wounds had healed and her bones had mended, and there was no way that she was going to stay in that hospital, or in this town. Sally wanted out of Laughlin. She wanted to be hundreds of miles away from any doctor who believed that her time was any shorter than that of a complete life. In spite of what the bogus tests showed, she was fine. In fact, all and all, she felt she was doing pretty well for a person who had fallen out of an airplane.

She put her key in the doorknob and tried to turn it. It wouldn't budge. She took the key out, looked at it, and then put it back in—nothing but a tight knob.

Sally looked at the number on the door again, wondering if by some chance she was standing in front of the wrong door. The elevator dinged, and she could hear someone running toward her. She turned to see Steven, the apartment manager, racing up the hall. He stopped in front of her. He was breathing hard, and his face was a deep shade of red.

"Hello, Steven," Sally said.

"Sally," he said, trying to catch his breath. "Harvey just told me you were back."

"I am," Sally said nicely. "My key's not working."

"Listen, Sally," he said with his gaze directed at the ground. "I rented your apartment out."

"What?" Sally asked, confused.

"I wasn't sure you'd be coming back."

"I told you I would be," Sally said, frustrated. "I've been sending you rent checks."

Steven switched his gaze from the floor to the wall. "I didn't cash any of the checks. I just didn't know for sure you'd be back."

"Why would you think that?" Sally looked confused. She glared at Steven. "Someone told you I wasn't going to make it," she declared angrily.

Steven directed his glance so far away that he was practically staring behind himself. "I just didn't know. Someone needed the apartment, and I decided to go with that. Your stuff is down in the basement. You didn't have a lot. I think all the furniture belonged to us."

"That's just great," Sally said, tears began to push up as she gave up trying to stay calm. "Is there another apartment?"

"You know there isn't," Steve whined. "The last thing this town has enough of is apartments."

"So I'm homeless?"

"You could sleep on my couch for a day or two," Steven said. He suddenly looked hopeful. "I mean it's not the greatest place, but I keep it pretty clean for being a bachelor pad and all. In fact, if you needed a week . . ."

Sally looked at Steven and laughed. She couldn't help it. She wasn't laughing at Steven, she was laughing at her life, and the state of it, as she stood on the doorstep of what used to be her world. In a way this seemed to make her even more certain that she was going to live. Heaven wouldn't have gotten her out of that hospital only to leave her homeless and alone.

Something good had to come from all of this.

Of course, the only good she could focus on was the small, nagging feeling that she had been spared for a reason, and she felt arrogant and pompous every time she thought of this. She had never really known God, or believed that he might have any interest in her. She couldn't think of a single thing that she had ever participated in or experienced that might make her life worth preserving.

So what if she had survived her mother's death and father's abandonment? So what if she had made it through the hard childhood that her adoptive parents had forced upon her? What good was it that she had worked her way through school? There had been millions of people who had lived lives much more complicated or valiant than she had, and yet she couldn't ignore the fact that those millions of people hadn't fallen out of a plane and lived to tell about it, thanks to an ant pile and modern technology.

She had to believe that there was a reason she was still alive. She needed to want to be alive. She needed to feel secure in living again. And she certainly didn't want to live in the big city any longer. She didn't want to feel unsure or scared. She wanted to be somewhere where people were kind and would take an interest in her. A place where she could have the kind of security that she so desperately wanted—a place like . . . like Elder Heybourne's home . . . a place like Seven Pines. . . .

Sally stopped laughing.

"Seven Pines," she whispered.

"What?" Steven asked, still not feeling too good over being laughed at.

"Does your bachelor pad have an atlas?" she asked.

"It's a couple of years old," he said, embarrassed. "The maps might be outdated."

"That's okay," Sally tried to smile. "I need to look up someplace that's been there for a while."

Sally knew there was nothing for her here. She had a few dollars in savings—at least enough to get her to Seven Pines and get her a place. There she could work at the library or at the school, or live off the kindness of others. Either way, nobody would ever find her there, and she would be out of reach of anybody wearing a stethoscope and carrying a chart.

"Steven, do you think you could help me carry a few things from the basement into my car?"

"Sure, I guess," he said. "Are you going someplace?"

"I think so."

"'Cause if you are, then I need to tell you that there were a few dings in the walls of your place, so I won't be able to give you your security deposit back."

"You gave my apartment away," Sally pointed out.

"Like I said, I didn't think you'd be coming back."

Sally sighed. "I'll just take my rent checks that you didn't cash."

"Actually, I'll need to hold on to two of them because I didn't rent your place out until a couple of months after the accident."

"You're kidding, right?"

"No, I think it was at least two months, if not three."

"He's lying," a gruff, female voice sounded from behind the door they were standing in front of.

Both Sally and Steven looked at the peephole on the door.

"He let me have this apartment soon after you left," the gruff, eavesdropping voice added.

Sally looked at Steven.

"Well, I could be wrong," he said, his face turning red again. "I'm not good with dates or numbers. It could have been a couple weeks."

"I'll take my checks, and my things," Sally tried to say calmly.

"Are you sure you don't want to take a few days and think this through?" Steven asked. "Like I said, my couch is available."

Sally smiled and shook her head.

Steven hauled up her stuff and loaded it into her car, which had been sitting there unused for all these months. It started right up. Sally took that as a sign that she was headed in the right direction and on her way to finding some real security.

CHAPTER ELEVEN

THE PARTS HAVE BEEN POSTED

Ryan pulled his car slowly onto the road. He had not been back in Wyoming since the accident. The green he had marveled at all those months ago now seemed ugly and suffocating. He didn't want to be here. He didn't want to be within a hundred miles of this place, but he knew that this was necessary. Ever since he had healed, he knew he needed to get to and touch the spot where his life had been changed forever.

His legs began to feel weak, and he could feel sweat on his forehead as he drove slowly up the one-way road. There was some reason he was here; he just couldn't figure out what it was.

"Please stop shaking," he said, looking at his legs. "Stop!" he commanded.

He pulled his car to the side of the road and turned the engine off. He offered a quick prayer, feeling that God must be incredibly tired of him begging and bugging him for strength.

Ryan had never been the kind of person to pester the heavens. His prayers were a little different than most. All through high school he had been great at keeping Heavenly Father up to date on everything he did. He would kneel each night, and after thanking Him for his blessings, Ryan would sort of report in—fill the Lord in on his day. Now, Ryan felt as though he had nothing to say. The guilt he was hauling around over all that had happened acted like a giant clamp on his pipeline to the heaven. He didn't feel like he could thank, report, or ask. All he felt he could do was pray for Todd to get better, forgiveness, and some proof that God still loved him.

Ryan leaned over and opened the glove compartment. He pulled out a picture of him and Todd taken just days before the accident. The photo had been taken at a church dance in their hometown. Ryan had one arm around Todd and the other around Katie Preck. Todd was smiling and making a peace sign behind Ryan's head. Katie Preck was looking at Ryan and smiling as if she had stars in her eyes.

Katie Preck.

Ryan and Katie had been friends for years before they discovered that they liked each other in other ways. Katie was the first to clue into the fact that love was in the air, but it took little convincing on her part to open Ryan's eyes to the romance at hand. Ryan had always just seen Katie as another blessing. He would write Katie on his mission, come home, and get married. She came from a good family, he knew her history, and she was completely devoted to him.

That was then.

After Ryan and Todd had been flown home from the accident,

Katie was one of the first people to visit. She had cried and told Ryan that she loved him and that she was so glad that he was alive.

Ryan had always thought Katie was an honest person, but within a couple of weeks she stopped coming around. She complained to others that Ryan was different now and that she didn't feel comfortable being around him. Then, right before Ryan was released from the hospital, Katie's parents had stopped by to visit Ryan and to make sure he knew where he stood with their daughter.

"She still cares for you, but she knows it's not right anymore, Ryan. You have to understand that."

"I just need to talk to her," Ryan said frantically.

"I don't think that's a good idea," Katie's mother had insisted.

"I just need to—"

"That's enough," Katie's father said kindly. "Please respect her feelings and let her be."

Ryan had laid his head back and just stared at the ceiling after Katie's parents had left the room. Ryan had not seen them or Katie since. Being abandoned by her was just one more piece of everything that was horrible about the accident. Katie was beautiful and full of life. She would smile and people from across the street would trample each other to get to her and find out what miracle was occurring to produce such a grin. When she walked into a room everyone with eyes or an esthetic compass locked onto her. She was virtuous, lovely, and of the finest of reports. She was good, and Ryan now was less than good.

Ryan pulled back onto the road and continued driving. His legs were still trembling, but he knew he could not turn around. He followed the bend in the road to where it opened up into the long, downhill straightway. In the distance he could see the place where his truck had flown off the road, into the river. He drove slowly along, feeling each inch he traveled, reliving the sudden appearance of the moose and the unavoidable collision. He parked his car just below where he and Todd had gone off. A metal guardrail had been put up on the bend, and there was little evidence that tragedy had ever touched this place.

Ryan got out and climbed down the steep slope to the water below. He stood on the bank of the deep, slow-moving river, staring at its blackness and remembering the terror of being trapped in the cab of his truck.

"I shouldn't be here," he said aloud. "I should be on a mission. I should be writing Katie. I shouldn't be here."

Ryan looked at his foot as if it were its fault. If it hadn't pushed down on the accelerator then everything would be as it should be. Todd wouldn't be in a coma, he wouldn't be drowning in guilt, and Wyoming would have one less auto accident on its records.

Ryan found a clear spot on the edge of the river and sat down in the cool grass. He stuck his hand into the water, wishing he could dive in and come out a different man.

"Please," Ryan begged, looking to the sky, "I need to know that you haven't written me off. I'll take anything. Any sign or indication that there is hope for me, or showing me what to do."

The water continued running, and the sun kept its course.

After a few minutes, Ryan climbed back up the slope and onto the shoulder of the road. His stomach hurt, and he could feel a headache coming on. He had no idea why he needed to be here. A yellow pickup truck pulled past him and stopped on the side of the road. Two men wearing reflective vests got out. One of them pulled a sign from the back of the truck and handed it to the other, then grabbed a shovel and digging bar from the bed. Neither of them seemed to even notice Ryan. They took turns, one using the digging bar and the other the shovel until they were ready to place the sign.

Ryan leaned against his car and watched them work. He found

some comfort in the distraction of their labors. They knew exactly what they were doing. That was a feeling Ryan longed to have again. After a time, the workers dropped the metal post into the hole and tamped dirt around it and then began to pile their tools back into the truck. One of them noticed Ryan and spoke.

"Beautiful day, isn't it?"

"Not bad," Ryan replied, feeling as if he were being less than honest. "Looks good," he said, pointing to the sign they had just put up.

"Yeah, it looks better than the old one," the older of the two workers said, wiping his forehead. "A car plowed through that one about eight months ago. The sign flew all the way to that rock ledge over there." He pointed to where he meant. "Some kids blew through this spot and ended up in the water."

"That's awful," Ryan said, his legs shaking again.

"You okay?" the worker said, noticing Ryan's shaking legs.

"I'm fine," Ryan replied, knowing that he was being less than honest.

The two men said good-bye and then got into their vehicle and drove off. Ryan looked at the sign. His eyes raised and focused on the words painted on it.

"Seven Pines 112 miles."

As signs go it was a pretty good one. And for the first time in months Ryan felt as if God had not yet completely written him off. As small as it was, it was an amazing feeling. It was a direction, and something inside of him seemed to feel that it could be an answer to what he had been praying for.

"Seven Pines," he whispered.

Ryan got into his car and headed the direction that fate had kept him from all those months ago. A mile down the road he began to feel guilty, so he pulled off the road and turned off his car. He closed his eyes and said a quick prayer, thanking his Heavenly

Father for what appeared to be a sign and praying yet again for Todd and for his own salvation.

He wanted to feel whole again.

As he finished his prayer he opened his eyes and looked up to see a huge moose standing right next to his car, so close that its breath created a wet pattern on his driver's side window. Ryan screamed—embarrassing himself and causing the moose to flinch.

Ryan fumbled for the ignition and quickly started his car. He remembered his uncle telling him about a moose that had been hit by a car and had stalked the vehicle for years, trying to get revenge on the tourist who had run over it. Ryan couldn't tell if this moose was the same animal he had hit, or if it was just a stronger sign from God for him to get going.

Either way, he didn't waste a second pulling back onto the road and racing out of danger and toward salvation.

CHAPTER TWELVE

GO ON, NOW

August looked out at the horizon and sighed. The sun hung in the sky like a big sticky sucker—heat dripping over the entire day. The heat didn't matter—August was free. He rubbed the back of his neck and was surprised to discover so much sweat.

It had been six weeks since August had been caught eavesdropping. And in that six weeks he had done a good deal of thinking. More than once he had doubted the secret he had overheard. He had considered that those whispering it might have known he was there and were just messing with him. Or maybe they were just talking big and trying to impress each other with lies. Or maybe it was a trick of sorts, designed to catch whoever was dumb enough to fall for it. As much as August thought or worried about it, no form of inspiration or confirmation came to him. He would have written off the idea of chasing after the information completely if it had not been for the fact that he had no other inspiration to direct him anywhere else. Sure, he could always forget it and just . . . August stood there in the prison parking lot, trying to decide what he would do now that he was free.

"I guess I could go swimming . . . see a movie . . . take a walk . . . I could see a different movie."

Freedom suddenly didn't seem as exciting as he had thought it was going to be. He had no idea what to do with his life. He had no family, no home, no future, and no sister.

No sister.

Thinking about Rachel seemed to change the scenery. He experienced the same strange, strong feeling he had felt when the two thugs had attacked him—the same feeling of invincibility that had been influencing August ever since Rachel had passed away. At first the sensation had been sporadic and fleeting, touching him like an annoying friend might tap your shoulder. But while he was in prison, the feeling had begun to linger, hanging around him like a powerful odor. He couldn't have told you what the feeling was months ago, but now he was pretty certain he had figured it out.

August was invincible.

Nothing could hurt him more than the death of his sister, and he had already survived that. Losing her had been his greatest fear, and with her gone, there was nothing left to dread. For a time following her passing, he had mourned the loss, feeling vulnerable and depressed, but as the days passed his strength had increased. He had withstood things that would have previously permanently wounded or destroyed him. He was confident that had he not possessed this new power, he would have died in the fight he had gotten into in prison.

Yes, he was invincible.

Of course, there was a catch. He had also noticed that the

feeling of power was strongest when he was focused solely on him-self. The moment he began to grow attached to or feel sympathy for someone or something around him, the feeling of invincibility would all but vanish. Caring for others left him vulnerable and weak. But when he focused only on his own needs, he felt the power.

August stood there thinking about what he had been through and enjoying the feeling as it grew.

"Most guys walk out of here a lot faster," a prison guard, com-mented, stepping up to August from behind. "Seems to me you'd like to get as far away from this place as possible."

August shrugged. "I'm not sure where to go."

"That's why we see most of you guys back in a short while," the guard said, shaking his head. "Well, try to find something con-structive to do. If not, stay out of my neighborhood."

August couldn't tell if he was joking or not, so he half smiled and half frowned.

"At least pretend like you've learned something here," the guard continued. "Just once I would like to feel like we are helping society and not just baby-sitting a bunch of misguided punks."

August smiled. He *had* learned something here. His silence and listening in jail had paid off in a number of small ways, but if what he had heard was correct, there was a possibility of his listening paying off huge.

"I've learned something," August confirmed.

"Good," the guard smiled, turning to walk away. "I just hope it's something constructive. Good-bye."

August stared at the horizon. The feeling of invincibility inside of him began to intensify as if it were a wave beginning to crest. If he kept his thoughts on himself and what he knew, he couldn't be harmed, so what was he waiting for? He had the kind of information that could make someone rich. Why not take advantage of the first real ace that life had dealt him?

After all, he was invincible.

A yellow taxi pulled up and August waved. The driver stepped out.

"You do have money, right?" the overweight driver said.

"Of course," August smiled.

"Of course nothing. The last person I picked up here stiffed me for over thirty-five bucks. Let's see it now."

August pulled out his money and handed the man a twenty-dollar bill.

"What if the fare's more?" the driver persisted.

August handed him another twenty. The driver seemed to be all right with that.

"Okay," he said, pocketing his money. "Where you headed?"

"The airport," August answered.

The driver handed August back twenty dollars. "The airport's not going to cost that much. Unless, of course, you're planning to tip me really well."

August gave him the twenty back and smiled. "To the airport."

"Yes, sir."

August climbed into the taxi and closed his door. He glanced back at the prison and wondered why he had ever questioned going after what he knew. August didn't need to worry about it being a trap; after all, he was invincible. And so what if it was a joke, or a lie? At least it was a direction. He had information, and it seemed foolish to ignore it.

The taxi driver dropped August off at the airport curb, and August made a point of walking off before the driver could say good-bye. He waited in line for over twenty minutes only to discover that he did not have enough money to fly to Montana. In fact, he didn't have enough money to fly anywhere.

"There's no cheap standby ticket or anything?" he asked the pretty desk clerk. She was wearing a dark navy uniform, and the highlights in her hair reminded August just how much he had missed being around the opposite sex. She kept her brown eyes focused on the screen in front of her as if the information there really mattered.

"Let me check again," she said, knowing full well that there was nothing available but wanting August to stand around for as long as possible. "Nothing," she frowned, looking genuinely sad.

"What about a box? Could I go as cargo?" August joked.

The girl glanced nervously around, as if August's looks were enough to make her consider such a thing. To heck with her job, or her future. She would most likely never again run into someone who looked this much like a movie star, with such nice hair, brown eyes, and straight teeth.

"I can't do that," she said sadly.

"Thanks, anyway," August smiled, picking up his bag and walking away from her.

"Next," she said dejectedly.

August stepped out of the terminal and past the departure curb. He studied a family of really short people, wearing turbans, standing near the pay phones, and a family with really lanky kids, sitting on a bus bench. He put his hand to the back of his neck, willing the feelings of invincibility to grow again. This was not a setback. Money couldn't really stop a person who has the ability to withstand anything.

"Taxi," August hollered as one pulled alongside the curb. It stopped and August got in.

The driver was wearing a cap that would make a better fashion statement in England than in the U.S. It was just a bit too jaunty looking for an American. He also had a pencil behind each ear and two books of crossword puzzles lying on the seat next to him. "Where to?" he asked in a very American accent.

"As close to Montana as ninety-seven dollars will get me," August said, knowing it was all the money he had in the world.

"That's not going to get you anywhere near Montana," the driver pointed out. "It might get you to our state line."

"That's fine, just drop me at the side of the road when I've spent around seventy."

"Whatever you say," the cabbie said, shaking his head and dropping the meter. "It all involves me staring out the window and turning this wheel."

If the cab driver was trying to be funny, August missed it completely. Not that he was slow, he was just too busy enjoying the feeling that was creeping up on him again—growing like a weed that had been well watered and now demanded light. He could feel his soul settling in for the long ride. It was almost as if inspiration were guiding him. Either way, he was free, and he was headed toward Montana and the town of Seven Pines. *He* had information. *He* had the wherewithal. *He* had the ability.

He, he, he.

PART TWO

CHAPTER THIRTEEN

SEVEN . . .

Had a person been there at the creation of this world, they might have been privy to some pretty cool viewing—when light was divided, when water was introduced, and when man and woman were planted. Those in Seven Pines, Montana, were of the opinion those occurrences paled in the light of the creation of their town. Seven Pines made Mayberry look seedy, Hometown USA, seem depressed, and gave heaven an equal. It was touched, as in the cosmos reaching out to poke something really spectacular. People rarely left, and if they were forced to go away for some reason, they complained endlessly and did all they could to find a way to get back.

Seven Pines was that inviting.

At least that's what the locals all said. And nobody had any cause not to believe them, seeing how everyone in Seven Pines was as upstanding as the straightest arrow you may have ever met. Honesty wasn't a virtue, it was a genetic trait, and character wasn't something you worked to have, it was a divine attribute that the heavens had poured liberally upon the brilliant heads of the residents of Seven Pines.

Again, according to the locals.

It was the right size, right spot, right temperature, right setting, right landscape, and it had the right history. The story goes that Seven Pines was set up shortly after this world was created. After they had worked the kinks out of the Garden of Eden, they planned the layout of Seven Pines. Of course, at that point it wasn't named Seven Pines. At first, or at least as far as anyone could remember, it was named Henton. There are those who insist that the root word of Henton is Hebrew for "God's delight," but there has never been any real proof of that aside from the fact that Chief Fellows promised and crossed his heart that it was true. And anybody who lived within the boundaries of Seven Pines knew that Chief Fellows was a man of his word.

Sometime, not long after the discovery of electricity, a man by the name of Wilton Wood moved to Henton. He did well there, building up a profitable dry goods business and marrying the eldest Stack daughter, Maria. Maria gave Wilton seven children: six fairly good-looking sons, and one beautiful daughter.

Of course, it wasn't the children's lives that are important to this story. It is actually their absence that gave Seven Pines its real beginning.

Wilton Wood was an uncommonly stubborn man, who had absolutely no feminine side whatsoever. He was more male than most men would ever be, and if you didn't believe him he would have invited you to meet him outside behind the lumber shed for a vigorous physical epiphany.

He didn't wear his heart on his sleeve, opting instead to keep it embedded down deep in his thick chest where it couldn't betray any hint of emotion or feelings. He had experienced a hard childhood, thanks to his emotionally cold father. That childhood left him with an inability to care for those around him. His favorite color was gray, his favorite food was meat, and his best feature, if absolutely forced to list one, was his ability to ignore almost anyone. His wife, Maria, was just the opposite. She was open and transparent. She would cry when the wind shifted. She responded emotionally to something as simple as the silliness of a limerick or the words of sappy song, often weeping uncontrollably.

She was the woman, he was the man, and together they produced seven different versions of themselves—six boys and one girl.

Wilton never played a role in raising the kids. In fact he rarely even made a cameo appearance. His father had been painfully distant and cruel to him, and he saw no reason why he should not continue the cycle. On a rare occasion Wilton would communicate something to Maria and she would pass his word along, but for the most part Wilton steered clear of his children. He considered the fact that he was financially supporting them, by means of providing food and putting a roof over their heads, enough of a sacrifice for any man and much more than his father had ever done for him. On special occasions Wilton had yelled at his kids, or slapped their wrists, but those demonstrations of high emotion were few and far between. So Maria had raised the children largely by herself, crying doubly for every achievement or milestone they passed in their lives and knowing the only support she would ever get from her husband was distance.

Then the oldest boy, George, had turned eighteen, and for some unexplained reason decided to leave his family and strike out on his own. He had slipped away in the middle of the night, hoping to avoid having to see his mother cry or feel his father's wrath.

A funny thing happened, however. First off, his mother didn't cry. In fact, for the first time in a long while she had felt somewhat relieved. When George left to make his own way it was as if she had finally spotted the light at the end of her personal tunnel. It was different for Wilton. In an uncharacteristic demonstration of grief he lost it. He refused to believe that his offspring would abandon him. He demanded that the law search George out and locate his abducted son. After all, there was no other explanation for family leaving family without him having given the command to do so. Yes, in Wilton's mind some thief too cowardly to show his face had stolen his firstborn in the quiet of night.

Wilton mourned. It was as if an emotional spigot inside his soul had been turned on full blast. Feelings he had suppressed and suffered at the hands of his fathers, and the emotions he should have felt at the faults of his own fathering had spewed forth with a vengeance. He mourned what he had missed. He mourned what could have been. And he mourned the fact that he now had one fewer non-salaried employee to work his dry-goods store. He dragged around town singing sad songs that made absolutely no sense. He lit candles to show his faith and in the throes of complete and utter despair he even read a book about suffering. He honestly didn't glean much from the book, except he seemed to pick up on the suggestion that for those grieving it might be a good idea to plant a tree in memory of whatever loss they may have suffered.

Wilton liked that idea. "It seemed so cleansing," he had said. Which in turn prompted his wife to gasp and say, "I don't think I've ever heard you say the word *cleansing*."

"I've become a different man," Wilton had insisted.

In actuality, however, he really wasn't that different. He still shunned his other children and played no role in what they were doing. He couldn't find it within himself to father them. It was as if, now that George was gone, he could safely love him and feel grief at the loss, but the children who remained still caused him to keep his distance. He couldn't deal with what lay directly before him. He was still the same Wilton, only now he was always crying or moaning. Which really wasn't a good look for the proprietor of an extremely successful business.

But Wilton didn't care what people thought. He went ahead and purchased a small plot of land on the northern border of town and planted a pine tree in memory of George.

Sadly, as each of his children turned eighteen they would mysteriously disappear and Wilton never really got it. He would mourn the disappearance of each one, cursing the heavens for removing his progeny, and always purchasing a plot of land somewhere on the border of town for another tree. Two weeks after his seventh child disappeared, Wilton planted his seventh tree, thus completing the ring of trees around the entire town.

No sooner had the ring been completed than the town began to experience a sort of cohesiveness and peace that they believed they had not know before. Of course there were those who pointed out that perhaps it was just that nobody was paying attention previously.

Either way, all the Wood children were gone, and Henton had evolved into Seven Pines.

🌲 🌲 🌲

"Is there anyplace cheaper?" August asked, wondering why all the hotel clerks that he had ever known looked like gentler versions of his second cousin Tim.

"There's the Inn," Clancy, the full-time bellhop, recently returned missionary, and part-time car detailer answered, "but they charge twice as much as us."

"So I guess it's safe to say that you're less expensive," August pointed out.

"Cheaper," Clancy clarified. "And we trust you with the pool towels. You have to dry off *at* the pool over there."

"I'm in," August smiled, signing his name on the registry.

"So, are you here on business, Mr. . . ." The clerk stared at August's signature. "Mr. Thatch?"

"I'll be honest with you," August said. "I'm not exactly sure why I'm here."

The clerk smiled wide, his face morphing from long and tall to wide and short as he did so.

"I know this might seem weird, but I'm Mormon. And I just got back from serving a mission to Italy. The one over in Europe," he clarified. "And forgive me if I haven't completely shaken the experience off. You don't know why you're here? Well, I think I can clear that up."

August stared at him. "You know, you're right," he finally said smiling. "That does sound weird."

August took his room key from Clancy and picked up his bags as Clancy's face returned to its tall, somber form. August smiled.

"Nice try, Clancy."

Clancy smiled back and August walked off toward the room that would be home for the next little while.

🌲 🌲 🌲

Sally entered Seven Pines with a sense of awe. It was the most beautiful place she had ever seen, in a picture or in person. The streets were clean and lined with tall, gorgeous trees and vibrant bushes. The mountains surrounding the city were gigantic, with large flat tops that broke off at the edges, sloping down gently into a wide, blue lake at the north end of the town. Homes had American flags flying from the porches, and kids were riding bikes and playing hopscotch while an ice cream man made his rounds, his vehicle playing a melodic song. Main Street was lined with nice shops and quaint buildings that showed the world what a real downtown should look like. A number of people waved at Sally as she drove slowly down the street.

"Unbelievable," Sally smiled.

At the first stop sign, a woman walking on the opposite corner hurried across the road and up to her car. She rapped excitedly on the driver's side window. Sally was concerned at first, but she finally rolled her window down, figuring that this late-sixtyish woman couldn't do her too much harm.

"Hello," the woman said loudly. "Hello."

"Hello," Sally replied cautiously.

"I didn't recognize the car," she smiled. "I got to thinking that you just might be new."

"I am," Sally smiled back. "My name's Sally."

"What a sweet name," she grinned. "I'm Candle, as in wax and wick. My papa called me that because I brought light into our family. And even though I've been told I'm sweet, please don't shorten my name by calling me Can, or Candy. It's tempting, seems to roll of the tongue a bit easier, Can, Candy," she said, rolling the words off her own tongue. "But my papa gave me the nickname Candle for a reason. It was his last . . ." Candle paused and slapped her forehead. "Listen to me going on about myself. Shameful," she smiled. "Absolutely shameful. But let me at least add that my husband, Aza, runs the bank and my only child, Ezra, is top in his class. The Fellows's oldest girl might have an overall higher GPA, but if you factor character into the equation, Ezra is number one."

Candle stuck her hand through the open car window to shake hands with Sally. Sally took it and shook back.

"Congratulations," Sally offered. "About your son," she clarified.

"Well, isn't that nice of you," Candle said sincerely. "I'm not just bragging, although I'm awful proud of both my husband and my son. Moreover, I just want to do what ever I can to make your stay here perfect. And it helps to know the wife of the banker in case you have questions, or were looking for someone to help."

"Help who?" Sally asked in confusion.

"You, of course. Coming into a new place can be awful daunting without friends. Of course, you're no longer friendless. Count Candle Hick as one of your confidantes."

"Well, maybe you can help me, then. Do you know anybody here named Heybourne?"

"I'll say I do! That's one of the foremost families in our happy little hamlet. Do you know them?"

"I met Elder Heybourne when he was on a mission. He painted such a pretty picture of this place, I decided to come see it for myself."

"Which one! All the Heybourne boys have been on missions."

"I don't know. All he ever called himself was 'Elder' Heybourne."

"When did you meet him? Recently?"

"Yes. In the last few months."

"Well, that'd be Josh. He won't be home until this winter. But I could introduce you to his family."

Sally sort of smiled.

Candle patted Sally's shoulder. "Now I don't want to smother you, I just want to spread a little kindness. Papa always said you don't drown a piece of bread; you dress it lightly with butter, and maybe add a dab of marmalade. Look at me, talking about myself again. You city folks probably don't even call it marmalade. What do you call it?"

"Jam," Sally answered.

"I see. Now that's fine, but I find it gets sticky when the

occasion comes up that you have to say you're in a jam. Just a bit confusing, that's all."

"I agree," Sally smiled, commenting on the entire conversation.

"Listen," Candle continued, "I . . ."

Candle stopped talking to look at a car coming up the road. Sally was blocking the intersection, but Candle was nowhere near finished talking. So she waved the car through. It pulled around and drove by.

"I don't recognize that face, either," Candle said with concern. "I hope nobody's let our little secret out of the bag. I don't know that we can be neighborly to any more than four or five new families a year, and you make the second I've seen this week. Although if you don't mind me saying so, you're just about the prettiest new face we've had here. The Lemon brothers are going to be very excited to see you. Very excited. No, I don't think you'll go many days here without someone on your arm." Candle smiled beatifically.

Sally was slightly concerned. Candle seemed sincere, but never in Sally's life had she met someone so instantly open and kind, or interesting for that matter. Candle was wearing a long skirt with expensive tennis shoes. She also had on a purple vest made out of felt with a little rose pin on the left lapel. She was kind looking with a wide face and thin lips. Her hair was red and turning gray. It was short on the sides but stuck up like a flame on the top. She obviously liked the concept of barrettes because she was sporting at least ten. She believed that they made her look young. She had nifty brown eyes that were protected by glasses and seemed to be yellow around the edges and perfectly black in the center. She was like the perfect mix of the grandmother we all wanted and the old lady who lived in the spooky overgrown house down the street that all the kids made up stories about.

Sally felt as if she needed to warn Candle about not being too trusting and friendly. For all Candle knew, Sally could have been a deranged psychopath who went around to small towns swindling and cheating old women with weird names out of their life's inheritance. Of course that wasn't actually the case, so Sally figured she would stay quiet for the time being.

"I don't know about a date, but I am looking for a place to stay," Sally said.

"There are some lovely apartments just south of the school," Candle clapped. "Lovely. They've just remodeled them, and I must say the kitchens make me a bit envious."

"Are they expensive?" Sally asked.

Candle bit her lip and frowned as if she had forgotten something. "Look at me, forgetting that I have a spare room. I'll put you up there until you've found something better. Can't beat the price. Free," she clarified.

"Really?" Sally asked nervously. She didn't know if she was incredibly sold on the idea of moving in with a lady that had just stopped her on the street. Sure, her son was full of character and her husband was gainfully employed, but she could have been making those things up. What if she were the town's crazy lady? What if she went around inviting anyone and everyone to come spend some time in her spare room? What if people from town discovered Sally was staying with Candle and started thinking she was crazy, too?

"Sure you can," Candle smiled.

Of course, it *was free.*

"I'll take it," Sally said, a sound of confidence creeping into her voice. It surprised her to hear it, due to the fact that it had been dormant for so long.

"Perfect. Now how about a job?" Candle inquired.

"Excuse me?"

"Do you have work yet?"

"No, actually I don't know that I'll be here that—"

"Is there work that would interest you?" Candle asked, resting her elbow on the window and leaning in closer. Sally could tell that the rose pin Candle was wearing on her lapel was scented. Another car pulled around the two of them and drove on. Candle waved at the driver.

"I like to teach," Sally replied. "In fact—"

Sally's reply was interrupted by the high-pitched shriek of an amazingly loud whistle. The cause of that pitch being Candle, who had two fingers in her mouth and was blowing hard.

"Bishop!" she yelled as the car that had just gone around them came to a stop. Its brake lights flashed on, and it backed up toward them.

Bishop Skablund, a man of about forty-five and wearing a three-piece suit, rolled down his window and tried really hard to smile at Candle and Sally. He had crooked teeth that were white enough to cause Sally to squint and a monstrous combover that originated just above his right ear. He looked like a man who wasn't sure if having a public conversation with two women in the late afternoon was appropriate.

His car was lined up right next to Sally's, with Candle standing in the road between them as if she were going to wave and start them drag racing. She didn't wave, but she did turn toward Bishop Skablund.

"Bishop," Candle said loudly. "This young woman here is looking for a job and seems to have some strength in the field of teaching. Didn't I hear that Georgia was quitting?"

"We don't know yet," he said authoritatively. "But if she does, I'd be happy to offer you her position." He focused on Sally. "I assume you have references?"

"I really didn't—"

"Well, don't worry," he interrupted. "We're not above giving people a fresh start here in Seven Pines."

Candle smiled. "I'll tell you what, Sally. God must have you on the top of his to do list because he's fixing you right up. Don't you think the Lemon brothers might be interested in her?" Candle asked Bishop Skablund.

"Careful," he warned. "I don't want another October 5th to happen. I'm still counseling those couples."

"I misjudged that situation completely," Candle said soberly.

Sally cleared her throat.

"I'll see what I can find out about Georgia," Bishop Skablund said. "I should know something about her quitting by the end of this week."

"I'm really not sure I'm—" Sally started to say.

"What a wonderful day," Candle interrupted. "Right on top of God's to do list."

Bishop Skablund pulled away, and Candle waved as if he were her only son and he was heading off to war.

"I don't know what to say," Sally said.

"About what, sweetheart?"

"About staying with you, and him giving me a job?"

"Bishop doesn't give anything," Candle said seriously. "But I've never known a man who offers more. In fact—"

Candle may well have gone on speaking for days if it had not been for the interruption. In fact, she might have still been talking months from then if the town hadn't been suddenly rocked by a tremendous explosion.

Candle was knocked off her feet, falling to the ground and landing on her skinny behind. Sally grabbed the steering wheel tightly as if that would help settle things down. She looked at Candle as she was laid out on the asphalt. The air quieted as a plume of dark smoke began to rise in the distance.

108

"What was that?" Sally gasped. People were beginning to spill out of the buildings into the streets, voices raised in concern and curiosity, everyone looking toward where the noise had come from.

"That's George!" Candle hollered.

"George!" Blaine Lemon, a full-time dentist and part-time artist with a yellow hat, yelled, as everyone began to panic and run toward the black smoke that was now touching the highest clouds.

"Who's George?" Sally asked as Candle got up from the ground and turned to run. Sally got no reply. Candle shot off like a bottle rocket screaming into the distance.

Sally stared at everyone around her as they ran toward something involving somebody named George. She began moving forward in her car, careful not to hit any of the people in the street in front of her. After almost knocking down her third person, Sally pulled over and climbed out. She then proceeded to run with everyone else. It occurred to her that this was all quite ridiculous. For all she knew, they were running toward the edge of the earth and any moment the ground would drop out from under her. She had remembered reading stories about how Native Americans used to scare herds of buffalo over the edge of a high cliff to kill them for food and leather. Now, as she looked around and listened to the sound of her feet hitting the earth, she felt a kinship to those buffalo of old.

Sally had felt so calm and encouraged about Seven Pines, but now the entire town seemed to be identical to a rabid mall crowd rushing to be the first to get a look at the newly marked down clearance items.

She wondered how her life had come to this.

Chief Fellows, a full-time cop and part-time fiddle player, almost ran Sally down as he raced in the direction of the smoke. "George!" he hollered.

Sally wasn't sure, but she had a feeling that George was one incredibly significant person.

🌲 🌲 🌲

Ryan had only been in town five minutes when he heard and felt the explosion. It was an awesome sound that sadly seemed to fit right into the mess of noise his mind had been emitting lately. He had just stepped out of his car when the blast knocked him off his feet and unto the sidewalk. Kendle Heybourne, a woman in a baggy sweater and carrying a small child, teetered in front of him. Kendle's sweater seemed to roll and bunch as the ground rocked. She looked like a balloon that couldn't decide if it wanted to deflate or expand. Her smallest child, Evan, eventually lost his balance and fell to the ground, rolling slowly into the doorway of the café Ryan had just parked in front of.

Ryan grasped for ground as he tried to stand up. His feet slipped on the asphalt, and it took him two tries to right himself. He looked around, embarrassed and trying to make some sense of what had just happened. Kendle grabbed Evan and, without even assessing whether he was all right or not, she took his hand and came running toward Ryan. Ryan thought at first that she was going to scream hysterically about her kid being hurt or that she was going to be crying about the end of the world, but he was way off on both accounts.

"Are you okay?" she asked him. "Did you hurt yourself?"

"Excuse me?" Ryan replied in disbelief. Her concern for him seemed so out of place. After all, the whole town was falling apart. Plus, this woman's child had just been hurt, and here she had run over to help the big man who had tripped.

"I'm fine," Ryan said defensively. "What happened?"

"I don't know," she answered sincerely, "but it's coming from George."

Ryan stepped out into the stream of people hurrying toward the rising smoke. He ran with the crowd to a smoking hole in the ground and stood there in awe, wondering why in the world he had been prompted to come to such a place. He kept looking around for hidden movie cameras, feeling as if the entire setup was too odd to be real.

Mark Lemon, the full-time auto mechanic and part-time stamp collector, was standing nearest the hole. "What do we do?" he hollered, his tiny head almost engulfed in the size of his gaping mouth.

"Where's George?" Mark's younger brother Blaine yelled.

"Gone," Aza Hicks exclaimed sadly. "Gone. Of course I can see bits and pieces of him still flying and laying about," he pointed.

People actually winced as if the bark and pulp of a demolished tree were much more gruesome than they actually were. Small flecks of George drifted down, landing in people's hair and on their shoulders. Evan Heybourne stood near his mother, sticking his tongue out and trying to catch some debris on the end of it.

"This can't be good," Candle exclaimed. "We need that tree."

"Well, of course it's not good," Aza pointed out. "I don't know what it is, but I feel pretty certain that it's not good."

Candle glared at Aza.

"I mean, of course it's not good, Honey," he corrected.

"The ring has been broken," Ezra Hicks, their top-of-his-class son, warned.

Everybody pretty much ignored Ezra's comment. Ezra had become hooked on J.R.R. Tolkien's books a few years back and now everything he said anymore referenced or quoted the writings. Two years before he had begun sporting a cloak and trying to get people to call him Master Ezra. So far the request had not been respect-fully accommodated.

"No ring has been broken, Ezra," Aza chided, once again embarrassed by his son. "Take that cape off."

"It's a cloak."

"It looks like a cape to me," Aza said.

Ezra looked at his father, whipped the cloak in front of himself, and then did some sort of wizardish leap away. It might have been impressive if he hadn't tripped over his cloak length and stumbled into Jane Welch. Jane pushed him away, and he fell back behind some trees and out of view.

"Do you think it will blow again?" Clancy the hotel clerk asked the crowd as he stood staring at the hole George had left.

"It isn't a volcano," Aza pointed out. "Somebody's blown up George."

The entire gathering gasped, everybody besides Ryan that is. Candle spotted Ryan's un-slacked jaw from across the crowd and moved over quickly to get near him.

"Now there's a face I don't know," she said, tugging on his arm politely.

Ryan turned to look at her.

"What a day to visit us," Candle smiled.

"Excuse me," Ryan replied, now feeling completely confident that he had followed the wrong prompting by coming here.

"I'm not sure we've met," Candle said holding out her hand. "The name's Candle, as in wax and wick."

Ryan didn't say anything.

"Are you all right?" Candle asked sincerely.

A number of other people began to listen in on the conversation, curious about the new face as well.

"Don't worry," Kendle Heybourne hollered. "I talked to him earlier; he's okay."

With Kendle's endorsement, everyone smiled at Ryan, and those standing right next to him even patted him on the shoulders.

A really old man with a cane poked him affectionately in the calf with the end of it.

"So, are you staying for a while?" Candle asked, stepping right up to him and practically standing under the overhang of his nose.

Ryan stepped back and cleared his throat. The attention wasn't exactly putting him at ease.

"A short while maybe."

"Listen," Candle smiled. "I know we have a lot going on here, but in a while this smoke will clear, and Seven Pines will go back to being the normal town it always has been—clean lakes and straight living. So, that being the case, I was wondering if you could do me a favor?"

Ryan looked around at everyone, again wondering if he hadn't stepped into some elaborate joke being played on him. Everyone cast their glances from Ryan, back to the hole. Candle was the only one to keep her attention focused on him.

"Do your loved ones call you something?" she asked.

"Ryan."

"What a whimsical name. You should mention that one to my son, Ezra," Candle said, pointing toward Ezra. "He's been searching for a new name for quite some time. Anyhow, back to my favor. You see, there's this new young woman in town, and I'm worried that she might have a difficult time adjusting. She's going to be rooming at my place, but I'm old and boring. I haven't bought a new piece of clothing in seven years. Aza gave me this vest, but that doesn't count, does it? So, since you're young, do you think you could maybe show her around? You know, take her to the park, or the theater, or to dinner. There are dozens of great restaurants here in town. Of course, don't go to the Kettle, unless you've got one strong constitution. Pete says he's cleaned the place up, but Justin was sick for a week after his last visit. What do you say?" Candle looked around and then discreetly handed Ryan a five-dollar bill. "This ought to help offset the costs."

"Thanks," Ryan replied, trying to hand her back the money. "But that sounds like a job for some other guy, a guy who actually lives here. I just pulled into town. I don't even know my way around."

"Oh, what's to know?" Candle waved. "We've got four big streets, twelve smaller ones, and that footpath that cuts behind the courthouse. Now, there she is, right over there," Candle pointed, completely ignoring Ryan's concerns.

"I appreciate you thinking . . ." Ryan stopped talking the moment his vision came in contact with Sally. There was no need to keep talking. Sally was beautiful. She was different in the sense that the sun is no ordinary star. Her blonde hair was pulled back, and her eyes seemed alive and thoughtful, even through the light smoke that still lingered. She had a kind of vulnerability about her that made Ryan want to run over to her and ask how he could help.

"I don't know a terribly lot about her," Candle said, filling the silence. "But I like they way she talks. Has a nice voice, not too lilty, and my goodness, if she doesn't look lovely in that red shirt. I always wanted to pull red off, but being an autumn I just can't do it. Autumn," Candle spat, "what kind of clothing options does that offer a person? Oh, well, it's not like I've bought a new piece of clothing in seven years."

"That's her?" Ryan gaped in amazement.

"Yes. That's Sally," Candle said as if she were a proud mother. "Poor thing, she doesn't know a soul here. Drove into town looking like one of the Heybourne's rabbits when Evan is after them. She's here for something," Candle said reflectively. "I just can't put my finger on it."

"We're all here for something," Ryan said, still gazing at Sally.

"So true," Candle nodded. "That would make a nice bumper sticker or refrigerator magnet. 'We're all here for something.'"

As Candle talked and Ryan gawked, people began to get down on their knees and stare into the tree hole. There was no fire or sign of heat. It was as if the tree had just burst. There were a few people pointing and covering their mouths, and Evan got so close to the hole that he fell in. His mother jumped in after him and his father followed her. All three of them were wedged down in there so tightly that a group of men had to form a chain and yank them out.

Unfortunately, Evan had had so much fun that as soon as he was out he jumped from his mother's arms and ran back to the hole. This time neither of his parents followed him.

There were those who seemed dazed about what had transpired, but most folks were acting as if this were no big deal. So a tree had spontaneously exploded. What does that have to do with the taste of sugar in Burley, Idaho? The idea that the ring of trees played any real part in making Seven Pines special was silly. That was just a myth, a tired old belief. So they lost one. They were capable people that could take care of their own fates. And Ryan, although still thoroughly confused, felt as if for the first time in months he could see what might be, if magnified and accentuated, a proverbial light at the end of the tunnel. He could still feel his soul decaying, but for some reason a simple glimpse of Sally had given him something to wrap his thoughts around—something besides what he had done to Todd and himself. It was as if God were beginning to redeem the dead. As if He were beginning to move things into place again.

Ryan put thoughts of Todd and his hurt aside to focus on the fact that from where he now stood he could see a beautiful girl, a quaint town, and a couple of potential possibilities.

CHAPTER FOURTEEN

SIX . . .

From his birth, George Wood had always been a real handful for his mother, Maria, and his father, Wilton. Some speculated that one of the reasons Wilton had never even begun to care for or appreciate his children was because George had gotten things off to such a bad start for the couple. George had been born angry, an angry child that grew into a hot-headed youth. He had a low threshold of frustration and a fiery temper that often exploded. One of his problems was the pressure that was put upon him as the oldest child by his overbearing mother and his distant father. With Wilton never playing a role in the family, George was made to feel as though he had to step up and assume the position. He constantly took on too much responsibility and in turn was always upset and close to a feverish boil. So when he slipped away on his

SIX . . .

eighteenth birthday and disappeared, a number of locals were actually relieved. They felt as though they had averted a tragedy or sidestepped a possible town massacre.

🌲 🌲 🌲

The morning after George was blown apart was warm, unseasonably warm. The cool, mild days that had been lingering all summer seemed to have packed up and migrated north. The local paper, *The Pines Monitor,* ran four stories about the destruction of George. One article covered the historical angle. It had a photo of the real George, a photo of his father, Wilton Wood, and two columns of simple facts—big tree, big explosion, big deal. Then there was an article on those who had not been able to sleep due to the absence of the seventh tree and who were nervous about losing the protection it had supposedly provided the town. This story also included a report detailing the scant evidence the police had found at the scene and speculating about what they thought might have happened.

In a third article, Rigby Fellows, the police chief, droned on and on in print about how the explosives had been well-crafted and ingeniously set. How if he hadn't known better he would have sworn it was the work of one of his own men, or of Tony the hermit, who lived on the lake and who liked to fish with hand grenades. Chief Fellows was careful to say that he had personally checked out the alibis of all his men *and* questioned Tony. "According to all of them," the paper quoted the chief, "they didn't do it."

The fourth newspaper article was written by the town's conspiracy expert, the aforementioned Tony the hermit. He claimed that at exactly the same moment George had exploded, the seventh rock from the north, not counting the first, and discounting the

117

third, at Stonehenge had quivered and threatened to fall. How Tony might have known this the article didn't say.

"All for nothing," August said to himself, commenting on the senseless destruction of the vandalized tree.

August set his newspaper aside and took another bite of his breakfast. The café he was sitting in, one of Seven Pines' many, was amazing. He had never been in an eating establishment (or any establishment for that matter) that was cleaner. And the service was equally impressive. He had dropped a fork on the floor for fun, and less than two seconds later Jane Welch had picked it up and placed a new one to the right of his plate.

"Careful," Jane flirted, handing him a fresh napkin to go with the clean fork.

Jane was so attractive that August temporarily forgot he wasn't too bad-looking himself, or that he had never really met anybody out of his league before. She looked terrific in her starched waitress uniform, but August couldn't help thinking that she would have looked terrific in anything she might have worn. Her eyes, which were now locked onto his, were a fascinating shade of green, and her smile was dazzling. Reminding himself that he had not come to Seven Pines for romance, August was the first to look away.

"I have a feeling that if I sneezed you guys would shut the place down and re-sterilize everything," he joked with her.

"You're right. Last week a guy lost an eyelash while wiping his face, and Chief Fellows sent twelve of his best men over here to secure the scene until we could find the missing lash."

"Wow."

Jane smiled again, thinking the exact same thing.

At a booth on the other side of the café, Ryan sat thinking about things of his own. While Jane was flirting with August and the rest of the town was talking about George and its demise, all Ryan could do was focus on the image of Sally. He kept thinking that meeting her was exactly what he needed. And now, as he sat awaiting her arrival, he could hardly contain himself. The cold, dark guilt over what he had done to Todd was still inside of him, but thinking about Sally had somehow taken away some of the pain. He lifted the baseball cap from his head and ran his fingers through his brown hair for the hundredth time, then brushed his napkin across his lips just to make sure that he would be as presentable as possible.

Sally entered the café cautiously, like Goldilocks opening the Three Bears' door, and looked around. Ryan waved to her, and she smiled and made her way to where he was sitting. He stood up, nervous, feeling a little light-headed, even breathless, wanting to make a good impression. Then it hit him—a rush of guilt that rose from his toes and slammed into his stomach. He tried to tell himself that it was only nerves—butterflies—that Sally was beautiful and that any guy would have to be legally dead not to be anxious in her presence. But that wasn't it. It was pure guilt. While he was here, excited to be alive and about to become acquainted with a fantastic girl, Todd lay in a hospital bed, unconscious. He wiped his lips again and pleaded with heaven to calm him.

Sally extended her hand.

"Ryan, right?"

Ryan nodded. "Sally?" he asked, as if he had not said her name over two hundred times since he first saw her.

She slipped into the booth across from Ryan.

"I guess we have Candle to thank for this," Ryan smiled, his anxiety calming some.

"She's great." Sally's blue eyes shined.

"Yeah."

Across the room, August stood up and fished a ten-dollar bill out of his wallet. He laid it on the table, and as he did so, glanced across the diner to where Sally and Ryan were having an animated conversation. He got his first real look at Sally.

All right, it's like this: Sally wasn't the incredible new car model that the dealer puts out front on the spinning turntable with flashing lights and a sign that says: "Picture yourself behind the wheel of this beauty." She was more like the model you personally discover parked back behind all the overstock and you wonder how in the world she could have been overlooked—a find you instantly feel compelled to wrap your arms around and claim before anyone else discovers her. Not that she would be a possession or a trophy, or that she was something to own. She was more like something you sense would make you complete. She was a happy pill that would never wear off, the comic strip that only you get, an old man with a ten million dollar check and a microphone knocking on your door, or a fountain of cool water bubbling up in a parched desert.

And she was gorgeous.

August knew he was staring, but he couldn't help himself. The feeling of invincibility that he had been enjoying was subsiding, and he reminded himself of why he'd come to Seven Pines and how he couldn't afford to let any attachment get in the way of what he had come to do. He took another look at Sally and shook her off, then walked out of the café and into the warm day.

"Do you know him?" Ryan asked Sally.

"Who?" she asked.

"That guy who just walked out. He was staring at you."

"I've never seen him before," Sally replied, trying to act as though August hadn't fazed her in the least.

All right, it's like this: August was the incredible new car model that the dealer puts on the spinning turntable up front with the flashing lights and a sign that says: "Picture yourself behind the wheel of this beauty." A car that would keep a buyer from looking around on the back lot or even caring that there might be other options worth checking out. August had that effect on women. They all wanted to wrap their arms around him and fight off anybody who might have similar ideas. He was something to own, a possession, a trophy to be displayed. He was a happy pill that would never wear off, a comic strip so clear that you didn't have to figure it out, an Adonis standing on your porch with flowers and a ten million dollar check preparing to knock, and a trunk full of cash while Nordstrom is running a sale.

And he was handsome.

And he was at least two inches taller than Ryan.

"Are you okay?" Ryan asked.

"I'm fine," Sally answered.

Ryan glanced at Sally's hands. She was using a dinner knife to saw through a packet of Sweet and Low. Sally looked at the mess she had made. She was as surprised at what she was doing as Ryan was.

"It's a habit I have," she lied.

Ryan was willing to overlook far more than that. In fact, even with all of the pain and self-loathing he was carrying around, he could feel that there might be room for someone like Sally in his life. Of course, there was no way that anything could come of Sally and him if he didn't begin to be the kind of person he knew he was supposed to be. The kind of person he felt had gotten lost in the accident. He understood that he couldn't simply throw a switch and change, but he had a hopeful feeling that change was possible. He had come to Seven Pines to find himself, and he knew all too well that the only way that could really happen was if he could shed what he had become.

"Do you want to order something?" Ryan asked Sally.

"I've never seen him before," Sally said, taking a drink of water.

"I believe you," Ryan said slowly, wondering why she was still stuck on the tall guy with the strong face and big hands. "Listen, why don't—"

The door to the diner burst open, and Gus, the slight pharmacist who was married to Chief Fellows's second daughter, and who was an expert horticulturist in his spare time, skidded into the entrance.

"Peter's down!"

Two people dropped their forks, and before the entire group could finish gasping, Jane had delivered them new ones.

"How?" one of the patrons asked.

"He was dug up last night," Gus explained. "Somebody's after our trees."

Two more forks went down.

This time Jane didn't react.

Peter was the most secluded of the seven trees. He had been planted on a piece of earth just to the west of town, up on the steepest part of Fairy Hill.

"We should go to him," Agnes Finch spoke up, her mouth full of Belgian waffle.

"Chief Fellows has the place roped off," Gus explained. "He's not letting anyone near this one."

Everyone began to whisper and talk. Had a poll been taken, the results might have come out something like this:

Booth nine thought it was teenagers who had done it.

Booth eight thought it was foreigners.

Booth seven figured it was someone with ties to that one group that hates trees, but they couldn't remember what the group was named.

Booth six didn't want to get involved.

Booth five was more concerned about their eggs tasting funny.

Seated at the counter, Tony the hermit was sticking to his Stonehenge connection and wondering if anyone smelled gas.

Ryan and Sally didn't know what to think. The small town seemed to hold promise for both of them, but the fascination with and commotion over the trees was a bit disconcerting.

"Does this seem odd to you?" Ryan asked.

"Extremely."

Ryan smiled—he and Sally had something in common.

CHAPTER FIFTEEN

FIVE . . .

When Peter slipped away all those years before, most people didn't even notice. He had spent his life in the shadow of his older brother, George, while trying to avoid the shadow of his father. He didn't like to be asked questions or singled out. He couldn't take his mother's sadness or his father's coldness, so he stayed in the background as much as he could. Consequently, he never stood out or was noticed by anyone. He was skinny and pale and would do what others told him or do nothing at all. He had no backbone or strength and let life blow him where it may—a real pushover. When he turned eighteen and left, the few who did notice his absence were not surprised. Everyone just figured that he was simply imitating what he had seen his big brother George once do.

▲   ▲   ▲

August had to admit that the mornings were phenomenal in Seven, make that Five, Pines. The daily sunrise over the nearby, forested mountains was spectacular, drenching the little town in light and warming the pine-scented air. Tucked away in a shallow mountain valley, the village boasted a quaint main street and cozy surrounding neighborhoods and was completely encircled by an encroaching forest of old, stately evergreen trees.

In spite of the little town's pleasant location, friendly people, and inviting appearance, August still wondered if he might not be wasting his time there. Yes, he had a little information he needed to research, but he didn't want to become too attached to the community. If what he was hoping to find turned out not to be there, he would need to move on. What worried him also was that the feeling of invincibility that he had come to enjoy so much in prison seemed connected to his focus. If he concentrated only on *his* needs and desires, he felt the power. But whenever he began to take an interest in others, he felt vulnerable and weak. He would have to take care not to get too entangled.

But for the moment he was here, and there were a few things that fascinated him enough to keep him grounded for a while. The two trees that had been destroyed interested him, to say nothing of the spot of light he had caught sight of the day before in the café. August was typically slow at love, but something about Sally made him want to pick up the pace. She was gorgeous, no doubt about it, but there was something else about her. He sensed that Sally would be a good thing for him—that she could help make him a better person than he was. This fascinated August because it involved him.

It had taken him only a couple of inquiries to discover Sally's name. It seemed to be common knowledge in town that Sally was staying with Candle Hick.

Luckily Candle's whereabouts were fairly well-known. She was said to be a Mormon and something called "The Ward Librarian"— an assignment she reportedly took very seriously. August's inform-ant had explained that a Mormon ward librarian normally shows up a few minutes before church and passes out a couple of erasers and pieces of chalk and copies of worn scriptures, begrudgingly makes a few photocopies, and then locks up. Candle, however, took a broader view of her responsibility. She kept the ward library open nine to four, seven days a week, taking a break only on Wednesday afternoons for her book club and from eleven to twelve Tuesdays and Thursdays when she volunteered to help the Meals on Wheels program. Candle figured that the library needed to be open on the off-chance that somebody would want to prepare their Sunday lesson earlier than Sunday morning. She had been man-ning the library for over a year now, and in that time only two people had actually stopped by on a weekday—one to borrow some chalk to draw a hopscotch course out on the sidewalk, and the other the bishop who had come by to try and convince her that she was going way too far beyond the call of duty.

"Have you ever sat though one of Scott H.'s lessons?" she had asked the bishop, abbreviating the name so that she wouldn't be giving the identity of the individual away.

Of course, the bishop, being the bishop, had a pretty good idea who she was talking about. And having sat in on some of those lessons, it was not as if he could argue the point she was making.

"Maybe, just maybe, someday Scott H. might wake up," Candle said passionately, her face glowing with the vision of her assign-ment. "He might wake up and discover that preparing a lesson involves more than locating your manual. And just maybe it will be a Tuesday afternoon around three when the Spirit hits him. And, Bishop, when that happens, I will be right here."

Nobody could fault her dedication, especially August, seeing how her going the extra mile made it easy for him to find her.

Candle was both shocked and delighted to have someone come into the small library. She jumped up off the stool she had been occupying and smiled. She had a thick pile of papers in one hand and a stapler in the other. Her graying red hair looked taller than it usually did due to the fact that the ceiling fan in the library was running in reverse and actually creating a pull that was now lifting her hair higher.

"Good morning," she sang out, her hands continuing to staple and sort as she spoke. "Now I'm pretty certain that I haven't bumped into you in these halls. "

"I'm not Mormon," August admitted.

"Listen to you," Candle smiled. "This isn't a confessional. We can't all be Mormons . . . yet."

August laughed politely, looking around the small room and wondering how on earth a person could fill their days sitting here when there was little or no possibility of anyone stopping by. It was obvious that Candle spent a lot of time organizing because everything looked properly placed and cleaned. There was a long counter that ran across one wall and a gigantic copy machine sitting about two feet behind the counter, in the middle of the room. Each of the other three walls had built-in shelves that held scriptures and visual aids and a plethora of videos. Sitting on the counter near Candle was a paper cutter that had a magic marker warning scribbled across the surface of it. The message read: "Be careful, or little fingers will become even littler."

Next to the paper cutter there was a clipboard with a sign-up sheet on it, with a yellow pencil attached to the clipboard by a string and duct tape.

"So this is a Mormon library," August said, trying to sound intrigued.

"A material center," Candle corrected. "Library is just a nickname that some of our enemies have given it. Like Mormon."

August didn't have the faintest idea what she was talking about. "And you stay open all week?"

"Except on Wednesday afternoons, and on Tuesdays and Thursdays, between eleven and noon."

"That's extremely dedicated."

"We all do our part," she said modestly, stapling a thick stack of paper. The staple couldn't make it through, and it jammed the stapler up. Candle popped it open, fiddled with the staples, and then continued. "Now, what would bring a nice-looking non-Mormon into a well-organized material center in the middle of the week?"

"Actually, I—"

"Don't tell me. I want to guess. But before I do, could you tell me what faith you practice now? If you're one of those people that just believes in darkness after this life, or that we began with a burst, then that would radically change the way I guess."

"Bang," August corrected. "They believe we started with a bang."

"That makes it even sillier."

"Either way," August smiled, "I believe in more than black. I'm Christian."

"So far, so good," Candle encouraged. "How about your parents?"

"That's not important," August said quickly, sounding more defensive than he intended. "What I mean is, they have always been confused about religion. I guess they passed on more of that confusion to me than I would like to admit, but I think I'm headed in the right direction."

"Well, I'm pleased that direction brought you here. And you came to Seven Pines because . . . ?" as Candle asked, she subtly directed August to take a seat on one of the chairs in front of the counter. August had no desire to spend the day shooting the breeze, but he also wanted to know whatever Candle could tell him about Sally. He was willing to invest a little time, figuring that someone as talkative as Candle would eventually get around to her attractive house guest.

"To be honest, I can't really tell you why I'm here. It was the next stop," he explained.

"On your way to where?"

"North," August shrugged, pushing his brown hair up off his forehead.

"You know," Candle said cautiously, "we normally don't get too many visitors here. We're not on any main routes. We're out of the way to almost anywhere important. And the locals hate to talk us up too much for fear of growing too big. So normally we might get a couple of new families every year. Maybe someone will decide to start a fishing store or sewing shop. But we've never really seen a burst . . . or a bang, in our population like we have in the last few days. There's that attractive woman from Nevada. Sally, I think her name is."

"Oh, really," August tried to butt in. "And who is she—"

"And then there is that sad boy. Handsome, but sad," Candle went on. "Ryan is his name. I can't say that he and I have had any heart-to-heart discussions, but I can see the hurt in him even when I don't have my eyes on."

Candle took off her glasses to point out what she meant by her last line.

"So let me get this straight," August attempted. "A hurt boy named Ryan . . . and who was the other?"

It didn't work. Candle just kept on going. "Then, as if two new faces isn't talk enough, here comes what has got to be about the best looking set of shoulders God ever assembled, walking right into my well-organized material center."

Candle smiled in such a sincere way that the shoulders remark didn't seem as creepy as it could have been. She definitely knew how to put people at ease. Her inflections and glances were so familiar sounding and looking that anyone careless enough to wander into a conversation with her couldn't help but give up a number of minutes of their time, and all the while feeling right at home.

"I'm guessing you're the same August that Jane has been talking about," she added.

"The waitress?"

Candle nodded and then whistled. "Three young strangers in the space of a couple days. Unbelievable."

"I could leave," August joked.

"Now that's exactly what we don't want," Candle insisted. "This is the kind of town that looks for ways to keep those we love around us."

August shifted uncomfortably. Talk of loved ones and staying and towns and Sally and Jane and normal life and shoulders caused the feeling of invincibility inside him to wane. He felt no power in joining the community. As he thought about that, his face betrayed him.

"I said something that's bothering you?" Candle asked.

"No," August waved. "It's nothing.

"Listen, August," she said, setting her smile aside to look as motherly as her age suggested, "I like this town. I like the fact that most folks would rather give up wearing gloves in winter than move out."

August looked at his hands and then stared at her, wondering if she had more to say. She stapled something and then looked up.

"I want you to be a positive to this town," she continued. "I don't care if you're Mormon, or that other religion. I just want things to be as good if not better for all of us when you and your friends leave."

"I don't know any of the others who have come," he tried again.

"You will. People your age don't just go about their business without exploring their possibilities."

"Do you talk to everybody you know like this?" August asked.

"Only the ones with nice shoulders. Now hand me those papers, and I'll fill you in on Sally."

August did just that.

"She's a wonderful girl," Candle admitted. "Wonderful. But I don't want you to get too excited over her just yet."

"Because . . . ?" His brown eyes widened.

"That third stranger I was telling you about earlier, Ryan, I think he has ideas about her as well."

"I don't mind a little competition," August smiled. "Actually, I guess that's not completely true. It would be easier without him."

"I think the thing that you need to decide is if this is more than just the next stop for you. Maybe you shouldn't worry yourself about any one person here if you're just going to blow out in a short while anyway."

"Are you always this straightforward?"

"Can't be what I'm not."

August looked at Candle and smiled. She looked old, but her flower barrettes were a good reminder of how young her soul wanted to be. He thought that even though she was a character, there were a lot of things that she wasn't. She wasn't hip in the traditional sense. She wasn't lovely in the worldly sense. She wasn't funny in the common sense. But she was making a pretty honest point. If he really got to know Sally then he might just be setting himself up to have to leave her someday. Those things in his life that had brought him to this moment and created the feelings in him were for a purpose, and he knew that. His strength came from being unattached and focused on just himself. He could only feel unbeatable when he thought of his sister and how he had survived her death. He had made it through that, and there was not anything that could hurt him further as long as he concentrated on himself. But somehow thoughts of Sally seemed more selfish than genuine. She was interesting and appeared like a small star that you knew could shine brighter.

"So will you help me with Sally?" he finally asked.

"Asking a woman if she wants to get involved in pushing two people together is like wondering whether a hot sweaty pig wants to wallow in cool mud."

"So, is that a yes?"

"It is a warm day," Candle smiled.

An hour later August left the material center. He and Candle had worked up a plan of sorts. There wasn't much to it; it just involved getting him and Sally and Ryan in a room alone together tomorrow during the Mormon church service. As far he could tell, it just might sort of work. Of course, it depended a little bit on Candle's ability to talk Sally into sitting in a classroom and being taught things about August. But August felt pretty confident that Candle could talk anyone into just about anything.

On another note, two hours later, Ralph, the third tree, and the only one that could be clearly seen in the skyline of Seven Pines, was plowed into by a beat-up old car. The driver had run off before anyone could get a look at him or her. The car had uprooted Ralph and knocked it two feet out of the ground. Both the tree and the car were totaled.

Chief Fellows ran a check on the car and found that it belonged to a man named Ray Smoother in Nephi, Utah. He tried to locate Ray, but he was nowhere to be found. His parents in Utah told the chief the last time they had seen him was weeks before, when he had taken off to find a new life for himself. The neighbors across the street from where Ray used to live had told Chief Fellows over the phone that Ray had always been a nice, quiet kid and had never shown any hostility toward trees.

Regardless of reason or Ray, Ralph was down.

CHAPTER SIXTEEN

FOUR . . .

Ralph had been born the smallest of the Wilton Wood children—four pounds, seven ounces. His father, of course, had not been there at the birth, but Maria had taken him and fed him pure cream for the first eight months of his life. The cream made him fat and slow. She tried to wean him, but it is quite the task to talk a cream-fed eight-month-old into going for rice paste and milk when he has been feasting on the fatted calf. Ralph cried and cried and cried. In turn, Wilton forbade Maria to stay in the house as long as the child still had the ability to use his lungs. Wilton, after all, was a shop owner with a successful business that required he always be alert and at his best.

So Maria had taken George, Peter, and Ralph and moved into the shed behind their home. There she could let Ralph cry all he wanted without Wilton losing a moment's sleep or potential alertness.

Ralph cried for three months, and by the time he finally settled down, Maria was content living in the shed. She had fixed the place up so nicely that there really was no reason to move back into the main house. So except for making Wilton breakfast, lunch, and dinner and cleaning, she spent most of her time in the shed, crying and taking care of her children, who were coming at the rate of at least one per year.

When Ralph turned seven, he became ill and spent an entire winter in bed. After that, he never really returned to his full health. He got slightly better, but he never was well. He would often just stand there, like a deer caught in the headlights, waiting for life to run him over. When he turned eighteen and slipped away from the town into a life of his own, his father worried more about him than the other two who had gone before him. Because of this, Wilton planted Ralph's memorial tree in an area south of town where it could be viewed easily and thus taken care of better. It sort of worked. It was easily seen, but all the care in the world couldn't keep that tree healthy. Ralph struggled to simply grow. His roots would curl, his needles were brown, and his bark was always scabby and green. Even after several years, Ralph was so fragile that it looked as though it might fall over at any moment. To protect it more fully, the city fathers had built a small fence around the sickly tree.

🌲 🌲 🌲

The fence around Ralph had worked for a number of years, but now, thanks to someone with no compassion for the sick, Ralph had been knocked out of the ground and left to die near the very spot he had resided all these years.

The residents of Seven Pines were beginning to wonder if something wasn't up. Even those who had little or no known affinity for the trees were worried that they were dealing with some kind of mass murderer. Chief Rigby Fellows went to great lengths to point out that trees were not actually people, and that despite what everyone wanted, they could not call these senseless acts of violence homicides.

Ezra Hick made a special suit out of aluminum foil so as to ward off any radiation that the dead trees might possibly be emitting. He then spent the afternoon closely inspecting the hole that Ralph's absence had created. He had some trouble with his cape getting caught on the ripped-out roots that still jutted out of the ground, but that was nothing compared to the wicked sunburn he got on the underside of his chin and around his neck from the sun reflecting off his tin-foil suit. His father claimed that he had never seen a brighter shade of red. Ezra, making the best of an odd situation, pointed out that the burn made a "ring" around his neck and wasn't that frighteningly eerie?

Yes.

Ezra Hicks was a nice seventeen-year-old kid. That's not to say he wasn't different, or unusual, but he was ultimately nice. Candle had given birth to him when she was forty-seven. It was a surprise to both Aza and her that she had even gotten pregnant. They had wanted a child for years, but had been unable to conceive. Then, late in life, when they had already moved into the autumn of their years, fate had given them the great gift of a first and only child.

They loved Ezra, but they really had no idea what to do with him. Candle had heard once that books were good for children, so she and Aza began buying Ezra tons of them. Soon Ezra was spending all his time reading. He read everything and he read constantly. His parents rarely saw him, so it was something of a surprise for Candle to look at him recently and realize that he was so tall and that if he would comb his dark black hair and stop wearing a cloak, he would be a nice looking young man.

Ezra struggled with having parents so much older than he was and with living in a small town where the library was so tiny it didn't even carry the complete works of Tolkien. But now, with the trees falling, Ezra was finding meaning. Finally something really odd and out of place was happening. It was like discovering an old friend. He knew a lot about being odd and out of place.

Well, that odd increased as the night settled on the very day that had seen the end of Ralph. A warm wind picked up and the farm of Clayton Peterson caught on fire, filling the entire valley with smoke. That smoke had reached such a density by the next morning that a couple of religions called off church. Not the Mormons, however, for whom the smoke seemed to be a nice reminder of why we should be sure of where we stand with heaven.

Sally didn't pay much attention to the smoky skies this morning. She was more interested in what Ryan had on his head. She had wondered why he always wore a baseball cap and figured it was due to one of two things, one—because he was balding, or two—because he was fully bald. She had also figured that by going to church with him, she would get an opportunity to finally see him without cover. Little did she know that Ryan was not about to expose himself this early in the relationship. He had seen August and therefore knew pretty well what he was up against. So, just to be safe, he had shown up at Candle's home to pick Sally up for church, wearing an English-style derby hat that the man at The Man's Hat Shop on Main Street had sworn would make him look debonair and confident.

Sally smiled at Ryan the second she saw him. She wanted desperately to laugh, but she valiantly fought the urge. Of course, to her, Ryan actually wearing such a hat was proof positive that he was losing or had lost his hair.

"Are you okay?" Ryan asked, taking her hand and feeling about as far from debonair and confident as a person possibly could.

"Fine," Sally smiled, taking the steps down from Candle's porch slowly. She looked at Ryan and tried to keep her glance from resting on his hat. She considered saying something, or complimenting him on it in an effort to make him comfortable, but the thought crossed her mind that it might actually be some sort of Mormon thing. She knew Mormons didn't drink, didn't smoke, and didn't get tattoos or pierce their bodies, but Elder Heybourne had never mentioned anything about hats. Elder Heybourne had talked about how much the Mormon religion respected Jews and how there were some similarities between the two religions. Sally wondered if the bowler might not be the Mormon version of the skullcap.

Ryan opened the car door for her, and she climbed in.

"I'm glad you agreed to come," Ryan smiled. "I think you'll like it."

"I'm not too sure," Sally replied. "I'm doing it mainly for the missionary who helped me in the hospital. And for Candle."

Ryan tried not to look excluded. He glanced into his rearview mirror and caught a glimpse of himself in the hat. He sighed deeply and then decided to just come out with it.

"I'm balding," he announced.

Sally reacted as though this was a normal conversational announcement.

"I can't spell very well," she said, trying to one-up him—her lovely pink lips giving way to a smile.

Ryan sighed. "I paid sixty dollars for this thing."

"You never know when you might need a bowler. Listen, Ryan," Sally said, touching his arm and looking into his green eyes, "I don't care if you're balding. Of course I don't even really know you, so I can't imagine why my opinion should matter. I came to Seven Pines because I wanted to feel a certain way. I didn't come here to date or to find me a man. In fact, that would be foolish, seeing as how—"

Sally suddenly realized that she had hurt Ryan's feelings. He had a wounded look on his face.

He would have pulled over and dropped her off if it had not been for the fact that he had not taken her to church yet. He was hoping that by showing her what his religion had to offer that she might look at him in a completely different light. That maybe she would realize that the way she longed to feel was somehow connected to his desire to be forgiven.

Ryan pulled into the church parking lot, parked, turned the car off, then tossed his hat into the back seat. Sally got out before he could help her do so, but she waited for him and looped her arm through his as they walked to the entrance of the building.

"Don't let me do anything stupid or rude," she said. "I have no idea how to act around Mormons."

"Just smile," Ryan joked, "and talk about families."

Sally smiled, but her smile intensified as she and Ryan stepped up to the door and August was suddenly there opening it for them.

"Thanks," Ryan said naively, his green eyes making it obvious that he had no idea that August was out to get what he currently had in hand.

"Good morning, you guys. I wanted to say 'Hi' at the café the other day, but I had to run. I'm August," he offered, extending his hand.

"Ryan," Ryan said, trying to look happy, still not confident or liking the version of himself that he had to present to people. "This is Sally," he added.

She had on a yellow dress that was giving the smoky sun a run for its money. Her blonde hair was pulled up, showing the world what a neck was designed to look like, and her smile certainly left nothing to be desired. Since seeing her in the café the day before,

August had wondered if he wasn't making Sally out to be more than she was. Now, he didn't think so. She was, in a word, *dazzling*. It might not have been love at first sight, but it was certainly like at first look, especially today.

"I'm not Mormon," Sally explained to August, shaking his hand.

"Good," August smiled. "Neither am I."

Sally was surprised to feel a little disappointed by this revelation. Ryan smiled as well, sensing a missionary opportunity. If he could get August interested in the gospel, it would go a long way toward making up for ruining his and Todd's lost missions. What he still didn't understand was that August was out to take something from him.

"So why are you here?" Sally asked bluntly as they all stepped inside. "I mean, if you're not Mormon."

August had that question covered. "I came to church because I'm working on a book."

"What's it about?" Sally inquired.

"Religions of the West," August answered.

Ryan smiled again, feeling as if he had fallen into something really good. This guy was obviously searching for something.

"So are you writing it for fun, or school, or do you have a publisher?" Sally asked.

August hadn't anticipated Sally questioning him this far. He had told Candle that he could create his own excuse for coming to church, but now he had put himself in a position where he would either have to lie or go with the truth.

"I'm writing it just for fun," August said lamely.

Both Ryan and Sally stopped smiling.

"Well, hey, let me know if I can help," Ryan offered, leading Sally around August and into the chapel.

August stood in the foyer, debating with himself over whether or not he should just walk out the door and leave Seven Pines for good. The information that had brought him there hadn't been real detailed, and he wasn't making any significant progress toward what he had hoped to find. More and more he was beginning to wonder if what he had heard was nothing but a joke.

Now, here he was, chasing after a girl he didn't even know. She *was* beautiful, and from what Candle had told him, August knew she was also searching for something. That made her vulnerable, and he kind of liked the challenge. But what if he succeeded in getting her to like him? It would just complicate things. He knew that liking often leads to *really* liking, and that really liking often leads to *love*. And the last thing August felt he needed was love. Still, Sally *was* gorgeous, and there was the excitement of the chase. It was a selfish enough thought to keep him feeling invincible, and he decided to stick with it for a little while longer.

August entered the chapel just as the congregation began singing a hymn. He spotted an empty seat over on the left side and two benches up from Candle. He walked over and took his place in the sea of Mormons. He could see Sally and Ryan sitting on one of the long center pews near the back. Ryan was sitting up straight and trying to look respectful. Sally was looking around in awe, like a child might look in a room lined from ceiling to floor with gum ball machines.

August liked the look in her eyes. It was as if the vulnerability he had seen earlier was subsiding to let in happiness. He couldn't imagine what she could be seeing to make her feel like that. So August glanced around as well, hoping to spot something that might make him happy.

What he saw was mostly families, some with ten kids, some with one. There were two solid rows of senior citizens near the back, and August figured that they were sitting together so as to avoid being stuffed between too many little kids. Carmen, the full-time zookeeper and part-time sign language interpreter, was sitting up front below the podium on a metal folding chair. She was signing the words of the song to two or three hearing impaired people directly in front of her. Above her was a pulpit with a box of white tissues sitting on one side of it and a potted flower that looked better suited for a funeral service on the other. Seated on the stand, behind the pulpit, were three somber-looking men. The one in the middle was wearing a three-piece, dark suit, but the men on either side were less formally dressed, one wearing a sport coat, the other a wrinkled blazer.

The song they were singing was catchy and made August wonder if he had misjudged Mormons all these years.

After the singing and a lengthy prayer, Bishop Skablund got up and walked to the microphone. His given name was actually Bishop. His father had given him the first name of Bishop because of the way he had come out of the womb. He had popped out with his arms folded and wearing the most somber expression Gary Skablund had ever seen. And so he was Bishop Bishop Skablund.

At age two, Bishop had been caught trying to put on a tie. At twelve, his school teacher had warned him that if he did one more book report on *A Marvelous Work and a Wonder,* he would receive a failing grade. At age eighteen, he had turned down a scholarship to a prestigious university because the last three digits of their fax number were "666." And at age twenty-one, after coming home from his mission, he had decided to wear only three-piece suits and had thrown out all of his other clothes. It didn't matter if he was helping someone move or teaching the girls at girls camp how to rough it, he always wore a three-piece suit. There had only been one or two times over the last twenty years when he had even unbuttoned the top button of his suit coat in public.

"There are only three things a year that I actually look forward to," Bishop Skablund was saying dryly. "One is the annual Bear

Festival. I think bears are important to this community, and I think it is a good thing for us to take a day a year to point out what's good about them," he said defensively. It was obvious that some member at some time had told him that they thought the Bear Festival was a bad idea, making him feel defensive and in need of defending it.

"Two," he continued, "I like it when Darlee Fellows makes her Christmas bread. I could eat that stuff three hundred and sixty-five days a year, twenty-four seven. She says it's the way she adds the yeast, but my wife has tried adding it that way, and the end result tasted a lot different than just poorly applied yeast."

The bishop's wife blushed and shook her head. You wouldn't expect that a man who constantly wore a three-piece suit and talked so somberly would have an attractive wife, and in doing so, you would be right. Sister Skablund could have been pretty if she had not decided to start frowning some thirty years before. Frowning was something she was good at, and she had perfected it over the years. Her frown was now so deep that when she spoke it looked like a little rainbow of unhappiness opening and closing. She had played the angel in last year's Christmas pageant, and when she declared that she was bringing them, "Good tidings of great joy," everyone began to weep.

"The third thing I look forward to," Bishop Skablund continued, "is the ward Primary program. And, well, if I'm not mistaken, today is that day."

August actually shivered, as if some unseen force was letting him know that something was coming. He looked around again, but everything looked sort of normal.

The congregation sang another song, and then the sacrament was blessed and passed. August had no idea whether or not he should take any of the bread or water, so he simply waved it away.

This, of course, caused at least three people to begin wondering about him.

After the sacrament, a woman wearing a pretty green dress and a red smile stood and introduced the theme of today's program. August tried to look interested, but he was lost. The church he had attended growing up was nothing like this. His father and mother used to drag him down to a really stuffy building that also doubled as a firehouse during the week. There August would sit for hours on the hard benches as their pastor would go on and on about how God visits those he loves most with deprivation and poverty so they will not succumb to the riches and evils of the flesh. The congregation's having nothing and no hope of having anything was the evidence their pastor cited of God's great affection for his little flock.

August had always thought that was a peculiar doctrine.

He knew of people who the heavens hated enough to give them air conditioning and backyard swimming pools. As a boy he often wished that God would begin to curse his family in that way. It never happened, and as August grew older he became even more confused by religion. He wanted religion to have some relevance, for what he was taught to make sense, but it didn't. He could still remember the day he first realized that Buttercrest was different and that polygamy was not the norm. It was the same day he discovered that his father had no real idea what faith was.

When August was sixteen, the year Rachel had left his family and gotten out, he had spent a full week praying for God to please let him know what to do. He didn't know *if* he should stay, because he didn't know *why* he should stay. He didn't know *what* to believe, because he didn't know *whom* to believe. He didn't know God, because he had never really been introduced.

Now as he sat here watching little Mormon kids get up and recite things they had memorized, he was mesmerized. Aside from a red-headed little girl who burst out in tears, it actually looked like they were enjoying and believing what they were reciting. Then the entire group of kids got up and sang together "I'm Trying to Be like Jesus." The song was so simple and so sweet, it caused August to glance around to see if everybody else was hearing what he heard. He looked to the vents to see if they were pumping in some sort of feel-good gas.

Where was Tony the conspiracy hermit when you needed him?

The good feeling was almost too much to bear. August had to get out of there. He stood up in the middle of the song and began to walk toward the back. His face was flushed, and the feeling of invincibility inside of him had disappeared. This was not a good place to be selfish.

As he headed for the door to the chapel, he passed Sally and Ryan sitting in their pew. Sally was gazing at the children in a way that August wouldn't have minded her looking at him. When Ryan saw August looking at him and Sally, he shifted slightly closer to Sally. August barely noticed. He then smiled and waved as he passed Candle's row. Candle smiled back.

A young man tending the door opened it for August, and he stepped into the foyer, grateful when the door closed behind him, partially blocking the singing out. He took a couple of deep breaths and then stood there, willing his sense of invincibility to return.

Sitting in the foyer was a middle-aged man named Justin. He was wearing a green polo shirt and jeans so new they still had the stiff crease in them. In fact, August was a little baffled at how Justin had been able to bend his legs to sit down.

Justin was sitting on a floral couch pulling on the hair on his right arm. He stopped pulling as soon as he realized that August was looking at him.

August leaned against the wall for a moment and then sat down in a chair directly across the foyer from Justin.

"Is it always like that?" August asked, referring to the feelings he felt.

"Kids screeching?"

"No," August replied.

"People singing?"

August shook his head and opened his mouth as if to explain.

"Sort of smelly," Justin tried, "like old cabbage?"

"Actually," August smiled, "I was talking about . . . never mind," he said, deciding not to mention what he was feeling after all.

"All right then. Are you new?"

"Visiting."

"I'm Justin Wride," he said, extending his hand but not getting up.

"August Thatch." August extended his hand, but there still was a good ten feet between the two of them. They both sort of waved their hands in the air as if completing the shake.

"So you're the non-Mormon with good looks, a checkered past, and dubious reasons for being here?" Justin observed.

August didn't reply, deciding instead to simply stare at him until he went on.

"Candle and I talk," he explained. "She likes to keep abreast of everything going on around here. Any luck with that Sally girl yet?"

"Wow, Candle really talks," August said.

"Don't tell her anything you don't want the town, the heavens, and everything in between knowing. She's given away more secrets than Santa has gifts."

Again August didn't reply.

"Of course Santa's not real," Justin answered, feeling like he needed to clear that up.

"So do they always let the little kids talk and sing in church?" August asked, motioning to the chapel doors and what was going on behind them.

"Seems like it," Justin replied. "You know, I'm not real active. I take care of the Memorial Gardens here, and I have a hard time working church into my schedule."

"There are a lot of burials on Sunday?"

"No," Justin waved. "But there are twice as many people coming out to pay their respects. Twice as many. That kind of crowd promotes trouble. So I stay on hand to keep the peace."

Justin liked to talk with his hands. He had made more hand motions in the last few minutes than Carmen, the sign language interpreter, had made the entire meeting. He had certain movements and gestures that he used repeatedly, but he also ad-libbed a lot.

Justin was forty-eight and one of the few immigrants to Seven Pines. He had come a number of years back from Bear Incident, Montana, an even smaller town fifty miles to the east. He was single, due to personality, and attached, thanks to his job. He took the act of dying very seriously and the responsibility of grooming the resting spots that the deceased now occupied even more seriously. He had been known to chew out families for bringing ugly flower bouquets or for not cleaning off dirty headstones.

Physically Justin was gaunt, white, and dingy. He was clean, but he was the kind of person who could put on a stark white T-shirt and moments later it would be the gray shade of his skin, never to be white again.

"How many people come by the cemetery in a day?" August asked, trying to be friendly but wishing he had stayed inside the chapel.

"Memorial Gardens," Justin corrected. "We've had as many as twenty in one afternoon," Justin said proudly. "Double that and you're looking at forty. So do you work?"

"Not at the moment," August answered.

"I could use a strong back," Justin said, as if he were dangling some fat piece of meat in front of a starving dog. "The pay's not bad compared to what Sam tosses those kids down at McDonald's."

"Thanks, but—"

"Flexible hours."

"How flexible?"

"You can come and go as you want as long as you get done what is needed. There's really no such thing as late."

"Can I think about it?" August asked, remembering that having a source of income might not be a bad thing—especially a source of income that didn't depend upon him being on time. He had lived off the kindness of strangers ever since he had been released from jail, but he knew that he couldn't make that last for too much longer. Besides, if he stayed around for any amount of time, he would eventually have to pay a hotel bill. He had been totally opposed to taking a job for fear of growing too attached to the town, but for some reason the prospect of working at a cemetery appealed to him. It would be a constant reminder of his sister.

"I suppose you can think about it," Justin said. "But I've got a hole to dig by four tomorrow."

"I'll be there," August smiled.

Candle stepped out of the chapel and sternly glanced at August and Justin. They both looked guilty, like two kids busted for skipping class or stealing candy.

"I thought you might have gotten lost looking for the restroom," Candle scolded August. "The meeting's almost over. And you, Justin, keeping him out here."

"I was just sitting here," Justin complained. "He started talking to me."

August stood, wondering again why he didn't just walk out the doors and keep going. This stop was already getting too complicated. He could go to some town where there were more people to move and hide around—forget his secret and start a new life some-where else.

"The Smith boy is about to recite his poem," Candle said, motioning August to follow her. He did so, slipping back into the chapel and sitting down next to Candle's son, Ezra, who was hold-ing a small pewter figure of what looked to be an elf. August had been seated no longer than a couple of minutes when the feelings of happiness began to attack him again. He tried to focus on Ezra's elf, but once Ezra saw that August was looking, he shifted so as not to share the pewter.

So August was left to listen to and watch the singing kids. He decided that maybe now was a good time to pray—him being in a church and all. The problem was that he didn't know what to pray for.

"Bless those who are sick and those who are needy, oh, and bless that the feelings of happiness will stop drowning out my feeling of invincibility."

August was deciding on how best to beg for something when heaven took the lead and offered some distraction.

As young Evan Heybourne came to the pulpit to do his bit, he accidentally knocked over the potted flowers that were there to brighten things up but in reality sort of made things look depress-ing. That is, of course, until he pushed them over onto Carmen as she was signing. That part was kind of interesting. Carmen jumped up and began dusting herself off, all the dirt from the pot having dumped down the back of her dress and over her arms.

People tried really hard not to laugh or gasp too loudly. A few people helped pick up the mess, and then the program continued. Unfortunately, it turned out Carmen was allergic to something in the soil. So as the children sang, she tried desperately to sign and scratch at the same time. It became a little confusing for those she was interpreting for. One of them thought that she was telling him to get up and turn off the lights. So he did. Once that was cleared up and the lights were back on, another watching Carmen thought she was being personally insulting and left. Then the third believed that maybe there might be a future for him and Carmen because of the flirty things she was signing to him. In the end Carmen ran out, sobbing, while the children continued singing "In My Lovely Garden." It was very dramatic.

Despite the distraction, August began to feel as though he would have to bolt again or lose his feelings of invincibility altogether. But just as he decided he could take it no more, the meeting ended. August began to clap, but nobody joined in. It did cause Sally to look at him, which wasn't an entirely unpleasant consequence.

After sacrament meeting, Candle rounded up Ryan and Sally and told them that she would be teaching a special "non-member-but-slightly-curious class" in the bishop's office down by the kitchen and across from the stairs leading up to the stage. Ryan and Sally blindly fell for it, following Candle and August to the bishop's office.

Once all four were seated in the office, Candle began talking. August and she had planned to have an informal class that they could then use to get to know one another, but apparently plans had changed. Candle was cutting to the chase.

"Listen," she said, "I'm old, and I've got a son out in the hall who is insisting I drive him home because his stomach feels queasy. So I'm going to get right to it. August and Ryan, forgive me, but, Sally, there are two boys in this room who both want a shot at you."

"What?" August said, acting surprised.

"Excuse me?" Ryan added, feeling like he too had to at least pretend that he wasn't so desperate.

"Ryan, I saw you pull up to church wearing a bowler," Candle pointed out. "If that isn't obvious, then I'm twenty and still have all my looks."

August winked at Candle, "And you thought I was here for Sally."

Candle smiled. "That's sweet, August, but I'm a married woman."

It was true, Candle was married. To a very peculiar looking man. Aza, bless his soul, was not what most women would have called a "catch." His pointy face was covered with a perpetual stubble of whiskers and a full-grown mustache that drooped down over a tiny mouth and receding chin. He made up for the scarcity of unruly hair on his head by a profusion of fur growing out of his ears. And his close-set eyes were a little crossed, which made it hard to tell where he was actually looking.

"Okay," August said dejectedly. "I'll settle for Sally." He of course said it in such a way that Sally didn't seem to mind.

"So do I have a say in this?" Sally asked. "Or is this how Mormons work? They get some unsuspecting woman into a small room and tell her who she is going to like?"

"Hey," August pointed out, "I'm not Mormon."

"And I didn't set this up," Ryan added.

Candle again jumped in. "I'm old, and I can see from the shadow under the door that Ezra is beginning to pace. I could stay here and point out that August wanted to trick you into getting to know him. Or I could comment on the fact that Ryan didn't ask Juliet Mavis to come to church with him, but he did ask you."

"Juliet Mavis?" Ryan questioned.

"She works at the tourist center," Candle explained. "Missing a couple of teeth and has that attitude problem."

"Sounds like the perfect person to be working at the tourist center," Ryan observed, his light hair looking even thinner under the lights.

"You may have a point," Candle agreed, "regardless, there was more than just Christian duty spilling over when you picked Sally to invite here."

"You told me to show her around," Ryan debated.

"You could have ignored me," Candle said to him.

"So I'm an assignment?" Sally asked.

"This is an outrage," August joked, reaching for Sally and acting disgusted. "Let's you and I get out of here."

"Hear me out," Candle said, holding both hands up. "I did ask Ryan to show you around, and I also felt compelled to help out August. So, Sally, maybe you should tell them a little more about yourself."

"What does that mean?" she asked suspiciously, feeling as if the question were way too personal. She had felt so confident in herself ever since she had arrived in Seven Pines. Now, with Candle firing questions at her with two guys she scarcely knew somehow competing for her, she became defensive. "I'm not sure I want to tell anybody anything."

Candle looked hurt.

"I mean, my business is mine alone," Sally added.

"Of course it is," Candle said softly. "But let me give you a little of my business." She sighed. "I don't know what it is. I grew up here and then spent some time away. While I was out in the world I realized that where I was needed was here. Well, I can't sing, I can't paint, and I think I've taken my calling as the ward material center person about as far as I can go. So a short while ago my husband asked me what it was I really wanted to do with my life. And I don't know if it was because I had just watched *Fiddler on the Roof,* or if it was divine inspiration, either way the word *matchmaker,* came out of my mouth. That seemed like it would be a fulfilling contribution. I've spent a lot of time trying to bring people together. So why not make it more than a hobby?"

"So this really isn't about any of us?" August asked, pointing at Ryan, Sally, and himself.

"It is in the sense that I need further practice," Candle explained, her wide face seeming to widen even further. "I've had some problems in the past, and I'd like to prove to my husband and the bishop that I can get it right."

Ryan looked at Sally, Sally looked at August, and August shook his head.

Aza stuck his messy noggin in the door. "Sorry to interrupt, but I'm taking the boy home," he said without much enthusiasm. "He says his spleen hurts."

"Make him some soup," Candle suggested. "And tell him that his lounging cloak is in the dryer."

Aza shook his head in embarrassment and left.

"You know, the one thing I've never liked about courting is all the frou-frou and fluff," Candle went on. "I say, if you see what you like, grab it. So I want to run my practice in the same manner. We could take a couple of weeks exploring things on the phone, gradually getting acquainted, but where's the thrill it that? I say, let's speed this thing along."

"People need to get to know each other," Sally said, feeling more uneasy every second.

"Of course," Candle agreed, reaching into her purse. "That's why I've set up some together time for the three of you." She handed Ryan two sealed envelopes. "Ryan you'll go first. Tomorrow morning." Candle gave August his letters. "August, you're up tomorrow night. Then we'll go through the rotation one more time the next day, and I think by then we'll know if there is anything real between any of you."

"So I really don't get a say?" Sally protested. "What if I don't want to spend time with either of them?"

"Well, you'll know for sure in a couple of days if that's the case.

As far as I can tell, not a one of you has a single thing to do. You're three strangers who have come to my town. So if you'll hear an old woman out and do her this favor, I'd be most happy."

"I think I should point out that Justin has offered me a job. My time's not all mine." August smiled, happy about all of this. He had no problem sharing Sally with Ryan. This was the perfect non-committal way of getting to know her.

"Oh, you can dig a hole any time," Candle poohed. "I'm sure Justin can work around your schedule. If not, let me talk to him. Any questions?"

"Can we leave now?" Sally asked.

"Not without getting a lesson," Candle insisted. "August's plan was for me to teach you three about some of his better traits. I think I'll skip that and tell you all about a little sin called vanity."

After church the three of them split up. Sally wanted to be alone. Ryan wanted to be with Sally but respected her wishes and headed over to the city park to do some thinking of his own. August invited them both to go see a movie with him, but Ryan said that he didn't go to movies on Sunday and pointed out that Sally shouldn't go with August alone because that was kind of like a date, and Candle's plan didn't call for that yet. So August went to the movies by himself.

Later that night, after most of the town was sound asleep, somebody chopped down Edward.

CHAPTER SEVENTEEN

SLIPPING AWAY

Edward was the middle child in the Wood family of seven children. He was the peacemaker and everyone's confidant. He helped his older brothers get along with his younger brothers and their sister. He was also the one constantly at his mother's side, helping, cleaning, and learning. Edward's head was always turned slightly to one side, so that he looked at people from a skewed angle, a look that his father blamed on the way he was born—that way being, in a car, traveling about seventy miles an hour. Wilton had refused to pull over so that Maria could give birth. He knew that if he stopped, he would be obligated to help deliver the baby, and there was no way in heaven or in heaven's opposite that he was about to do that. So he had done his part by ignoring his wife's screams and simply pushing harder on the gas.

He made an heroic effort, but it didn't prevent the child from arriving. Ten blocks from the doctor's office, Edward appeared. Wilton accounted for Edward's daft look by saying the boy sized up his first surroundings and became confused by them, which is understandable, given that his first view was the underside of the dashboard of a car. Wilton was always irritated by Edward's seeming refusal to look his father full in the face, and he used to make Edward chop wood for hours as punishment. But no matter how many logs he split or trees he chopped he always came in from the chores with his face still looking odd.

Most folks had thought that, unlike his older brothers, Edward might stick around instead of sneaking off at eighteen. They figured he was too loyal to his siblings or too attached to his mother to break off from the family tree. They figured wrong, and on the night of his eighteenth birthday, he followed the family tradition and slipped off, never to be heard from again.

Well, by the time Edward left, Wilton had already suffered through three missing children. Now his middle child, whom he had made fun of and teased over his odd manner, was gone. Taken like a fat pie from a low window ledge. That reference of course being extra applicable due to Edward's size. You see, while Edward was making peace, he liked to eat. He also had been told once that his face seemed to straighten out when he was chewing. As a result, he more "rolled off" than "slipped away."

Regardless, he was missed. It was the first time Maria cried when one of her kids left. Wilton, distraught as usual in his own peculiar way, but still not having it in him to manifest his love to his remaining children, bought a piece of land to the southwest, back behind some other trees. There he planted the fattest pine he could find. Edward (the tree) had maintained its weight beautifully. All the way up until some unfeeling hoodlum cruelly felled it with an ax.

🌲 🌲 🌲

Seven Pines was running scared. Somebody or something was out there, systematically reducing the ring of protective trees that supposedly had brought this town so much security and peace. There were only three of the original seven trees left now, and people had begun locking their doors and spending the night on their front porches with guns. Committees were formed and assignments given to guard the remaining three trees. The town of Bear Incident sent over a load of relief quilts, but the women of Seven Pines nitpicked the stitching on the quilts and Justin overheard the criticism. He told his family, who still lived in Bear Incident, and about one hour later a truck full of angry men pulled into town looking to take back the quilts from the ungrateful people of Seven Pines.

People didn't trust one another as much anymore. Neighbors were wondering what their neighbors had done wrong to bring this upon all of them. And no one could understand why a group of such wonderful people would have to be put through this.

The morning after Edward was toppled, seven wells turned up dry. Deep wells, wells that supported multiple homes and ranches and businesses. Wells that were believed to contain so much water that they would never dry up. Those wells were now dust. And as if that weren't disconcerting enough, the manmade pond in the city park at the center of town turned purple. It really freaked a number of people out until Ezra confessed that he had dyed it in an effort to scare people into believing. Believing what, they had asked?

"Believing that the ring has been broken, and no good will come from it," Ezra thundered.

Well, in a sense, everyone *already* believed that. A couple of people pointed this fact out to Ezra, who in turn began pouting and complaining that nobody took his warnings seriously. Embarrassed by his son's behavior, Aza sent Ezra home with instructions to finish vacuuming the living room or he would be grounded. He had been warned many times about prophesying before his chores were done.

Chief Fellows began distributing flyers, asking for anyone with any information about the trees to come forward. He passed the flyers out and posted them on buildings and trees throughout the town. It was in vogue to tell Chief Fellows not to put a flyer on any of the three remaining trees because it would just turn up missing. Chief Fellows laughed at the joke the first time he heard it but actually locked up the unlucky, seventy-third person who said it to him.

Chief Rigby Fellows was a large man in the sense that he was huge—big arms, big legs, big smile. He had thick, wavy gray hair that stuck out from under his cap like a leafy wreath. He walked bow-legged, talked straight, and played a mean fiddle during his down time. He and his wife lived in a big house that touched the east edge of Lincoln Lake. He had always lived here, always would, and was determined to make the time in between serene and enjoyable. Up until now, he had experienced little or no trouble from his town. People had gotten along, and life had been easy.

Things were considerably different now.

August read the morning paper and sighed. The café was busy as everyone worked on consuming what they had been told all their lives was the most important meal of the day. Jane gave August a fresh glass of orange juice and one of her dazzling smiles.

"You all right?" she asked. "You look a little tired."

"Fine," August smiled, thinking that he couldn't remember ever being told that. But he didn't mind. He liked Jane. Not love-like, but like-like. Which is actually a pretty powerful thing.

"Shame about the tree," Jane added, deftly wiping a spill off August's table. "You never realize how much you're going to miss something until it turns up missing. I'd only seen Edward three or four times," she said sadly. "He was the most hidden and hardest to get to. Now he's gone, and I feel awful."

Even her pout was becoming.

"All for nothing," August agreed sadly. "It seems so pointless."

August finished his orange juice and stood up. He put some money on the table and smiled one last time at Jane. He wasn't going to do this anymore. He had stayed in Seven Pines too long. He could list on three hands the people he needed to avoid so as to not have to actually say good-bye. Attachment seemed to drain him of any feelings of invincibility and put him in a spot where he could be hurt again. So he had decided late last night that enough was enough. Ryan could have Sally, Justin could find another strong back, and he would move on. The information that had brought him here was obviously a joke. He felt confident that those inmates he had overheard were just trying to mess with him by sending him on a wild-goose chase.

Jane waved, but August got out before she could say anything to him. He flung his bag over his shoulder and began walking north. But before he had gone even forty steps, a car pulled in front of him, blocking his progress. Candle got out of it and waved frantically.

"I need your help."

"Sorry, Candle, I'm—"

"Hop in," she ordered nicely.

August sighed, threw his bag into the back seat, and climbed into her car. She threw the car into drive and sped down the road toward the church.

"I really needed to do some thing," August said trying not to sound too bothered. "I was on my—"

"Listen," Candle ignored, "I've had an emergency come up, and I need someone to fill in for me at the material center."

"Me?"

Candle nodded.

"Can't you just close it for an hour?"

She shot him a disgusted look. "I don't know much about your past, but I can tell you weren't taught responsibility."

"That's true."

"Two hours," Candle declared. "I'll be back in two hours."

"I have no idea what to do."

"Don't worry, nobody will show."

"Then why stay open?"

"Do we need to go over this again?" Candle said, disappointed, her tall hair seeming to frown as she knitted her eyebrows. "Two hours. That's all. If someone does need something, just stall."

"For two hours?"

"Most people here like to talk."

"That's true," August said for the second time.

Candle pulled into the parking lot and jumped out of the car. August grabbed his bag out of the back seat and followed, only not quite as enthusiastically. She opened up the building and then led him to the material center.

"Are you sure this is legal?" August asked. "I'm not even Mormon."

"Chalk's the same in every religion," Candle said, unlocking the door and flipping the light on. "Now have a good time." And with that, Candle was gone.

August stepped into the library, realizing that he could simply just leave. He could lock the doors and walk away from all this. But he really hadn't thought out where he would be going. And if Candle needed help, he guessed he could postpone the unknown for a couple of hours.

August walked behind the counter and turned the copy machine on. No sooner had the lights begun to flash and the copier beep than a frantic looking woman came through the door carrying a pile of papers and the weight of the world on her shoulders. August recognized her as Sister Shick, the woman who had introduced the children at church the other day. The one wearing the green dress and red smile.

"Where's Candle?" she asked in a panic.

"She had something to do," August explained.

"I need these cut and hole punched," she said, banging a stack of papers down in front of August. "And if you could cut off the edges that would be great," she said in a huff.

"Can you give me four hours?" August asked.

Green dress laughed. "Sister Fellows is expecting me at her place with these pages in twenty minutes. We're finishing up scrapbooks for all the Primary children. These pages are crucial to the last week of their lives."

"I really don't know how to do all that," August admitted. "And Candle won't—"

"Give me those," she growled, grabbing her papers back and coming behind the counter to do the work herself.

"I could probably hole punch," August offered. Before she could answer, Bishop Skablund entered the library wearing his three-piece suit and holding a manual.

"Where's Candle?" he asked.

"Busy."

That seemed sufficient for him. "I need to find video number 7229. It's the fifth Sunday this week, and I'll be teaching combined priesthood and Relief Society."

"Congratulations," August said sincerely.

"Thank you," Bishop Skablund replied, seeming genuinely flattered. "Anyhow, number 7229 will supplement my thoughts perfectly."

"I have no idea where it is," August said honestly.

"I suppose I could find it," the bishop said, as if he had just figured out the riddle of the ages.

"It's all yours," August motioned.

Bishop Skablund came behind the counter and began looking at the videos. Apparently the movies they had on hand were sort of like memory lane for Bishop Skablund. As he looked at each title, he would comment about how much he had liked that one, or how long it had been since he had seen that one, or he didn't know they had a video about that subject, or "Why don't they make videos like this anymore?"

August honestly didn't know, so he honestly didn't answer.

As the bishop searched and as Sister Shick begrudgingly cut paper, Ryan and Sally stepped through the door. Sally looked beautiful and less vulnerable than she had appeared the day before. August was a bit upset about this, seeing how he hadn't done anything to help bring about this change in her. And whereas Sally looked beautiful, Ryan looked happy to simply be near Sally.

"What are you doing here?" Ryan asked, obviously not quite as happy to be near August.

"Helping," August said quietly, so as to not get an argument about that from those he had not really helped. "What are you two doing here?"

"This is where we are supposed to come for our day date," Ryan answered. "The instructions say, 'come to the material center right about ten, you'll find a TV, a VCR, and a friend.'"

August had been set up. "I guess that's what she's talking about," he pointed. There in the front corner of the material center was a small TV sitting atop a rolling cart. Beneath the TV on another shelf was a VCR.

"What about the friend?" Sally asked.

August waved.

"I don't want to sound mean, but this is supposed to be our date," Ryan pointed out.

"Not a date," Sally clarified. "Together time. At least that's what Candle called it."

August snorted. "Either way, I'm sure Candle will work it so that you show up during Sally's and my together time tonight."

"No wonder she wants practice at matchmaking," Sally added. "She's awful."

"Well, it looks like she set up two chairs for you," August said. "So you might as well see what it is she wants you to watch."

Ryan and Sally sat down and turned the TV on. August couldn't tell what the heck was playing, but he heard Ryan say, "Johnny Lingo."

Ryan turned up the volume.

Bishop Skablund found the video he was after but stayed to watch the film Ryan and Sally had started.

"This is a powerful story," he whispered to August, pointing toward the screen.

August really didn't understand Mormons.

Aza Hicks came into the material center holding a huge bowl of popcorn and wondering where his wife was.

"She had something to do," August explained.

"Always does," Aza said. "Well, she wanted me to drop off this popcorn."

"Over here," the bishop waved from two feet away. He then took the popcorn from Aza and offered some to Ryan and Sally.

"What are they watching?" Aza whispered.

"Some movie about cows," Sally replied.

The hole punch got jammed, and Sister Shick began banging on it.

"Shhh," the bishop said.

"I've got a deadline," she huffed. August moved to help her while Aza found a place to better view the movie.

"Give me a handful of that popcorn," he said to Ryan.

It was at that moment that August first heard the noise in the hall. It grew louder and louder until there was a large group of school-aged children gathered right outside of the material center door. Yvonne Yawney, a blonde, friendly looking girl, stood in front of the children, wearing a reflective vest. She looked like a novice school crossing guard who had accidentally directed a large group of children here.

"Can I help you?" August asked.

"Shhhh," Aza hollered, which was a good thing because Sister Shick was experiencing trouble with the hole punch again and may have said a couple of words that were less than child-friendly. Aza's Shhhing had covered things nicely.

Yvonne turned and told the children to be quiet. She then turned back to August. "Candle promised us a tour of a real, working material center."

"Candle's not here," August pointed out, quietly.

"Could you turn off the lights," Bishop Skablund asked. "I'm getting a glare."

Aza hopped up and turned them off. If it had not been for the TV and the hall lights, the room would have been completely black.

"If you could just show us around quickly," Yvonne said. "It takes quite an effort to gather all these children up and get them safely here."

"They're watching a movie," August explained, motioning to the TV. "And it's dark."

"We'll be quiet. Won't we, kids?" she asked.

"Yes!" they all hollered.

"Shhhh," both Aza and the bishop said simultaneously.

August shook his head and then pulled open the bottom half

of the divided door to the media center. August then led the children on a short tour, whispering so that they wouldn't disturb Ryan and Sally's date.

"It looks like this is where they keep the scriptures," August explained with no real authority.

Seven hands went up.

"Let's keep the questions until the end, and you can ask them out in the hall," August whispered.

All seven hands stayed up.

"Yes," August sighed and pointed.

"I have some scriptures," a skinny, freckled-face kid commented.

"That's great," August said, ignoring the other six hands and moving on. "Now here's where they keep the . . ." August pulled out some pictures to make sure he was giving correct information. "Yes, here's where they keep the pictures."

Seven hands went up again.

"Let's play a game," August suggested. "Today is opposite day, so if you have a question, don't raise your hand."

Every hand went down.

"Now here's the copier," August said, pointing to the big machine. "And right next to that is a hole punch."

One of the children recognized Sister Shick and called her name while waving.

"Shhhhhh," Aza said impatiently.

"Here's where they keep the videos," August continued.

One hand went up.

"Yes," August said, dejected.

"I don't have a question," the child explained, "so I raised my hand."

August quickly wrapped things up. "Here's the chalk, erasers, pencils, and tape." He then escorted them all out from behind the counter and back into the hall.

"Now, children," Yvonne said, "how do we say thanks for the tour?"

The kids broke into a song that August thought was much more thank-you than he deserved. Feeling a little guilty about the quick tour, he gave them each a small piece of broken chalk as a souvenir. They all acted as if he had just handed them the key to the city.

"Thank you," Yvonne said.

August stepped back into the material center and began to trim the edges of the papers Sister Shick was frantically finishing up. He noted that the movie everyone was watching was coming to an end.

"That's the ugly girl?" Aza asked those he was watching with. He was pointing at the screen, obviously in disbelief about the ending.

"Impossible. I've given Candle thousands of dollars in gifts, and she still looks the same," Aza reasoned.

The bishop flicked the light on just as Sister Shick was finishing up. Bishop Skablund slipped out quickly, claiming that he had something in his eye. Sister Shick was right behind him, and Aza, after getting his popcorn bowl back, followed suit.

Ryan stood up and shut off the TV.

"What's next?" August asked them.

"That's it," Ryan answered. "No more instructions for today."

"We had breakfast," Sally added, slipping her arm through Ryan's so as to let everyone know that she hadn't had a terrible time. "So that movie was made by Mormons?" she asked Ryan.

"A long time ago," Ryan said defensively.

"Interesting," was all Sally said.

"You know, we could take a walk or something," Ryan suggested. "It's not like we have to instantly split up."

"I'd like that," Sally smiled. "I'll see you tonight, August," she waved as the two of them left the library and headed out.

Despite the fact that Sally had left, her impression lingered. August knew that there was something about her that he needed to know. At least he wanted to pretend that was the case. It felt noble thinking that it was something beyond her looks and personality that was keeping his mind fixated on her. He tried to shake the feeling, but that only caused it to settle deeper into his heart. He stared at the empty doorway until he realized how pathetic he must look.

August was alone.

He folded up the chairs and picked up pieces of popcorn until the floor was clean again. He straightened the hole punch and realized that he had not had Bishop Skablund sign out the video he had taken.

He almost felt bad.

There was something about these Mormons that created a new sensation in him. It was a sensation that seemed to crowd out his feeling of invincibility. He couldn't tell if it was good or bad. But he had a feeling it wasn't pain free.

He also now felt compelled to stay in Seven Pines a little longer. Sure, he had been ready to pack it in a couple of hours ago, but seeing Ryan and Sally getting along sort of made him jealous. He couldn't just let Ryan win by virtue of a forfeit. And it couldn't hurt to do a little more checking on the information that had brought him here.

Candle came back exactly two hours from the time she had left him.

"How did it go?" she asked.

"Nothing happened," he answered, acting bored and not willing to give her the satisfaction of knowing her plan had worked.

"Nobody stopped by?"

"I don't know, I wasn't really paying attention."

Candle looked puzzled. "Well, thanks for filling in. I suppose you had better get back to what you were doing when I stopped you."

"Oh, that," August waved. "It was nothing important."

"So nobody came in?" she asked again. "That's frustrating."

"Tell me about it," August agreed. "I don't know why people don't take advantage of this place."

"I knew you were a perceptive one," Candle smiled, liking the idea that someone besides herself recognized the importance of staying open. "Just once I'd like to really give this copier a workout during the work week. Just once," she said patting the machine.

August could sense that Candle needed to be alone with her material center, so he left, shouldering his bag and walking down the hall and out into the open. He couldn't help noticing the many chalk lines that someone had drawn on the walls leading to the doors. There was also a hopscotch course drawn out on the side-walk leading into the chapel.

Chalk really was the same in every religion.

August thought Seven Pines was an all right place. But he was also a little afraid that his soul just might pay dearly for feeling that way.

CHAPTER EIGHTEEN

THREE . . .

August spent much longer getting ready for his date than he had ever done in the past. He even said a prayer, wondering just who he was actually talking to the whole time. He tried to pattern his prayer after the ones he had heard at the Mormon Church. The effect was much more rewarding than he had anticipated.

He didn't want his life to be lonely, but he could already feel bits and pieces of the pain he would ultimately feel when he had to pull away from this place. He wanted God, wherever he was, to keep him invincible but allow him to be fulfilled.

A person can dream.

August set aside his thoughts and opened the envelope marked "No. 1" that Candle had given him. The instructions were simple but frightening.

Purchase five dollars worth of clothing from the thrift store for each of you. Change into said clothing and then proceed to Bruce.

All his primping had been for nothing. He would be spending the evening in somebody else's old clothing.

He met Sally in front of the café.

"You're late," she said, looking beautiful, her blue eyes causing August to wish he had been on time.

"Sorry, I usually am."

August shared Candle's instructions with Sally, and the two of them walked toward the thrift store. It was a depressing night. Smoke from the lingering forest fires hung in the air, giving everything a gloomy feel and making it difficult to breathe. The lush landscape that had been here days before had wilted in the hot, sticky weather. August looked down at Sally as they walked and was surprised to see her smiling.

"Did you have that good a time with Ryan?" he asked.

"It was nice."

"Nice like a toddler waving an American flag? Or nice like winning the lottery?

"Those are your definitions of nice?" Sally laughed.

"I don't know," August said, pushing his brown hair up off his forehead. "I guess I'm not as familiar with nice as I should be."

"We had a great time."

"I'm happy to hear that."

"Happy like finding a new penny?" Sally asked. "Or happy like inheriting ten million dollars from a relative you didn't know you had?"

"Actually, neither. Happy like I'm not telling the truth."

"Oh," Sally replied.

August would have commented on that "Oh," but they had reached the thrift store.

"Do we really have to do this?" August pleaded. "We could act normal and just have dinner and go to a movie."

"This is for Candle. Besides, it'll be fun," Sally replied.

That made August wonder if Sally were really as discerning as he had originally thought. Once inside, August picked out a shirt that looked old enough for Moses to have stitched personally. He then found a pair of pants that he thought weren't too awful, but they were seven dollars and thus out of his price range. So he settled for an ugly, two-dollar pair to go with the shirt, which cost a dollar twenty, and a pair of shoes that were only seventy-five cents.

Sally made it easy on herself and just bought a four-dollar dress and a twenty-five cent pair of flip-flops. They changed in the restrooms and then headed out to see Bruce.

"You look fabulous," August told Sally. The dress she chose might have been used, but it didn't detract from her beauty in the least. It just made her look a little more earthy, which in August's mind wasn't all that bad.

"You look homeless," she replied.

August had on a light-orange, button down shirt with fading navy blue slacks. And the tennis shoes he was sporting were green with white stripes. The entire ensemble was as outdated as loincloths.

"I was working on a tight budget," August explained.

Sally's pink lips formed a delicious smile, and she held his hand as they walked.

"So can I ask you something?" she asked.

"Of course."

"Just between you and me, what do you think of Mormons?"

"I think I may have misjudged them all these years," August answered. "You know, I never really knew anything about them. I saw a couple on bikes once, and some friends of mine had told me that they don't drink and that they all look alike. But I don't know, they're really not that weird."

"I agree," Sally smiled. "All I had ever heard was that they have ten wives."

August stopped.

"What is it?" Sally asked.

"Mormons have ten wives?" he asked, suddenly uneasy.

"No," Sally waved. "I guess some used to. But not now."

"Are you sure?"

"Yes," Sally insisted. "That's what Ryan said, and I don't think he would lie to me. Why? If they did, would you be more interested in joining?" she joked.

"No way," August quickly said.

Sally stopped and looked at him. The early evening was hot and dusty. The sun sat low in the sky, red from the smoke in the air that the fires were bringing. A flock of birds scattered across the horizon like slow-moving buckshot. Sally squeezed August's hand and smiled.

"Are you all right?" she asked.

August was torn. He preferred leaving his past a complete mystery instead of spelling it out. He had made it a rule to not tell anyone anything about where he came from or what his family was like. Now, however, as he looked at Sally, it was as if he felt a need to speak. He wondered if his sister weren't somewhere compelling him to do so.

"I come from polygamists," he said casually.

Sally laughed. She stopped as soon as she realized he wasn't joking. "They're polygamist now?" she asked.

"All right, I'm completely embarrassed by it, but yes." August could feel the feeling of invincibility growing inside of him. He had nothing to fear from telling the truth. This was about him and the things he had endured. He had no reason to dodge it any longer. He had made it through worse things.

"Isn't it illegal?" Sally asked, her blonde hair blowing gently in the growing breeze.

"Yes, but the state of Michigan has more pressing things to do than to break up families," he said flatly.

"So do you get along with your parents?"

"I haven't seen them in years. I left home when I was eighteen and have never gone back. They never really liked me hanging around. I asked too many questions and disagreed too often. Then when I was eighteen they announced that I would be marrying the Stoutfingers' daughter. You know, Becky Stoutfinger wouldn't have been the worst person to marry, but I knew that along with her came the tradition of finding another wife as well. I couldn't take that. When I carve my name into a park bench, I want to be listed with only one other person. Not August plus Becky plus Susie plus Wendy equals true love forever."

August stopped talking and turned to look at Sally. The dusty night and low light of the evening made the blue of her eyes look especially deep. He thought seriously about kissing her, but the talk of multiple wives had sort of ruined the moment.

"Enough about boring old me," he joked. "Tell me something you wouldn't normally share with others."

"There's nothing to me."

"That's about the biggest understatement I have ever heard. What about your parents?"

"My mother died at birth, and my father abandoned me shortly after," she said, pushing her hair back behind her ears.

"I'm sorry to hear that," August said, literally feeling his strength desert him as he said it.

Sally laughed but not in a happy way. "Isn't it interesting? You had too much family, and I didn't have enough. I've always been

NEVER CAN SAY GOOD-BYE

jealous of people who have a normal home life. I suppose that's why I came here. I used to listen to a Mormon missionary talk about this place and how his family was so close and did all these fun things together. I guess I was hoping to find security and peace here."

"Nothing like exploding trees and raging wildfires to give you a real secure feeling," August joked.

Sally looked up at him and smiled sadly. "I've learned not to notice too many of the bad things around me."

"So can you even see me then?" August half joked.

"Dimly," Sally smiled back.

"So, who raised you?"

"I was adopted by some really uncaring people, ran away at sixteen, and almost died jumping out of a plane last year. That's my whole life."

"You're amazing," August said, honestly.

"You think so?" Sally stopped walking so as to better look at August. She had never had anyone say such a thing, in such a way. There had been those who had marveled at her surviving the fall, but the way August said "amazing" made it clear that it was for her and not for what she had been through.

"We're a lot alike," Sally smiled. She put her arm through August's, and they continued walking toward Bruce.

They spotted the crown of Bruce and began walking faster. It seemed as if the wind was following their pace. Aza and Justin were standing about twenty feet from the tree when they got there. Aza had a gun and Justin was practicing making mean faces in case anyone tried to attack or take out the tree. Near the pine, lying on the ground, was a blanket spread out with a couple of plates and a basket full of food. It wouldn't have been such a bad sight to August if it had not been for the presence of Ryan already sitting there. He looked about as uncomfortable being there as August felt having him around.

"I guess we shouldn't be surprised," August said, trying not to sound disappointed. "After all, I sat in on your video this morning."

"Ezra told me that someone was trying to dig up Bruce," Ryan explained. "So we ran over here, which by the way was awkward because of Ezra's cape. It kept blowing behind him and whipping me in the face. When I got here I realized that I had been tricked, and Aza has refused to let me go."

"Someone should sit down with Candle and explain to her how matchmaking really works," Sally laughed.

Sally and August took a seat on the blanket with Ryan.

"Actually, I'm glad you're here," August said honestly. "I've wanted to ask you something about Mormons."

Ryan smiled, and Sally was amazed at how good-looking he was. It was as if that one smile had released a thousand pounds of pressure.

"Shoot, " he said.

"Do Mormons have more than one wife?"

"No."

"Really?" August persisted.

"All right," Ryan said, "in the early days of the Church, some of our members had more than one wife. We believe that the Lord used polygamy . . ." Ryan said *polygamy* as if it were a big word that Sally and August might not be familiar with. " . . . He used polygamy to raise up a righteous generation of church members, but we no longer practice plural marriage or condone it. It was the Lord's right to use it when he saw fit."

"So if I became a member and wanted a second wife, could I do it?"

"I guess, but you'd be excommunicated from the Church."

"Weird," August sighed.

The hot breeze that had been steadily blowing now escalated into a strong wind. The blanket that the three of them were sitting on started to flap like mad at its loose corners and tipped over the picnic basket.

"Where did this come from?" Ryan asked, looking at the sky that was suddenly a threatening, inky black color.

"This place has the oddest . . ." August was stopped by a paper plate that whipped up and smacked him in the face.

Everyone tried not to laugh as they attempted to hold things down with their empty hands. It was as though the wind became angry at them for trying to hold it back. In no time at all there were plates and napkins blowing everywhere.

"This is really strange," Sally said nervously.

"Maybe we should take this picnic inside somewhere," August suggested.

"I don't think Aza will let us leave," Ryan said seriously.

August stood up and walked over to Aza.

"We're going to take the food indoors!" August shouted.

"Candle told me to keep you all out here until you were finished," he shouted back.

"Well, I'm done," Ryan said, standing.

With both Ryan and August off of the blanket, the wind was able to pick it up and pull it out from underneath Sally. It blew right into Justin, who danced and struggled with it for a few moments before he was able to rip it off of himself, screaming.

"Let's get out of here!" he hollered to Aza.

It was at that exact moment that lightning struck. There was a blinding flash of light and a simultaneous clap of thunder, so powerful that it knocked Justin off of his feet and caused both Aza and Sally to scream.

"Run!" Ryan hollered. "Run!"

Everyone took off. August and Ryan each took one of Sally's

hands, but in the end August was the gentleman, letting go so that they could all run to safety. August dove under a large stone ledge as Sally and Ryan rolled beneath the overhang of a cluster of tall pines. August had no idea where Justin and Aza had made it to, but when he looked out to see if there were signs of them, all he could see was another terrific flash of blinding light, accompanied by the rip of thunder. The bolt of lightning struck Bruce, exploding it into a billion pieces. Debris from the pulverized tree was swept away by the wind that smelled of heavy ozone.

Bruce was gone, and for the first time in a long while August was a little nervous.

The storm swept on, lightning flashes and thunder moving away over the nearby mountains, tearing apart the sky with violent fits of light and noise. Then, as quickly as it had all begun, the hoopla and glitter was gone, leaving the night still and calm.

August ran to the hole where Bruce had once stood and called out for Aza and Justin. Aza came running, followed closely by Justin. Justin looked at the hole where Bruce had been and swore. He then apologized for swearing and promised that he would try harder to have a clean mouth. Ryan and Sally came up behind him and announced their presence. The scare startled Justin, and he swore again.

"Unbelievable," Ryan observed, looking at the ground. "That tree was huge. Now it's nothing," he said, dusting bits of Bruce off of himself.

"I saw the lightning hit," August said.

"Me, too," Aza added.

"So did I," Justin announced, wanting to be included.

"We couldn't see anything," Ryan said lamely, still holding Sally's hand.

"I hate to say it, but I think we're in trouble," Aza whistled. "God's gotten into this now."

"It's just a coincidence," August laughed. "An unbelievable coincidence."

The air was completely quiet now. It was a peaceful, serene night with the sounds of crickets in the air. Aza lifted his gun into the dark quiet sky and fired three times. Within a few minutes half the town was standing around the hole, finding it hard to believe that what they were seeing was true.

CHAPTER NINETEEN

TWO . . .

Bruce Wood was a big troublemaker. He had been born with ·an amazing ability to mess up everything in a funny, entertaining, and ofttimes interesting way. He had ruined his eighth birthday party by feeding buckets of cooked mushrooms and kidney beans to the ponies his mother had rented for the kids to ride. That had been a real disaster. As a young boy, he had mailed ransom notes to Santa, demanding better presents and threatening there would be one less child to spoil in the Wood household—and he wasn't talking about himself. At twelve, he had begged his father to give him a job wrapping Christmas gifts at his dry good store for customers. Impressed by his son's willingness to work for free, Wilton gave him the job. Unfortunately, Bruce had wanted the job because of the power for mischief it provided. In his richly deviant mind he had envisioned what might happen when unsuspecting people opened packages that had been wrapped weeks before. Bruce gleefully slipped a book about hygiene into a husband's gift for his wife. He also wrote little notes and put them in with new dresses or other clothes that people were giving as presents. Notes that said things like: "I doubt this will fit, but they didn't have a bigger size" or "These earrings should divert people's attention from your ugly nose."

Needless to say, he was not a nice kid, and the day after Christmas was not a happy time at the dry goods store.

At seventeen, drawing upon the fact that he looked much older than his age, Bruce had run for mayor of Seven Pines, wearing a disguise and promising everything under the moon. Nobody ever thought to check his credentials, or even to ask where he lived.

He won by a landslide, and at his swearing-in he took off his wig and false mustache and told the audience what he really thought of them. The townspeople wanted to have him arrested, but he really hadn't broken any laws on their books. Apparently, impersonating a politician was perfectly legal.

The runner-up stepped into his place and spent his entire term trying to run Bruce out of town. He would have met with absolutely no success if it had not been for the fact that Bruce turned eighteen during his term and slipped away from Seven Pines of his own accord. The whole town had rejoiced, their only disappointment being that they had never really gotten a chance to see Bruce get struck down and put in his place.

With Bruce's disappearance, once again Wilton had mourned. The pain of his loss was almost too great for him to bear any longer. With the escape of his latest son, Wilton had finally begun to understand what he had lost in being the kind of father he had been. The pain he felt in realizing this was greater and more devastating than any of the heartache he had ever suffered. The realization that he had let the best time of his life go by without ever knowing his children ate at him like acid resting on a bed of porous salt. He could see and feel the hurt and pain that his father had passed on to him and that he was now passing on to his children. Sadly, despite what he understood, he could still not make himself change.

He planted Bruce's memorial tree close to town on the southwest side. The tree didn't do well at first. In fact, more than a couple of times, Wilton thought about digging it out and planting a healthy one. But as the second spring of Bruce's disappearance broke, the tree began to grow—its progress could be seen by everyone as the crown crested above the rest of the forest, pointing to heaven and reminding the world that Wilton had wanted to love his mischievous boy.

🌲 🌲 🌲

Seven Pines was no more. It was now Two Pines, and the panic and chaos that accompanied the name change was huge. Nobody felt safe. Nature was out to get them. Everyone looked constantly over his or her shoulder, judging and wondering who they could blame. There was no sense of community anymore. The town had forgotten what it once had and who had ultimately provided them with it.

With the bloom off the lily, people who had lived there forever were making plans to leave. Those who were planning to stay were stocking up on food and ammo. Ezra Hicks put on his best cloak and spent the morning walking around and waving his hands as if he were blessing the place and warning people that the ring was in disrepair and they had better watch the skies. A couple of townspeople were so unnerved by Ezra's warnings that they called Aza and told him to get his son off the streets before they found a use for all the ammo they were hoarding. Aza wasn't necessarily mad about Ezra wandering the street in costume, chanting, he was just ticked off because Ezra was supposed to be at his piano lesson. Aza raced down to town and hauled his boy over to Paula Lemon's to work on passing off "Red River Valley."

August had tried twice to slip out of town unnoticed. He knew that he had already stayed too long. The secret he had come to town to discover remained hidden, and he was already beginning to see the hurt leaving some of these people would bring. He needed to feel invincible. It was all he had. This worrying about others and being concerned about his neighbors was ruining the cold, hard strength he had found in concern for his own needs. He could clearly see that, so he tried to get out. Both attempts failed miserably.

First, Justin stopped him near the border of town and begged him to help dig a grave for the Rodchesters's Great Dane. The old dog had died trying to learn a new trick and now the family wanted him in the ground before he began to stink and ruin all of the happy memories they had of him. Justin would have dug the hole himself, he said, but he had twisted his wrists while fighting that blanket in the big wind that preceded the demise of Bruce.

August protested but eventually gave in and returned to the cemetery to dig a big hole for a Great Dane.

The second time August tried to sneak off was early in the morning. Before the sun was even up, he had begun hiking out of town through the forest. He figured that if he stayed off the road, he would have a much better chance of not running into someone he knew. But he ran smack dab into Bishop Skablund. The bishop was in the thick part of the woods, dressed in his three-piece suit at five in the morning, picking Morning Sparkles.

"August," he had said with no surprise.

"Bishop," August answered, not having any idea what else to call him. August had then glanced at the flowers in his hand.

"They're for my wife," Bishop Skablund said sheepishly. "Morning Sparkles are prettiest when picked in the early morning.

August pictured Sister Skablund receiving the flowers and the bright smile she would emit.

"That's nice of you."

"I've been remiss."

August didn't know what the heck the formally dressed man meant by that, so he just smiled and said, "Haven't we all?"

Bishop Skablund blinked, then closed his eyes, as if contemplating something incredibly profound. "Haven't we all," he repeated softly. "Thank you, August."

"You're welcome," August said.

They looked at each other for a few seconds. There was even a brief moment when each considered hugging the other, but neither was certain the other felt the same way, and so the moment was lost.

"So what are you doing out here?" Bishop Skablund finally asked.

August blinked and closed his eyes as if Bishop Skablund had just said something incredibly profound himself. What *was* he doing out here? August wondered.

He had always struggled to find any real meaning in life. Growing up with three mothers and then losing his sister, the only person he could remember ever having truly loved, August had insulated himself from additional hurt by drawing into himself. He could see that now. So long as he didn't love anyone or anything too much, he couldn't be hurt by its loss. And having endured the loss of Rachel, the thing he cherished most, he knew he could never be hurt that much ever again. That had been his source of strength and peace. So long as he focused on himself, he felt strong and secure—even invincible.

But now, here in Seven Pines, and especially here in the woods with Bishop Skablund, he felt another emotion. Thinking about the bishop's wife and the bright smile she would emit when her husband would hand her those flowers was strangely appealing, and it filled him with a sudden rush of happiness. It was as if August's feet were lifted off the ground and the forest were circling round him like a chain of children dancing. He could see equations in his mind and feel the answers in his soul. Morning light streamed through the forest, and he knew that there was no more important place he needed to be right then than right here.

August had been remiss. But maybe that could be fixed.

"I came to walk you home," August lied.

Bishop Skablund looked at him and smiled. August could see the change in himself by the way the bishop looked at him. It was as if the Bishop Skablund had been standing in the shower, fully dressed in a three-piece suit of course, and August had rolled open the frosty glass door so that he could clearly see out.

"There is something about you, August Thatch," the bishop said, shaking his head. "Now tell me, why aren't you a Mormon?" he asked as they began to stroll slowly back toward town.

"I've never owned a three-piece suit," August joked.

Bishop Skablund laughed, then actually loosened his tie and unbuttoned the top button of his shirt.

The town awakened that morning with the dark realization that it was in trouble. People were afraid. *The Pines Monitor* reported on a case of looting that involved a single family and their own children. They also did a whole half-page article on how it was twelve degrees warmer this year than last, how the reservoir was low, how the skies were filled with smoke—thus causing the moon to turn to blood—how the fifth tree had been obliterated by the hand of heaven, and how, for some reason, subscriptions to the paper were down. Tony the hermit had a short column in that edition as well, where he ranted about nature taking away what he felt was his job–to alarm people.

The high school set up a triage for potential victims and wounded. Of course, nobody had actually been hurt or wounded. In fact, aside from five missing trees, a couple of fires, dried up wells, some people pulling up stakes and abandoning town, and the spate of unseasonably warm summer weather, life was not too much different than it had always been in Seven Pines. Say something like that in the open, however, and you would have been asking for a heated argument. It seemed to everyone as if things were falling apart and that the town had no real ability to fix itself.

August wandered around town, wondering what he was going to do. He had no clear sense of right or wrong anymore. He couldn't remember life before Seven Pines almost as much as he couldn't picture a life after it. He had the ability to leave, but for some reason the town wasn't easily letting him say good-bye.

Apparently Ryan didn't feel that the town falling apart was any reason to call off the dating game he and Sally and August had been playing. As he passed the café, August spotted the two of them having something to eat. They were laughing, apparently enjoying each other's company. He smiled at them and then pretended he had someplace to rush off to. It was while rushing that he realized he had absolutely nothing to do. He did not know why he was here, why he couldn't leave, or what to do next. Like grass, the town had sprouted up around his ankles and given him reason to sit and stay a while. And even though he didn't mind hanging around, he knew that this was not where he was supposed to put down roots or call home.

It was in this state of mind that August spotted Ezra Hick coming out of his piano teacher's home, carrying his songbooks.

"Hey, Ezra," August waved.

"August," Ezra answered back. Ezra liked August all right, he was mainly jealous of his name. August seemed like a warm, fiery name that any self-respecting citizen of middle earth would have.

"How was piano?" August asked.

"I passed off "Red River Valley," he said glumly.

"Congratulations," August offered, noticing that Ezra seemed out of sorts. "Are you okay?"

Ezra wiped his eyes with the hem of his cloak. "I'm all right."

"Sorry about the earth not ending yet," August said sincerely.

"Really?" Ezra perked up.

"I'm sure once the other two trees are gone, things will really go downhill."

Ezra smiled. "We've got to do something."

August was all for that. It had been a long time since he had solved any of his made-up mysteries. In fact, he couldn't remember a time since his sister had passed away that he had even noticed a single insignificant detail between point A and point B.

Maybe it was time to begin looking again.

"I'm glad I ran into you, Ezra," August smiled.

"You are?" Ezra said, surprised.

"Let's go check out the trees."

August and Ezra walked to the Northwest edge of town to look at Joseph, one of the two remaining seven pines. It stood straight and tall and looked to be twice the size and strength of any of the other seven pines. Nobody was guarding the tree anymore because, quite frankly, ever since it seemed heaven had gotten involved in destroying the trees, people were a bit nervous about standing too close to either of the two that were left. August and Ezra just stared at Joseph for a while.

August's thoughts were considerably different than Ezra's.

August could see how dry the needles on Joseph were. He could smell the smoke in the air and could feel the difference in the town and himself that five missing trees had made. Ezra, on the other hand, was wondering if today would be the day that the mail carrier would deliver the special Hobbit snow globe he had ordered.

"So who's taking the trees?" August asked Ezra.

"It has to be . . ." he began to speculate. He stopped and put his piano books under his cloak. He then continued. " . . . it has to be either a warlord or an unseen black force that was released by the changing of the seasons."

"So the normal teenage hoodlums theory is out?"

"Unless you want to be boring."

"So do you think that the unseen black force will take out Joseph?"

"Nobody could move Joseph," Ezra said reverently.

"God could," August observed.

Ezra flinched.

"You know, there's a place in heaven for people who like Tolkein," August said, wondering why on regular, or middle, earth he was talking about heaven. He was about as far from an expert on the subject as anybody God had ever put down here.

"Do you think there really is a place?" Ezra said hopefully.

"My sister loved those books, and she's in heaven," August went on. He didn't like even bringing the subject up, but he thought it might help Ezra.

"How do you know she's in heaven?"

The feelings August had felt that morning with Bishop Skablund began to grow again. He didn't know if he could survive another similar experience. That morning he had almost collapsed under the weight of it. He couldn't even express to himself how he felt. He knew that the death of his sister, Rachel, had impacted him in ways that he still had not noticed or did not understand. But he wished that he could control his life in such a way so as to not be afraid of what he was about to feel. The feelings of invincibility he had so much treasured were inferior to the power of real emotions.

"Some things are just known," August replied, wishing he had a real answer to give him. "I didn't know you would be coming out of your piano lessons and wanting to talk to me, but here we are."

"Wow," Ezra said. "You should be a Mormon."

"I keep hearing that."

"You want to know something, August?"

"Sure."

"My parents are old," Ezra lamented, changing the subject but keeping the conversation honest.

"They're still good," August pointed out.

"My mom's never even read *Lord of the Rings*," he confessed.

"Maybe not, but she runs a mean library."

"Material center," Ezra corrected.

"Your parents love you," August said. Again, it was really quite silly of him to be saying such things. The knowledge he had of parents loving their kids was nil. He knew nothing of what a father should be like to a son, or a mother to a child. He had heard Aza yell at Ezra. He had seen Candle mending his cloak. He had seen his own father stepping away from him time and time again so as to not be bothered. He had seen his own mothers argue over whose responsibility he really was.

"I know they do," Ezra said, breaking up August's thoughts.

"You're a good kid," August said honestly.

Ezra stared at August. He looked down at himself and then up at the tree. "I hate the color black," Ezra said, staring at Joseph as his black cloak rippled in the hot wind. "I hate Seven Pines."

August could feel Ezra looking at him out of the corner of his eye. He knew that what he had just told him was what he had wanted to tell somebody for a long time.

188

"It's just a place," August finally answered. "There are other places."

"Do you think you could tell my parents what I just said?"

"Don't you think they would rather hear it from you?"

"I don't think they would like to hear it from either of us," Ezra moaned. "My parents love this place. It's as if they would not exist if they didn't live within the borders of this town."

"It's where their son grew up."

Ezra looked around and then realized that August was talking about him. He liked the feeling of someone having noticed that he was grown up.

"So do you think you'll stick around here forever?" Ezra asked.

"I don't think so."

"You could marry Sally and buy one of the homes up for sale at the moment."

"You're talking like I have my own life figured out, Ezra."

"You don't?"

August smiled. "The only thing I know is that I'm glad I ran into you today."

Ezra looked at Joseph and then turned to look in the directions where the other trees had once stood. He could barely see where George and Peter had been. There was nothing visible of Ralph's resting spot, and Edward and Bruce's plots were hidden by forest as well.

"You know, this place used to be different," Ezra finally said. "It did seem secure and magical just weeks ago. Those trees did something for us."

"You still have two," August pointed out, the tender feeling inside of him diminishing some.

"I hate Seven Pines," Ezra said again.

"I miss my sister," August added.

🌲 🌲 🌲

August really did need to go. He couldn't take another conversation with anybody. He couldn't stand feeling for these people who he knew he hadn't been honest with, and there was no strength in opening himself up. He knew that he felt something for Sally, but he was smart enough to know that she could never be truly interested in him. He felt something for Seven Pines, but he was smart enough to know that he had emotionally worn out his welcome. He had set himself up to be hurt. The secret he had carried with him here was a joke, and the strength he had possessed just days before was being replaced by unpredictable waves of lightheadedness and confusion.

He walked back to the hotel and picked up his things for the third time in twenty-four hours. He was glad that he had never officially checked out. It would have been embarrassing by this point.

He walked through the lobby, careful not to make eye contact with Clancy or anyone else. He stepped out into the street and there was Sally. She was wearing a white shirt with long sleeves that were loose around her wrists. Her hair was shining under the light of the hotel's neon sign. She stood like a person who had been told they were beautiful but still didn't know if they should believe it. August temporarily lost his breath.

"You're late," she said, as he breathed in.

"For what?"

"Our together time," she smiled. "Don't tell me you forgot," Sally added, acting disappointed.

"Of course I didn't," August lied. The feeling of strength he had felt just moments before, knowing he was finally walking out of Seven Pines, was disappearing. Despite Sally and the amazing way the light rested on her, he needed to get away. He knew that if he didn't focus on himself, then he was doomed. "Just let me go change into my orange shirt," he said, thinking it might give him a chance to slip out the back door of the hotel, even though he was holding a bag with everything he owned in it.

"You're fine just how you are," Sally insisted. Her voice was out to get him. He had never heard someone be so vulnerable and in control at the same time. It was as if she were admitting to liking him simply from the sound of her vowels. "So where are we going?" she asked, cleverly using every vowel but U.

August had not read the instructions from Candle. He had never even opened his second letter. He had no clue where he was supposed to take Sally. "It's a surprise," he said with little confidence, taking her hand and pulling her down the street.

There weren't as many restaurants to choose from as there had been when August and Sally had first come to town. Over half the unusual spots were closed due to worry. Those still open were doing a booming business. People needed places to meet and speculate.

August spotted the Bubbling Kettle and headed toward it as if he were doing exactly what the instructions he had never read had directed. Once inside, they were seated, and August took a moment to realize that running into Sally wasn't a setback. It was a bonus. He could have a nice meal with her and then drop her off at Candle's. Then he could head out for good. She might be a little hurt by him leaving, but if he had stayed around for every girl who had ever been interested in him, he would have never gotten anywhere in life. Although a person could argue that he really hadn't gotten anywhere yet. August casually picked up his menu and read aloud a few of the things that sounded good. Sally had things besides entrees on her mind.

"So can we talk about stuff other than food?" she asked.

"Sure," August answered without thinking. "Where's their drinks," he said flipping the menu over.

"Or liquids," Sally smiled, her pink lips curling up in the most amazing way.

"Right," August replied, his brown eyes still taking in her curling lips. "Completely nonnourishing conversation. I'm all for that. What should we discuss?"

"Tell me about your sister," she said.

It was a shock. If August had been drinking milk he would have blown it out his nose, mouth, and ears. He had been very careful not to say anything about his sister or anything connected to her. He had made up things about himself simply to avoid having to talk about his Rachel's death. It was sad and miserable. It was weird. It was a brother grieving over more than just a sister. It was a person realizing that he had lost everything that would ever be honest to him.

"Which sister?" August asked, never taking his eyes off the menu and still wondering how Sally knew.

"The one reading books in heaven," Sally said sincerely.

"Ezra," August cursed.

"So, tell me."

"There's not much to say," he bristled. "She passed away this last summer."

"I'm sorry to hear that."

"I was sorry to live it," August added, sounding more biting than he would have preferred. This was not a conversation he had ever wanted to have. The light seemed to be hitting Sally differently as she brought up things he didn't think needed to be brought up.

"If you don't want to talk about it, then I understand," Sally offered.

Again August realized that it wouldn't hurt him to talk about it. His sister's passing had made it possible for him to withstand anything. And even though his mind was clouding up with darkness from Rachel's memory, he answered Sally.

"She had a weird disease," August explained. "It came up suddenly and took her life before I could really grasp the reality of it."

"I'm sorry," Sally said sincerely. "I know what it's like to be really sick."

August always hated this part. It seemed as if whenever Rachel's death came up, everybody always had a tragedy or trial to top it. Just once, August wanted someone to say that they had no clue how he felt and that they were certain that they would never experience the kind of hurt he had.

"So how was the funeral?" Sally asked.

"Fine," August waved. "Afterwards I accidentally burned down the school where she taught. They put me in jail for it," August nonchalantly motioned the waiter to their table. "Ready to order?" August asked Sally.

She closed her jaw and nodded. "I'll have the soup of the day and a house salad."

"I'll have the same," August said. "Only make mine slightly bigger than hers."

"Yes, sir," the waiter replied, taking the menus and walking off.

"So how was your date with Ryan today?" August asked, surprised at how uncomfortable he was feeling.

"You were in prison?" Sally finally was able to ask, surprised at how much she wanted to know.

"Just for a short while," August said flippantly. "I wasn't guilty."

"I don't think I've ever been out with an ex-con."

"Now you can check that wish off."

"People make mistakes, August," Sally said, trying to be kind despite August's belligerent attitude.

"That's true. But I bet Ryan's never been in jail."

"I don't think he has."

"Stick with him then." August rubbed his forehead and took a deep breath. He had not felt this weak in months. He suddenly wanted nothing more than to be away from here.

"Are you okay, August?" Sally asked as the waiter served them their drinks.

"Fine," August said, reeling under the ugly feeling that was making his head foggy and his thinking confused. "I just need to get out of this town."

"Leave?"

"I didn't come here to stay forever."

"You've barely been here a week."

"Listen, Sally, you're beautiful," August said, giving in to the ugliness inside of him. "You're sitting in a dumpy restaurant in a small town that's falling apart, and you're still gorgeous. I bet I could turn off all these lights and you would still shine. But that doesn't help me at all. You could light me up with spotlights, and I still wouldn't glow."

"What are you talking about?" Sally asked sadly. As she sat across from what was arguably the most attractive man she had ever met, listening to him talk about her beauty, she felt ugly.

"You're perfect," August jabbed.

"Knock it off, August," Sally insisted, not comfortable at all with what was happening. "I didn't come on this date to feel awful."

"What?" August motioned. "You mean Ryan doesn't talk to you like this?"

"All right," Sally said, embarrassed, putting her napkin on the table. "I think I'd better leave. I'm sorry about your sister, but I can't help it if I'm finding what I came here to find and you haven't."

Sally stood and looked long and hard at August; his brown eyes looked black in the poor lighting of the restaurant, and he looked whiter than she had ever seen him. She acted as if she were going to say something and then decided against it.

She walked out the door as if that too had been one of the instructions Candle had given them. August sat there feeling the mess inside his soul rush out and let in the reality of what he had done.

"Good," he said to himself. "It'll beat having to say good-bye." August had the waiter bring him both meals anyway. August finished them off without any problem. Then he picked up his things and left the Bubbling Kettle, disgusted both with himself and with how much he had just eaten. Then just as he began to feel like he might need to throw up, there was Ryan standing outside the restaurant doors waiting for him.

Even in his pre-vomit condition, August thought Ryan looked taller. He wasn't as stooped over or pale as he had seemed before. August figured it was simply the lighting of the night.

"Are you okay?" Ryan asked.

"So Sally told on me," August tried to smile. "Listen, Ryan, just leave it alone," he said sadly, not wanting to hurt anyone anymore than he already had. "I just want to leave."

If Ryan had stopped and thought about it he might have responded differently than he ultimately did. With August gone, his chances with Sally were that much more assured. But the emotions that Ryan had been feeling over the last couple of days wouldn't allow him to just drop this. He had come to Seven Pines because of a road sign and because he was hoping to find forgiveness for himself and for what he had done to Todd. In Sally he had begun to see hope again, and in that hope the feeling of self-loathing had receded to a point where he could look himself in the mirror and begin to worry about somebody other than himself.

"You can't leave," Ryan said kindly.

Ryan's sincerity was so honest that August almost threw up from the impact of it. He could feel his invincibility being doused. August stared at Ryan as if he were an alien with ten eyes and big funny ears. This was what August had wanted. Not the alien part, the honesty. This was what he had needed from his father, from his mothers . . . from his life. He needed honesty. The truth had never set him free because the truth had always been something to bend or avoid. He had hated his family because no matter how they explained or justified what they did, they were dishonest. Now here was this Mormon boy from Sharfield, Arizona, giving him his first glimpse of real honesty, and he almost couldn't stand due to the blow of it.

"I can't stay here forever," August pointed out, his insides really messing with him now. He had to get out of Seven Pines.

"I'll help you back to the hotel," Ryan offered.

But August waved him away and began walking off behind the restaurant to see if he could make himself feel any better. The time had come for him to go.

Unfortunately, he didn't make it four steps before he fell to the ground and passed out.

CHAPTER TWENTY

ONE . . .

When August finally awoke, it took him a full ten seconds to discover where he was. He thought for a moment that he was back home, or that he was in prison, or that he was simply laid out in one of the waiting rooms of heaven waiting for someone to come and tell him that he had been delivered to the wrong place.

He sat up and looked around the room. He had been eating dinner, and Sally had left him and Ryan was there and . . . nothing. August looked at his arms and pulled back the sheets to see if his legs were still hooked on. Everything looked okay. Jane came in wearing her waitress uniform. August blinked, figuring that he was still asleep and dreaming. Jane took his wrist and put a hand to his forehead.

"Haven't I seen you before?" August joked.

"You're delirious," she smiled.

"But—"

Jane shoved a thermometer into his mouth to shut him up. She then walked around the bed and opened the curtains. Light burst into the room, exposing every nook and cranny. The place was almost as clean as the café.

"What happened?" August mumbled.

"You passed out in the Kettle's parking lot," she said as if it were an everyday occurrence. "It was not your finest moment. The hospital was full, so they brought you here."

"This isn't the hospital?" August said, surprised.

Jane laughed. "This is my spare bedroom," she explained. "The café's just on the other side of that wall. If the hospital fills up, I help them out by taking in their least banged up patients. I guess they think I keep my place clean."

"So I'm going to live?" August joked, letting his brown eyes show that he wasn't serious.

"I suppose," Jane smiled. "Although your reputation might be bruised for sometime."

"I don't care about that," August lied. "I'm sure most people have passed out before."

"And then lost their stomach all over the people trying to help them up?"

"I did that?"

"And then began taking off your shirt because you were delirious and thought you were too hot. What was your exact quote?" Jane thought for a moment. "Oh, yes, 'I'm melting.'"

"At least it was only my shirt," August tried.

"Did I say that?" she said fluffing his pillow. "I might have left some of the details out. I don't want to make you feel too bad about yourself."

"So I passed out, threw up, and then disrobed?"

"I also left out the part about you weeping like a baby."

"Just great."

Jane walked around the room, wiping down a couple of things and looking even more beautiful than August had originally thought. Her long, dark hair was a pleasant mystery, the kind of mystery where nobody dies and you figure it out all on your own. She also had the most alluring stance. It was as if she were the only person who had ever stood that way.

"So, Jane, this is how you decorate your home?" August asked, trying not to sound too opinionated. "It's stark."

"We all have our phobias," she pointed out. "I like things clean."

"How often does the hospital fill up?"

"Not often. But a lot of people were hurt last night when Joseph fell."

August sat straight up. "Joseph fell? Joseph the tree?"

"He got the trunk blown out of him," she explained. "There have been pieces of him spotted as far east as Elk Street. Most of the injuries were splinter-related."

"So I got bumped for people with slivers?"

"Well, the top of Joseph fell on the Heybournes's home and did a number on Horton Heybourne's remodeled bathroom and Horton's left leg."

"How could Joseph blow up?" August said in disbelief.

"Justin did it," Jane said as if it were no big deal. "What I'm hearing is—"

A loud buzz went off.

"Sorry, August," Jane apologized. "I've got an order up." Jane quickly left the room.

August crawled out of bed. He grabbed his clothes—which had been washed, pressed, and folded and were neatly stacked in a chair in the corner—and threw them on.

He had to go see Justin.

August found Justin in jail, and he was only partially happy to see August. The jailhouse in Seven Pines didn't get used much. The cell door kept popping open the entire time August was talking to Justin.

"I can't believe it," August said, shaking his head.

"Don't lecture me," Justin complained, his gray skin nicely complementing the dark bars. "I thought I was onto something. I thought I was being smart."

"By blowing up a tree?"

"*Trees,*" the deputy that had led August to the cell corrected.

"I only blew up the one," Justin said adamantly. "I only did the one, August. Just Joseph. I promise I had nothing to do with the others."

The deputy walked off, leaving Justin and August alone. The cell door popped open and Justin dutifully pulled it closed. He then asked August if he would mind leaning against it so as to keep it from doing that. August leaned against the bars and smiled. It wasn't necessarily a happy smile. It was the kind of smile someone executes when they are stumped, stuck, or stupid. At the moment August felt like he was all three. He should have gotten out of Seven Pines days ago.

"What were you thinking?" August asked. "What could you have figured out that led you to blow up a tree?"

"Okay," Justin said, "it's like this. I figured that somebody was removing the trees because of something hidden inside or underneath one of them. Then I got to thinking that just maybe they hadn't found what they were after. I thought since we had already lost five trees it wouldn't really be a big deal to clear out one more and see if I couldn't find it."

"Find what?"

"Whatever it was that was in the tree."

"And that was?"

"Something worth breaking the ring for."

"So, you figured that all out yourself?" August asked.

"Candle helped," he said with embarrassment. "I told her part of my story, and she began to believe what I was saying and started me wondering if there might be something under one of those trees."

"So did you find anything?"

"Only dirt," Justin lamented.

August shook his head. "You should remember that Bruce was removed by lightning," August pointed out. "You were there. Besides, what could anyone have possibly hidden underneath any of those trees? They were planted years ago."

"I don't know," Justin said sheepishly. "It was stupid. I remembered that I had all that dynamite from back when I had experimented with digging graves with explosives."

"That seems like a bad idea," August said shaking his head.

"It was. It got the job done, but it did a number on some of the nearby headstones. If you knew what—" Justin stopped himself. "Anyhow, I used way too much dynamite. Joseph blew all over." Justin smiled for a second as if he had done something kind of cool. Then he caught himself and frowned insincerely.

"How long are they going to keep you in here?" August asked.

"I think they were going to let me out on bail, but they just discovered that I'm using an alias."

"Justin's not your real name?"

"I changed it when I left Bear Incident. It seemed like women like men named Justin better than Francis."

Knowing that Justin hadn't done particularly well with the ladies with either handle, August laughed lightly.

"They're wondering if I might have a past," he sighed. "Of

course I don't, unless you count that owl thing. I'm sorry, but when a bird sneaks up on me I take action."

"We all have a past," August pointed out.

"Tell them that," Justin begged. "That's powerful. They'll listen to you."

"I'll see what I can do," August lied, thinking of nothing but getting out of town. He felt foolish for having come to visit Justin.

"Listen, August," Justin said, his eyes darting back and forth as they looked to see if they were alone, "I need some help. The Smiths are burying a loved one today at six. I'd sure hate to have them show up and not find a hole."

"I'll take care of it," August said resignedly. "But that's it. After that, I quit."

Justin looked shocked.

August left before Justin could say good-bye.

CHAPTER TWENTY-ONE

NONE

Joseph had been Wilton and Maria Wood's sixth child and sixth boy. His birth had been uneventful, but his growth thereafter had been noteworthy. That boy could grow. By age ten, he was taller than any of his brothers, and by age sixteen, he was closing in on seven feet and easily the tallest person in Seven Pines. He was also the first child to tell his parents that he was not going to disappear on his eighteenth birthday. His father, who by that time had been weeping for many years, was so miserable and broken that Joseph's announcement did his heart good. Then Joseph turned eighteen, and everyone watched with bated breath to see what would happen. Well, on the day after his birthday, Joseph was still there.

The town had been amazed.

Both Maria and Wilton had been ecstatic. Their euphoria

didn't last long, however. No sooner had Joseph made it clear that he would stick around than his father began acting like his old self. While he continued to cry for his five children who had bolted, he bossed Joseph around, took him for granted, planned out his future, and treated him like something he had won and now owned. Joseph put up with it for a while, but then one day while his father was picking on him, he just exploded. He voiced every hurt and feeling he had endured and then ran out of town for good. Wilton and Maria were devastated in ways that they had never been before. Wilton recognized almost instantly what he had done and the chance he had blown. For the first time in his life he began to pray for forgiveness and for his children wherever they were. He wanted God to change him. He wanted God to let his children know that he loved them. He knew he had lost the opportunity to see them, but he just wanted them to know that he knew that he had been wrong. During this same time Maria became ill and moved from the shed back into the main house with their only remaining child, Mary.

🌲　🌲　🌲

The air in Seven Pines was smoky and gray. The town bore only a weak resemblance to the idyllic setting August had stepped into a week before. He could spot three separate forest fires and seven "closed" signs, and felt constantly the intense heat in the air. In a large way, the magic of Seven Pines had vanished with the destruction of the trees, leaving in its stead a place most people would rather never even know about, let alone live in.

August walked straight down Center Street, looking at the horizon and willing the feeling of invincibility to return. He had not felt even a stirring of it ever since his final date with Sally. He felt like running his fist through a glass window to see if he would bleed, or walking off a tall cliff to see if he would bounce.

"I'm alone," he said to himself as he walked through town. But somehow, the words didn't seem as honest as before. He had been alone because his sister had died. If he walked out of Seven Pines now he would be alone of his own accord. August was so caught up in his own thoughts that he didn't notice Ezra come out of the café and fall in step beside him. Ezra looked different. His hair was washed, and he had on a rather odd looking ascot tied around his neck. He also was sporting his summer-weight cloak.

"I've been looking everywhere for you," Ezra said. "Yvonne wanted me to give this to you."

Ezra handed August an envelope. He stopped walking and opened it. It was a thank-you card from the children who had come to the material center for a tour while he was there. Everyone had signed it, and a couple of the children had drawn little pictures.

"Just great," August said aloud, wishing this town would just leave him alone.

"Bad news?" Ezra asked.

"No, just bad timing."

"Where are you headed?"

"I'm not sure," August answered. "Someplace cooler."

"I don't remember it ever being this hot," Ezra said, wiping his forehead with the hem of his cloak. "We could sure use some rain to clear out the air."

"Maybe you should put that cloak away until winter," August suggested.

"I was going to," Ezra said sadly. "But the ascot hooks on to the fastening brooch in such a way that I can't wear one without the other."

"I have no idea what you're talking about," August admitted. "I've never actually worn a brooch."

The smoke from the fires made the air hard to breathe, and it burned a person's eyes. The sound of a fire or police car siren sounded in the far distance, and August could see a family loading their car with luggage as if to get away for a long while.

"I can't believe this is the same town," Ezra said. "I used to think the green and beauty of this place were ugly. Now, I wish it would all come back."

"It will someday," August said.

"There's only one of the seven trees remaining," Ezra pointed out. "There's no protection or hope in a single tree."

"There was no protection or hope in seven," August insisted. "Towns don't fall apart because someone digs up some trees. They fall apart when people forget who created those trees in the first place." August stopped and looked away, embarrassed to be saying what he had.

Ezra stared at August. "You really should be a Mormon."

"I keep hearing that," August said lamely.

"So where are you headed?" Ezra asked.

"I've got a grave to dig for Justin. After that, who knows?"

"Good luck, August. Wherever you're going." Ezra said. "I've got to go baby-sit the Heybourne kids." Ezra veered off to the north, leaving August to walk alone again.

August was a nobody. He was less than that. He hadn't made this town better, as Candle had challenged him; he had made it worse. August looked out into the distance. From where he stood he could see the huge sign at the edge of town that read: "Thanks for visiting Seven Pines. Stop in anytime."

He could also see the roof and steeple of the Mormon chapel to the west. August walked across the church lawn and then down toward the Memorial Gardens. Two minivans drove past him with bags and suitcases strapped to the top.

"This town is history," August said to himself. "Six trees turn up missing, and everything falls apart."

The Memorial Gardens were empty, and the hot, smoky air gave the tombstones an eerie look, even in the light of day.

August walked to the caretaker's shed and opened the long skinny door that led into Justin's office. There on the desk was a pair of gloves and a map of the cemetery showing the plot where the Smiths were expecting to find an open grave. August found a shovel and walked out across the lawns toward the far corner, near a huge leafy tree.

August checked the map again, wondering why any person would buy this plot or choose to stick a loved one here to rest for any amount of time. The Memorial Gardens were beautiful, but this lone back spot was out of the way and the landscaping incomplete and rough. August began to dig. He had done this twice before—once for a dog and once for a person. The labor of digging a grave caused him to talk to himself much more than he usually did.

"Digging a grave," he said, disgusted with himself. "Why can't I just have the guts to walk out of here and forget all of this?"

Soon, however, the act of digging began to be almost pleasurable. There was a certain satisfaction in seeing the hole deepen, and with each shovelful of dirt August seemed to be able to think more clearly. In spite of the heat and his perspiration, the methodical process was having a kind of therapeutic effect on him. August wondered if Justin had ever noticed that before.

"I'll be honest," he said aloud, suddenly feeling as though he needed to confess. "Rachel, I don't think I miss you as much as I miss feeling secure. I mean, I loved you as a sister and all, but it's knowing that you are not around that I feel the greatest loss over." August wiped his forehead and kept digging and talking to himself.

"I know what's wrong with me," he said, as if Rachel were right there listening to him. "I have never been totally honest."

The shovel sliced through the dirt, beautifully punctuating his thoughts.

"I wasn't ever honest with Dad. I wasn't ever honest with Moms. And I wasn't ever honest with myself. I lied to Dad my whole life by pretending to accept what he believed. I lied to Moms my whole life by never telling them what I really felt or explaining who I was, and I lied to myself by thinking that everything only involved me."

Dirt was flying.

"I came here thinking I had an in, and here I am with no way out. Talk about useless information," August complained. "Just once I would like my life to be smoother."

The shovel thunked.

August repositioned the shovel and tried to take another bite of dirt.

It thunked again.

Something was down there.

August dug furiously and within a short while he had uncovered the entire top of what looked to be a wooden coffin. He looked at his map. He looked at his map upside down. He looked at it sideways. He stuck his head above the hole and surveyed the cemetery. Then he climbed out of the hole and walked off the distance again. This was the Smith's plot. As far as he could tell he had dug in the right place. And as far as he knew there was a coffin where it shouldn't be.

August ran across the cemetery and down the footpath that cut through the woods behind the courthouse. He climbed the steps of the jailhouse and asked the deputy there if he could visit with Justin. The deputy thought about getting up and showing August the way again, but it seemed like entirely too much effort.

"Go on in yourself," he waved.

August walked back through the double doors and over to Justin's cell. Justin sat up and smiled.

"How'd you know I was lonely?" he asked.

"That's not why I'm here," August said, panting from his run. "Listen. I dug the Smith hole, and we have a problem."

"Roots?"

"No, there's already a coffin down there."

"Impossible. You must have dug in the wrong spot. They wanted that cheap plot in the back, the one near that big tree."

"That's where I dug."

Justin yanked the map away from August. The cell door popped open as he did so. August stepped inside the cell and sat on the edge of Justin's bunk as they both looked the map over.

"That's where you dug?" he pointed.

"That's it."

"And you're sure it's a coffin, not just some rock or a root?"

"I think I can tell the difference between a root and a long wooden box."

"You're probably right. Did you open it?"

"I'm not going to *open* it," August said with conviction.

"You'll have to," Justin said, equally convicted. "Listen, August, if you dug where you're showing me, then there's a coffin that's not supposed to be there. The Smiths paid good money for that plot, and they're not going to want to share their hole."

"What good would opening it do?" August whispered loudly, surprised by the fact that he was suddenly curious about doing so.

"There might be some sort of indication as to who it is."

"What would that help?"

"Well, we could figure out if it's someone who is supposed to be there, or somebody who is supposed to be somewhere else in the cemetery. There's probably a serial number or something on the underside of the lid."

"Coffins have serial numbers?"

"I'm not sure," Justin admitted. "Just open it and find out."

"Isn't that against the law?" August whispered. "Shouldn't I tell Chief Fellows?"

"It's only against the law to dig up a coffin, and you've already done that. There isn't a law about opening a coffin to find out who's in it."

"This is ridiculous, Justin."

"Please, August," he begged. "The Smiths will be heartbroken if things don't go as planned this afternoon. And I don't want the whole community thinking that I run a shoddy greens."

August made his way out of the jailhouse, back behind the courthouse, and up the crooked footpath that opened up into the prairie just below the Memorial Gardens. He could not believe how hot it was. In his entire life he had never perspired this much.

The cemetery was still empty as August made his way over to the coffin he had uncovered. He was uneasy doing the ghoulish thing he was about to do. But there was a small part of him that loved this. It reminded him of the made-up mysteries and imaginary investigations he had enjoyed so much in his earlier life.

He climbed down into the hole and looked closely at the coffin, brushing away the dirt, halfway hoping to find a serial number on the outside.

There was nothing.

The box was really old-looking and square, kind of like a coffin invented before serial numbers.

He worked for a while to dig a place to kneel, off to the side of the coffin, so he could lift the lid. There was a large brass latch on each end that popped open with relative ease. August then hefted the lid to see if he could even budge it. It moved in his grip. He let go of it and kneeled there, imagining what hideous thing he might see when he actually lifted the lid.

He held his breath, hoping that the feeling of invincibility he had come to rely on might give him the strength to do what he needed to do. There was nothing. August felt empty and weak. So much so that he needed to lift the lid, if only to prove to himself that he *could* open it. When he tried, the lid came open so easily that it seemed to jump up at him.

The coffin sat there opened.

August was dumbfounded. Then, he wanted to throw up. Then, he wanted to run into the woods and never come back. Then, he wanted to get this coffin out of the ground and someplace where nobody would ever see it.

He dug voraciously. He cleared the sides of the box and then worked a rope underneath it and rigged up a pulley over one of the limbs of the tall leafy tree above the grave. Using the pulley, he lifted one end of the box until he raised it above the lip of the grave, then got into the hole, under the box, and pushed it up and clear of the hole.

He couldn't prove it, but he felt pretty confident that his sister was right beside him helping him. And for a moment, feelings of perfect control surrounded him again.

Once the coffin was completely above ground, August struggled, pushing and pulling it over to the caretaker's shed. He was finally able to drag it into a small garage attached to the shed where he locked it in with a padlock he found in Justin's office. Then he ran like the wind back to the jailhouse.

If August had stunk before, it was nothing compared to the way he smelled now. With permission he walked back to Justin's cell, hot, sweaty, and excited.

"Did you open it?" Justin asked, through the bars.

"You were right," August said sadly and out of breath. "It was only a root."

"See," Justin said proudly, "you don't work in the business as long as I have and not know a few things."

"Sorry to even alarm you," August shrugged.

"No problem. We can have a good laugh about this over a meal at the café this afternoon."

"What?" August asked, suddenly panicking.

"Chief Fellows is working to get me out. He figures I'm not a flight risk. Isn't that great?"

"Yeah," August lied.

"I'll be back in time to fill up that hole you just dug. You're still quitting, aren't you?"

"Listen, Justin," August said quickly, "I've got to go."

"No problem. I'll see you later today." The cell door popped open again, and Justin dutifully closed it.

August walked down the hall and through the double doors into the jail office. Chief Fellows was there talking to his deputy. August didn't miss a beat.

"Is there a place out front of the jailhouse that I can park? I need to get as close as possible."

Chief Fellows looked at August with a tilted head. "There's parking just to the west," he pointed.

"Would it be okay to leave an idling car there for a few hours?"

"Excuse me?"

"Justin wants me to leave his car there idling."

The chief and the deputy stared at August, who went on. "I guess he figures the extra change of clothes he wants and the couple of hundred dollars in small bills will be safe in the car since it's in front of the jailhouse and all."

Chief Fellows stood up straight and tall. "Let me get this straight. Justin just asked you to park his car out front with a change of clothes and money for him in it?"

"And keep it running. Is that okay?" August played dumb. "He said something about hoping to catch a sunset in . . . what's that big country above us?"

"Canada," both the chief and deputy said.

"I always want to say Upper America for some reason."

"Listen," the chief said seriously, "If I were you, I wouldn't worry about leaving a car out there. Justin won't be going anywhere anytime soon."

"That's odd," August said, scratching his head. "Justin said if the fat one doesn't set him free, then he can always just pop open the door and help himself. I figured he was talking in code. You know those caretakers, they have a language all their own."

There was steam coming from Chief Fellows' ears, and his big face was turning bright red. "Get me the welding supplies," he sputtered to his deputy. "I need to weld something shut."

August walked out feeling a little bad but also wearing a big smile. The feeling of invincibly within him was coming back to life. He had learned very well how it worked: as long as he was able to block out any desire to be honest or any concern for anyone but himself, there was nothing he couldn't do. He lifted his gaze to the smoky skies and tried to remember why he had even ever worried about anything.

August walked straight over to Ed Lemon's Ford Land. Ed Lemon, himself, an older man wearing a striped dress shirt and a checkered tie, approached him.

"Can I help you?" Ed asked August.

"I need a truck," August replied.

"Well, we have a nice selection of trucks and some really good financing plans, thanks to our fire sale."

"That won't be necessary," August smiled. "I have cash."

"I see," said Ed, smiling back. "Right this way."

A short while later August drove off of the car lot in one of the nicest trucks there. The price painted on the windshield still said twenty-three thousand, five hundred and seventy-two. But August had gotten a cash discount, bringing the total cost down to somewhere around twenty-one thousand.

Life was finally working out.

August pulled onto Main Street and maneuvered his new truck around a couple of cars and a woman taking a picture of the café. He spotted Bishop Skablund and his wife coming out of the Bubbling Kettle. Sister Skablund had on a beautiful new pink dress and was laughing at something her husband had just said. August sped down the road, not wanting to look too long at anything or anybody he knew.

The feeling of power inside him was huge. He had one stop to make, and then he would be out of Seven Pines and on to the next step in his life, wherever and whatever that might be. With his thoughts focused on nobody but himself, he was once again invincible.

He turned onto Aspen and then right onto Bison Drive. It was a bad move. There, far down the road but directly in front of him, was Mary, the last of the seven memorial trees. August tried to ignore it. He even took a couple turns, trying to avoid seeing her. But no matter where he turned or drove, she always seemed to be there, either waiting for him, or following him.

Mary was a tall and majestic tree. And backlit by the sun shining through the mist of smoke from a not-too-distant fire, she looked even more ominous than usual. August felt drawn to her. He thought of Sally, of Ryan, of Ezra, and of Candle. He thought of his mothers. His father. He couldn't stop thinking of painful things. He turned on the radio, but none of the buttons were preset, and he couldn't pick up anything but static. He pulled to the side of the road and turned off the truck. His head was pounding and his eyes burned. After a few minutes, he restarted his new truck, pulled back onto the road, and drove toward Mary.

He parked near the base of the tree and climbed out. There was nobody anywhere near. August walked up and touched Mary, as if doing so would help him to decipher reality. His life had changed so much in the last while. What he had grown up to be was gone. What he had been taught to be was forgotten. And what he had always wanted to be, he was turning his back on.

Standing in the long shadow of Mary, August felt all right about disclosing to himself what he honestly felt and desired. But that was not the way he had chosen to live. He knew that he would continue to wrestle his entire life with the choice between thinking of himself or thinking of others. Unless he did something about it today. Clearly, it was the fault of Seven Pines and those he had grown to care about that he was even having this struggle. These people had gotten under his skin, and he needed to be rid of them. He needed to get back on his own. He needed to be in control again.

"Forget it. What do they know?" a cold voice within him whispered. "You have survived things that would have killed others. Being honest and caring about people is not what matters to you." He thought back on what he had been through in the last week and what he had just discovered in the graveyard. He couldn't be hurt now.

August smiled. It wasn't a pretty, toothpaste ad smile. Nor would it have been the kind of smile that you might enjoy if, say, the boy picking your daughter up for a date was wearing it.

August got into his truck and turned in the opposite direction of the tree. He drove about a half of mile and then turned the truck around so that he was aimed directly toward it. Mary stood tall at the end of the long straightway. From that distance, she looked small and breakable. There was not another car or person in sight.

August nodded his head. He could do this. He *would* do it, to prove to himself that he was still in charge, untouchable—that the

strength that he had gained from having lost so much was sufficient. He experienced a wave of disgust. He was disgusted with
himself for ever having let people penetrate his soul and expose his
vulnerability.

He put the gearshift in neutral and pressed on the gas and listened to the engine rev. He gripped the wheel and wondered why
he had ever let himself listen to himself. He revved the engine
again. Then he wavered. For a moment he wished he was more
like Sally, more like Ryan, more like Candle and Ezra, and
more like Bishop Skablund. Actually, he really just wished he was
less like himself.

He pressed on the gas again, and the powerful new engine of
his brand new truck roared. Within seconds he was flying straight
toward Mary.

He could see his father frown. He could see his mothers knit
their brows. He could remember Sally as she stood and walked out
of the restaurant, and Ryan as he asked him if he was okay. He
could see Rachel dying. He could see her take her last breath and
remembered the loss he had so instantly felt. There could be
nothing worse than that.

August *was* invincible.

Mary was only a few hundred feet away now. August kept the
wheel straight. He couldn't tell how fast he was going, and he was
too nervous to look down and check for fear of drifting off course.
Then, as if he had planned it all along, he felt his hand reach for
the door and his shoulder push it open. He dove out of the truck as
it continued to race forward. He hit the ground hard, rolled off the
road, down an embankment, and slammed into the thick trunk of
a tree.

He had chickened out.

He saw green, and then yellow, and then black.

And then only black.

CHAPTER TWENTY-TWO

FAMILIES ARE FOREVER

August didn't want to get up. That's not completely true, he didn't want to do *anything*. He wanted to just lie there with his eyes closed forever. It was so still and so comfortable. He probably would have just stayed right there, resting, if it had not been for the sound of his sister's voice.

"Driving a truck into a tree," Rachel scolded. "I'm glad I wasn't alive to see that!"

August sat up, startled and amazed. "Rachel?" he said in disbelief.

Rachel smiled, and August knew that he was dreaming. She looked a little older and well. He tried to think hard. It seemed to him that someone had said something at some point about how dreams could be visions.

"Am I having a vision?" he questioned, wanting to put a label on what was happening to him.

"No," she answered.

"Am I dead?" he asked.

"No," Rachel smiled.

"Near death?"

"Not even," Rachel sighed. "I guess I shouldn't be surprised that the first thing you've asked me are questions about whether or not what you're seeing is true."

"All right then, how are you?" August asked, trying to appear less self-centered.

Rachel smiled, having seen right through him. "I suppose it's just a result of your head hitting that tree so hard." She sat down next to August, and for the first time he noticed his surroundings. They were in the back of the little chapel that they had attended while growing up—the same one that doubled as a fire station on weekdays. It wasn't comforting to be there. In fact August might have thought he was in hell if it had not been for Rachel.

"You're not doing too well, are you?" she said kindly. "With life, I mean."

August shrugged.

"I really liked that school," she said.

August was confused for a moment before he remembered. "I fell asleep. I didn't plan to burn it down."

Rachel smiled, and August was reminded how much he missed having family around.

"You never told our parents that I loved them," Rachel frowned.

"I was clear with you on that from the start," August said defensively. "I'm not talking to them."

"One phone call," Rachel complained. "That's all it would have taken."

"They would have hung up on me."

"No, they wouldn't."

"Is this one of those arguing visions?"

Rachel smiled again.

"I miss you," August admitted.

"I know you think you do," she pointed out. "But what you really miss is having someone around who believes in you being good."

"People believe I'm good," August said defensively.

Rachel looked at him skeptically.

"You're probably right. So is heaven nice?" he asked, changing the subject.

"It is," she said.

"Can I ask you something?"

"Of course."

"Are the Mormons right?" It was a question that had been bothering August for quite some time. All right, it had been bothering him for the last seven days. He had even considered praying about it, but now with Rachel sitting right next to him it seemed like an opportunity to get a direct answer.

Rachel smiled. "If I said yes, what would you do?"

"Join, I guess."

"And if I said no?"

"I probably wouldn't."

"So what kind of dumb question is that?" she laughed. "Come on, ask me something helpful. I've only got a couple more minutes."

"This is timed?"

"In a sense. Any moment now Aza's going to find you down by that tree and carry you over to the hospital. They're going to be filled up because of your truck, which missed the tree and kept on going until it ran into the petting zoo."

"Missed the tree?"

"Completely. You weren't quite as successful as when you ran down Ralph a few days ago," Rachel said, looking up at her brother.

"You saw me do that?"

Rachel nodded. "Not your finest moment."

"I didn't even get a scratch," August bragged.

"You were lucky," she chastised. "Just like when you blew up George without killing yourself."

"I'm invincible."

Rachel frowned. "You're wrong."

Rachel checked her watch and sighed. "Well, this has been far less productive than I had hoped."

"So what am I supposed to do?"

"About what?" she asked.

"About me, about life?"

"August, do you remember the glasses you got when you were nine?"

August nodded.

"You were so proud. Nobody in our family had ever had glasses, but you begged and begged until they bought you some. Then you wore them one day and never put them back on."

August remembered the story all too well. He had whined and pleaded to get glasses. Finally, one of his mothers had taken him to the big city and ordered him some. August had waited and waited for them to come in the mail, and when they finally arrived, he was thrilled. He put the new glasses on and wore them to school, thinking that his whole life would be better now that he could see clearly. Things might have been different if it had not been for the fact that the first day he wore them was also Halloween. Everyone at school and in the neighborhood thought they were his costume and commented liberally on how funny he looked.

"Good one, August."

"A four-eyed freak. Clever."

"Those make a good mask."

At the end of the day August had gone home, taken off his glasses, and flushed them down the toilet. Of course, glasses don't flush easily, so he took a hammer and busted them into little pieces that then seemed to float away effortlessly. His father spanked him unmercifully for losing his glasses. But the pain of his whipping was nothing compared to the hurt August had felt at knowing what he had chosen was stupid and worth laughing about.

"What do my glasses have to do with anything?" August said, frustrated.

"Nothing," Rachel smiled. "I've just always thought it was sad."

"That people were honest with me?"

"No, that you weren't honest with father."

"I wasn't about to tell him I had crushed them with a hammer."

Rachel checked her watch again, then said, "I've always wondered what it would have been like if you and I had been honest with our parents from the start. If we had told them that we didn't believe."

"Nothing would be different," August insisted.

"I wonder."

"Could we talk about something else?"

"I need to go," Rachel frowned. "They've just put you up in Jane's extra room. You'll be coming to soon."

"Wait a second," August panicked. "Do they know I was aiming for the tree?"

"No, but they're still kind of mad at you."

"Because of the hurt animals?"

Rachel checked her watch again and then shook her head. She sighed deeply. "After the petting zoo was destroyed by your brand new truck, everybody gathered to try to collect the wounded animals. There were peacocks and goats everywhere. Candle had gotten the news over the phone that the zoo had gone down, and as soon as she was able to find someone to fill in for her at the library—"

"Material center," August corrected.

"That town's growing on you, isn't it?" Rachel smiled. "Anyhow, as soon as she found a substitute, she came over in her van to help out. Well, they started throwing all the wounded animals into her van. They stuffed it full of any animal that was in need of attention. Then, in her haste to rush the wounded to the hospital, and due to a couple of frantic roosters clawing at her, Candle accidentally threw the van into reverse and slammed hard into the tree. Mary just popped out of the ground and collapsed. The tree's gone, August. And to make things worse, when the tree fell, so did Candle. She got out of the van to assess the damage, took one look at the fallen tree, and collapsed right there on the spot."

"Is she okay?" August asked desperately.

"I'm not sure," Rachel said. "All I know is that she got the hospital bed that would have been yours."

"I need to wake up," August said frantically.

"Go ahead," Rachel offered.

"I'm not sure I want to."

"Suit yourself," Rachel smiled. "But I'd better go."

"So that's it?"

"That's it."

"No mysteries revealed, or gushing appreciation for all the sorrow I've felt over your death?"

"Nope. I love you, August."

"I knew that before this vision."

"Then stop worrying about it and move on. Good-bye August."

"I—"

Rachel got up and walked off. August tried to follow, but he seemed stapled to the spot he was sitting. He struggled for a second and then began to feel his body waking up. The vision faded, and there was Jane staring at him.

"You're awake," she smiled.

"I need something to drink," August rasped.

Jane pulled out a pad of paper from her apron belt and took the pen from behind her ear. "What can I get you?"

August ordered water, as well as an explanation as to what had happened and how he had gotten there. It seemed as if his vision had been right on. He finished his water and then set out to see Candle.

Aza led August into the hospital room and presented his wife as if he worked for a game show and was sadly displaying a refrigerator.

"Is she going to be okay?" August asked, his head still hurting from the hit he had taken earlier.

"They don't know yet," Aza said soberly. "They're not even sure what's wrong with her. She just collapsed." He smoothed her tall hair.

Candle looked peaceful lying there. August was surprised at how concerned he felt over what had occurred.

"So what happened?" Aza asked him, trying not to sound accusatory. "Did you just lose control of your truck?"

"Yes," August lied.

"Where'd you get that new truck anyhow?"

"The dealer."

"It's a pity to lose control of such a fine looking vehicle." Aza began to cry. He wasn't losing liquid over the truck, he was honestly worried about his wife. "I've never been anything," Aza admitted. "I was a nothing before I met her and came here."

"I'm sure you were something," August tried.

"Oh, I had that car and a couple of nice suits and a successful business, but it wasn't until Candle walked in that I realized what I was missing. She thought my name was interesting—that it sounded Egyptian."

August stood there trying to look compassionate. It was new territory for him. He ran his fingers through his hair, shifted his weight from one foot to the other, then reached awkwardly to pat Aza on the back.

"Thanks, August," he sniffed. "I know you haven't been here for very long, but I think that Candle looks upon you as more of an extended visitor than just a stranger."

"Thanks, Aza."

"And that boy of mine respects your opinion."

August nodded.

"Of course, he is also convinced that there are magic rings hidden all over the world."

"A compliment's a compliment."

Aza wiped his nose on the end of his own sleeve. "You know what one of the saddest things is?" he asked rhetorically. "Candle wanted this town to be as magical as it was. She brought me here despite my objections because she said she could feel it was right."

"I'm sure she enjoyed living where she grew up."

"Candle didn't grow up here," Aza said, looking confused. "She grew up in Washington state somewhere.

"I thought she said she grew up here?"

"You must have heard wrong. No offense, but you younger generations have a hard time focusing on anything that isn't directly connected to you."

Aza went on talking, but August didn't listen. He was distracted, thinking back to the conversation he had had with Candle a few days before.

"Do you mind if I sit with her?" August asked. "Just for a while."

"That would be great," Aza said. "I need to get something to eat anyway."

"You go," August insisted. "I'll stay right here."

Aza kissed his wife on the forehead and ordered her not to leave him alone on this earth. He then thanked August and walked slowly from the room.

August sat alone with Candle, thinking.

CHAPTER TWENTY-THREE

GATHER 'ROUND

August didn't move from Candle's side. He felt a connection to his sister and to the vision he had had by simply sitting there. The hospital noises were comforting for some reason. The beeping and ticking of machines as well as the oinking and cooing of some of the patients seemed to calm him, despite what was happening to the town around.

Seven Pines was doomed. Fires were closing in, people were moving out, and Candle was in a coma. Fire crews from all over the state were battling the blazes, and most of the outlying areas had already been evacuated. The last of the seven memorial trees had fallen just as Candle had, and there seemed to be nothing left to hold the town together. Nobody was helping anybody out. In fact, it was a free-for-all as everyone scrambled over each other to benefit themselves and see themselves safely away. Ezra had almost been right.

The friendliness and prosperity that the town had enjoyed just weeks before was gone, and August knew he was to blame. As much as he wanted to walk away from this one, he couldn't. He was connected whether he liked it or not. The only people sticking things out were the Mormons. Bishop Skablund had counseled his ward members to do as they saw fit, but then added that nothing was going to make him and his family leave.

August played out the last week over and over in his mind. Seven days ago all was well here. Seven days ago the town held nothing but hope and possibility. Sally had come here for security, Ryan had come here for forgiveness, and August Thatch had come here to find some fabled money that was supposedly buried beneath one of the seven pines.

August had overheard the story in prison, right before he had gotten into his only fight. He had heard one inmate whisper about a town in Montana by the name of Seven Pines, and how there was a fortune buried beneath one of the trees there. Apparently that prisoner had been through Seven Pines sometime before and had overheard Ezra Hick telling the tale to Jane in the café. Ezra had known of the secret but had never believed it—apparently it seemed too far-fetched for him. The secret being that a sad old man by the name of Wilton Wood had mourned the loss of his children by planting the seven trees. He was said to have also left a substantial amount of cash buried beneath one of them.

Prompted by his feelings of invincibility, August had thought he could march in, find the cash, and walk out without too much effort or any involvement. He had blown up the first tree easily with some explosives he had purchased in a small town on the way here. There had been nothing under George. He had dug up the second with a bit more effort, but with no results. It had been then that he had put his invincibility to the test.

As August was thumbing his way to Seven Pines, he had run into a man from Utah by the name of Ray Smoothers. Smoothers was a man on a mission to give his things away. He had read a book on how to become a minimalist and had seen the borrowed light. He actually didn't have much to leave behind in Utah, but Ray figured he would work himself up to Canada where he could be a minimalist with better social benefits. It was August's luck to be picked up by Ray just as he had decided to free himself of the sin of owning a car. He handed August the keys at their last stop and wished him well with his "life of being a slave to objects and ownership." August had thanked him and wished that Ray had possessed a better car to give away.

It wasn't too many days after that that August had driven that old car straight into Ralph. August had walked away without even a scratch and with an even deeper conviction of his ability to survive anything. Once again, however, the tree had housed no money.

It was then that August first began to wonder if the story he had overheard had any real validity.

He took Edward out, and again no sign of money. It was at that point that August began to think seriously about leaving town. He wanted to get close to the fifth tree, but he knew that everyone was keeping too sharp of an eye out. Apparently, however, even Seven Pine's sharpest eye couldn't stop the skies from ripping Bruce out of the ground.

That was enough for August. He knew that heaven had obliterated Bruce for the sake of showing August who's who. August got the hint and became committed to leaving. Then Justin had done the dumb deed of blowing up Joseph and leaving August to dig that grave.

"Justin," August whispered.

"What was that?" Aza asked, walking into the hospital room and kissing his wife on the forehead.

"Nothing," August lied.

Ezra came in and asked August what a certain machine on the opposite side of the room was. While August was looking and answering, Ezra secretly kissed his mother.

"Is she doing any better?" Aza asked quietly.

"I think about the same," August answered, having absolutely no idea how she really was doing at all.

"It's too bad the town is disintegrating and everyone's leaving," Ezra frowned. "Mom always hated standing over at that material center alone. It'd be nice for there to be some people to stop in."

"Most of the Mormons are sticking it out," August said. "So there should still be people who need to prepare things."

"That's a nice thought," Aza said, sitting down. "Ezra and I used to go to the material center and ask for lesson helps just to cheer her up," Aza smiled. "Of course, she knew that neither one of us had a teaching calling. But, you do what you can."

That simple statement made August feel weak in the knees and a little dizzy. The hospital lights glowed and pulsated with the echo of Aza's words.

August had never done what he could.

He had never even done what he *kind of* could. He had used the oddity of his childhood as an excuse to never stand up and be counted. He had accepted his good looks, his selfishness, and lack of concern for others as the compensation for a mixed-up life.

He had never done what he was supposed to or could have.

It was during this period of painful introspection that Ryan and Sally walked into the hospital room with Clancy, the hotel clerk. Ryan shook hands with Aza. August noticed instantly that Aza shook Ryan's hand more earnestly than he shook his. August looked at his hands and wondered what was wrong with him.

"August," Sally said genuinely, extending her hand to him.

"I didn't mean all that stuff at the restaurant," August tried, paying attention to how she looked as she shook his hand. She looked good. No, she looked *great,* but it had nothing to do with his handshake.

"It's okay," her blue eyes smiled. "I'm happy you're feeling better."

Clancy moved over to the head of the Candle's bed. He took out a little plastic bottle that looked like it was filled with dish soap and poured a drop on Candle's head. August looked around at everyone—they all seemed to understand what was going on. August thought it was unusual behavior for a hotel clerk. Clancy closed his eyes and put his hands on Candle's head. He then said a short prayer clarifying that it had not been dish soap but oil he had anointed her with. He ended the prayer and then looked at Aza.

"Ready?" Clancy asked.

Aza nodded and stepped up to where Clancy was standing. They both put their hands on her head and then Aza began to bless his wife. August would have made fun of it all if it had not been for the fact that he had never witnessed anything like it in his entire life. He didn't catch every word, but he knew when Aza said "Heavenly Father" that those were not just made-up words.

Heavenly Father?

Aza blessed his wife that she would get well, that she would recover fully, and then reminded her that her Heavenly Father was mindful of her and watching. Aza ended the blessing and then shook Clancy's hand with the same respect he had shaken Ryan's.

August wanted someone to shake his hand like that. Sally stepped up to August as Ryan and Clancy and Aza were conversing.

"Can I talk to you for a moment?" she asked.

The two of them slipped out into the hall.

"Did you hear that?" August asked in astonishment.

"Mormons can give blessings," Sally said respectfully. "Bishop Skablund gave me one this afternoon."

"Why?" August was baffled.

"A couple of different reasons."

"Do they come true?"

"If it's what God wants."

"Unbelievable."

"Listen, August," Sally said seriously.

Here it comes, August thought. He had been in this spot a million times. The pretty girl admits that she can't live without him, and he tells her that she is going to have to. As beautiful as Sally was, August knew they had no future together. She held his attention like a long-running TV show with strong cliffhangers. He enjoyed being with her and always felt emotional and connected at the end of each encounter. But just like with TV cliffhangers, August always forgot what he had been drawn to by the time he connected with her again. In Buttercrest, he had been constantly approached by parents and peers wanting to line him up with some young woman who was in their estimation just right for him. Now here was Sally about to tell him that she had thought it over and she didn't care if he had been abrupt with her, she saw the diamond in the rough and loved him. August smiled at her.

"I want to say good-bye," Sally said.

August didn't know what to say.

"Are you okay?" Sally asked.

"You're leaving?" he finally got out.

"We're going tomorrow. Ryan's got a friend back home in the hospital that he needs to get back to, and I have some things I need to finish up myself."

"You're going with Ryan?" August questioned, his brown eyes betraying how shocked he really was.

Sally smiled, her blue eyes revealing how happy she really was. "He's giving me a ride back home."

August looked through the open hospital room door at Ryan in awe. August had never been so intimidated. Ryan carried himself like a person might think August should have. He seemed taller, even though he wasn't. He seemed to have more hair, even though he didn't. And he seemed to have more soul, largely because he did.

"Be careful that he doesn't turn you into a Mormon," August tried.

"Too late," Sally smiled. "Bishop Skablund baptized me this morning."

August didn't know what to say. He had never had anyone fall in love with someone else while he was standing nearby.

"So I guess Ryan won?" August said.

"Won what?"

"The matchmaking thing."

"We're not getting married," she smiled. "We're just driving across country together."

"That's how these things start," August tried to joke. "So is it because of my past?"

"What?" Sally asked confused.

"My parents, me being in jail," August clarified, still confused over how Ryan had won what August actually hadn't wanted to win.

"That has nothing to do with it," Sally grinned. "If I let the past influence my decisions, I would never be happy again."

Ryan came out of the hospital room and looked at August as if to say. *"Ha! I may have less hair than you, and maybe I'm a couple inches shorter, and my shoulders don't do that really broad thing, but I still got the girl!"* At least that's how August interpreted Ryan's look.

All right, it's like this. It's not that Ryan was the incredibly new car model that the manufactures put out front on the spinning turntable with flashing lights and a sign that says something like, "Picture yourself behind the wheel of this beauty." Likewise he wasn't a model that any self-respecting dealer would have kept hidden in the back. He was the solid, best-selling, dependable model that kept people coming back. He wasn't a possession, or a trophy, but he had value. He was a happy pill that dissolved evenly, the comic strip that you go to the effort of cutting out and pinning up, the kind of person you would open your door to regardless if he was holding a check for ten million dollars or simply knocking. He was an umbrella as the sky was falling, the right answer to the difficult questions, and he was the one who had found his own soul and had won Sally over while August had selfishly looked out for himself.

"Good-bye, August," Ryan said, taking Sally's hand.

August could only wave. He then stood in the hall watching Ryan and Sally disappear and thinking how completely envious he was that they had found what they needed from Seven Pines and were now moving on.

"Nice kids," Aza said, nodding his head.

August turned back into the room and saw Candle lying there. Ezra was sitting next to her with the hood of his cloak pulled up so as to hide his tears.

"Everyone's leaving," Aza observed, looking out the window at the town. "Not much for Candle to come to for."

"Don't say that," August said sharply, surprised by how strongly he felt. "Isn't that blessing true?" he asked.

"God works in his own way and time," Aza insisted. "No one can tell heaven what to do."

"So that blessing was just for looks?" August said, confused.

"No," Aza answered kindly. "But it takes faith and prayer."

"I don't know about the faith. But I think I can help with the prayer. Is the library open?" he asked Aza.

"No, I think the town's keeping it closed until the fires die down."

"Not the town library," August corrected. "The material center."

"Probably not, I think Candle's substitute went home a while ago. But if you need to work on a lesson, Ezra's got keys. They made him assistant librarian a few months back."

August motioned to Ezra who jumped up and came over.

"What do you have in mind?" Aza asked.

"Do you think it would be okay if we made a few copies?" August asked.

"There's a can next to the machine," Aza informed him. "Just leave a buck or two there."

August and Ezra left the hospital and went directly to the material center. Ezra opened things up and asked, "What are we doing here?"

"We're going to challenge heaven."

"What?"

"We're on a quest to right the forces of wrong before evil can take root and destroy the Shire," August tried, using one of the themes he remembered from *Lord of the Rings*.

"All right!" Ezra said enthusiastically. "What do you need me to do?

"Do you have nice penmanship?"

"I've been told I write like a girl on several occasions," Ezra bragged.

"Excellent. It's not much, but I want it to look nice," August said, handing Ezra a pen. "Now take this down."

Two hours later Ezra and August turned off the copier and headed out of the church. Each one had thousands of flyers, a stapler, and a couple of rolls of tape. August had made sure to put enough money in the can next to the copier to make up for all the "materials" they had used.

Once out of the church, August and Ezra split up—two in direction, but one in purpose.

CHAPTER TWENTY-FOUR

ERE YOU'RE STUCK IN A SMALL TOWN THAT IS FALLING APART, DID YOU THINK TO PRAY?

Mornings were a beautiful sight in Seven Pines—normally. The way the sun would rise over the Trudge Ridge Mountains and light up Lincoln Lake like a glowing mirror was second only to the smell and feel of the air. It was as if Seven Pines were the source of all oxygen. As if beneath its velvet prairies and green stained forest was the vacation home of Mother Nature. A place where on occasion she would rest and contentedly breathe life into the entire planet. Of course, that vacation home seemed vacant as of late. Either that or Mother Nature had neglected warning labels and wisdom and had taken up smoking.

Sadly, these days, the mornings were more like London, than Montana, except it was smoke, not fog, obscuring the landscape, and there were no cheery piping people in raincoats, just sour locals who couldn't believe the magic of their town had disappeared so quickly. Of course, this morning was different than any other by virtue of the fact that everywhere an irritated eye looked there were flyers posted to poles, buildings, trees, and fences. As far as a person could un-clearly see, there were sheets of white paper stapled and taped up. At first notice, a few were outraged at the staggering amount of waste and litter. But then people read them and could sense the importance of the four words:

Pray for Candle Hick

If August had expected the town to go wild and follow instruction, he was wrong. If he had in mind that they would read the note and then come around to the hospital to investigate and see if their prayers were really merited, then he was wrong again. Nothing fancy like that happened. All that happened was that people would read the notice, drop what they were doing, and return home to pray for Candle, in private or with their family. Folks leaving town stopped to realize what they were leaving. People predicting the end paused to pray for somebody who reminded them of a beginning. The streets became empty as everyone spiritually regrouped and focused their thoughts on Candle. It was the reminder that everyone had needed. Flowers were sent and cards were delivered to the hospital, but not a single soul came to visit because, in all honesty, they were too busy praying.

Suddenly home wasn't a place where people were forced to be because of the air quality or the heat outside. Home was a sanctuary that they could hole up in to pray for a person whom they either knew, had heard of, or loved dearly. And in doing so most were spiritually made aware of what they had forgotten. It wasn't the trees that had protected the town, or the location on which Seven Pines rested on a map. They had been blessed and they had forgotten. Now people were wearing out their knees in an effort to make things right.

All the while August remained by Candle's bedside with Aza and Ezra.

Well, two things happened—that's not exactly true, a lot of things happened, but not necessarily what you might think. Two days passed, and even though the prayers were still being offered, Candle had not shaken whatever it was she had fallen into. Plus, the fires continued, and the weather heated up. The air became smokier, and those fighting the fires began to give up hope. The order was given for the entire town to begin preparing for an evacuation.

This posed a problem.

Moving Candle was not as easy as one might suppose. She was in a fragile condition and any disruption, the doctor said, could cause a major complication, or worse. Despite all that was going on, August stayed by her bed, willing the blessing Aza had given her to come true. He wanted Candle to live for so many reasons, not the least of which was the fact that if she came through, it seemed to him like that would signify that there really was a Heavenly Father. The term was so frightening and exciting to August, he could think of little else anymore.

On the fourth day of Candle's condition, Chief Fellows announced that the remaining townspeople needed to clear out. Two of the fires were closing in, he explained, and if the winds held the pattern they were taking, Seven Pines would be toast by that afternoon.

The hospital was practically empty already. All the injured pigs and goats had gone home days before. And a number of the staff had cleared out as well. A few nurses ran around counting pillows and aspirin as if in the event of a fire it might be nice to recall what all they had lost. Aza and Ezra and August stayed in Candle's room, staring at each other and wondering what on earth they were going to do.

"We've got to go," August finally said. "Let's take the chance that if we move her out she'll be okay."

"No way," Ezra said. "She won't live, I know it."

"We have no choice, son," Aza said sadly. "Chief Fellows said he would remove us personally if we didn't get going. She'll be fine if we move her."

"People have prayed," Ezra said with conviction. "She should stay here."

Both August and Aza looked wounded. People *had* prayed, but the reality was Candle was in a bad spot, and she needed to be moved. They called the doctors in to ready the portable machines and get Candle onto a gurney. As August and Aza began to gently lift her, Bishop Skablund and his wife stepped into the room. There was a loud noise in the hall, and August turned to see at least a fifty people crowding in behind them.

"We've come to stay with Candle," Bishop Skablund announced, holding his arm around his wife.

"Me, too," Tony the hermit said. "I've been praying for her for days, and I'm not about to let some little fire ruin my faith."

"We figured that Chief Fellows can't personally haul all of us out," Sister Skablund said with conviction, her upside down mouth looking nearly straight across these days and helping to display the new necklace she was wearing. To August she kind of looked like that girl in the video that those Mormon cows had made so beautiful.

"This is ridiculous," the doctor said. "That fire's going to burn down this entire building."

"We have hoses," Jane yelled. "The hardware store let us take what we wanted. If we all get at it, we might have a fighting chance."

Everyone naively began unwinding hoses and screwing them onto any faucet they could find. A couple men got onto the roof of the building and began spraying water all over. The doctors, resigned to the fact that they weren't going to be able to talk any-body out of this, began handing out white surgical masks so people could breathe better. August grabbed a hose and climbed out the window opposite Candle's bed and onto the roof. Ezra detached the faucet ring on the sink inside and hooked the hose up.

"Turn it on," August yelled.

August could feel the water surging through the hose. The stream was powerful and shot out about fifty feet. From on top of the roof August could see the fire moving quickly in their direction, jumping from the crown of one tree to the next. He couldn't believe how close it was. Suddenly faith didn't seem sufficient to save them all. He frantically hosed down the roof where he was standing and sprayed water into the air around the building. August looked across the roof at hospital employees—holding hoses and spraying the air as if they all actually had a clue about what they were doing and were not frightened in the least.

The fire seemed to pick up speed as it touched town. It was as if it knew it had a challenge on its hands and wanted to get at the hospital as quickly as possible. Flames leapt from pine top to roof top, igniting buildings and trees at random.

The Seven Pines hospital sat right in the middle of town. It was a three-story structure with two small wings and a main section. The roof was made out of concrete, but there were dormers that shot up every fifty feet, and those dormers were covered with wood shingles. Thanks to the height of the building, those standing on top were about level with the crowns of the pine trees all around them.

August looked out and could see the fire swelling as it blew across wide streets and jumped from tree to tree. He could feel the heat even though it was still a ways off. August had spent the last three days praying, but to be honest the prayers he was offering now were considerably more intense.

A finger of fire raced around the back of the hospital and licked at the shingles on a large dormer. The second the flame touched the wooden tiles, both August and Jane doused it with their hoses.

The fire circled the hospital and began to split itself in what seemed to be a hundred directions. August heard and felt a huge spark pop and knock his left shoulder. He turned to see the ember smoldering on the roof. The reality of how real this all was washed over him with a heat ten times more intense than the fire was throwing off. He sprayed the ember down and shot water out onto a couple of the treetops that were closest to him. He felt as if he were going to melt, and he kept wishing that someone would spray him down. He heard a scream and looked around, wondering where it was coming from. It took him a second to realize that it was himself. Fire had caught on his back, and he couldn't see or get to it. Before he could yell again, a stream of water dumped down on him from a very vigilant Jane. In the midst of such heat and chaos, the water felt like heaven.

August's back smarted as he sprayed the dormer to his left and worked on the trees again. Those on the roof teamed together beautifully, maneuvering the water to keep the fire off the building. Water was also being sprayed out of almost every hospital window as those inside joined the hard fight with them.

August was so busy doing what he thought he should do that he almost didn't notice when the fire began moving away. He wasn't the first to cheer, but his was the loudest. He sprayed himself in the face and down his back and down his front and in his face one more time. Everybody on the roof gathered and squirted their hoses into the air in victory. Except for Jane, of course. She was too busy cleaning herself up. The entire crew sprayed water onto hot spots and smoke for the next two hours.

August finally climbed back through the window to see how those inside had fared. Everyone seemed fine. The power generators had worked perfectly, keeping Candle going and dimly lighting the inside area. Slowly everyone began to work their way back into Candle's room.

"That was so stupid," the doctor said. "Stupid but amazing."

"Is she all right?" Jane asked, curious about Candle. "I don't want all that praying to be for nothing."

"I think she's about the same," Aza observed. "We should probably all stay here for the night. There aren't many beds, but the floor's not bad if you lay out enough blankets."

So the hospital staff and the volunteer fire fighters all made themselves at home in the halls and on the floor in Candle's room. A couple of groups of people stayed up late recounting the horrific experience. A few stayed up telling ghost stories that seemed to pale in comparison to what had just happened. But everybody else remained silent in prayer, having noticed the familiar flyer that hung on all the hospital bulletin boards:

Pray for Candle Hick

August had no idea how long he had been asleep before he heard her voice.

"What the heck is going on here?" she asked.

He turned to see Candle, sitting up in her hospital bed, bewildered. It was very early morning, and a faint light was creeping in through the windows.

"Candle?" August whispered in amazement.

"August," she replied.

August smiled, feeling much like he had when he had seen his sister, Rachel, in a vision.

"Am I dead?" he asked Candle, still not sure if he was awake or having another vision.

"No, I don't think so," Candle replied.

"Near death?" August asked.

"Maybe," she said groggily. "I have no idea of your physical condition. I mean, you look all right."

"So tell me something," August smiled, asking her the same question he had asked his sister. "Are the Mormons right?"

"Of course," Candle declared.

"Candle's okay," August announced loudly.

Those who had been sleeping on the floor began to open their eyes and gasp.

"Candle!" Aza hollered, jumping up from the floor and wrapping his arms around his wife.

Aza had a small conniption compared to how Ezra reacted to his mother's recovery. People began to rise from the floor like dirty zombies with bright smiles.

"What the heck is going on?" Candle asked again, gawking at those who were gathering around her bed.

"We prayed for you," Ezra declared. "The whole town did."

"Well, couldn't you have prayed that I'd wake up somewhere normal?"

"We didn't know if you'd ever wake up," Aza cried.

"Oh, I wouldn't have left you here with Ezra," she guffawed. "He still needs nurturing. I just had a couple of things to take care of that's all."

The room was suddenly quiet and everyone looked at her with wonder.

"Things like what?" Tony the hermit whispered reverently.

"I don't know," Candle waved. "I'm just trying to get Aza to stop crying."

Aza dried his eyes as everybody cheered.

PART TWO AND SEVEN-EIGHTHS

CHAPTER TWENTY-FIVE

THIS IS THE MOMENT

By the time their last child, Mary, turned eighteen, Wilton and ·Maria Wood were a couple of emotional and physical wrecks. Maria was so ill that she couldn't get out of bed by herself, and Wilton was not even a shell of a man–he was more like a chip, or a fleck.

He had wasted his life.

He had learned far too late that the best time of his life was the breath he was drawing at any given moment. He had never really known his children, he had never been a real husband, and he had never experienced the happiness that results from rejoicing in someone else's good fortune.

As an eighteen-year-old young woman, Mary could clearly see what had happened to her parents. She had been a first-hand witness to the devastation her father had created because of his inability to love what he had. Her mother was dying of a broken heart, while her father was spending his sad, lonely days, caring for the six trees that were such poor substitutes for his lost children. More than once Mary had caught him sitting in the shade of those pines, having the kind of conversation with the trees he had never had with his boys.

She understood why her brothers had all fled. She had experienced the same sadness and loneliness that her parents had imposed on all their children. But as their only daughter, she felt sorry for her parents. For her entire life she had known nothing but a father who wept constantly for children he had never loved. She had been right there, wishing that he would turn and love her. And she had watched her mother wither under that same neglect.

Two weeks after Mary's eighteenth birthday, her mother, Maria, passed away in her sleep. At that point, Wilton stopped talking, stopped eating, stopped everything but caring for the trees. He would walk from tree to tree, scratching at the soil around its roots, trimming branches, and watering the ground. Mary tried to comfort him—gave him every chance to forget what he had lost and love what he still had the chance to love. But there was no response.

As the summer of Maria's death came to a close and the first signs of winter were being felt, Mary decided that she too must leave.

She found her father sitting next to Bruce, digging the ground with a garden trowel and pitching small rocks off into the distance.

"I have to go," she said.

"I know," Wilton admitted somberly.

"I want to stay," Mary cried.

"You can't," Wilton said, his voice cracking.

"I love you, Daddy," Mary said, meaning every word but

knowing that she could never stay and watch her father deteriorate in misery.

Wilton looked at her and wanted so desperately to hug her, but he didn't have it in him. Instead, he began to cry.

"I want to be your father," he said, his gray hair and deep worry lines making him look more like Mary's grandfather than her dad.

Mary also started to cry. She set down her bag and stepped closer to him.

"We all loved you," she cried. "You just wouldn't let us."

Wilton couldn't argue with that.

"I think it was easier for you to care for these trees," Mary sobbed. "In a sick way, my leaving will make it possible for you to now love me."

Wilton had had enough. He felt as if God had given him eight hearts for the express purpose of being able to break them all simultaneously. He looked at his hands as he worked the soil; he looked up at the tree he had planted for Bruce; and he knew that what Mary was saying was true.

He had already picked out the spot where he would plant Mary's tree. Had picked it out long ago. He had written off his present in favor of a future he could better prune.

"Good-bye, Daddy," Mary sobbed.

She picked up her bag and turned to go, taking three whole steps before he spoke.

"I wanted to name you Candle," he cried.

Mary turned.

"I wanted to name you Candle, but your mother thought that was foolish."

Mary walked back and sat down by her father. She put her arms around him as he dug at the ground. He dropped his trowel and patted her back. She then stood and left everything she had ever known.

Seven Pines looked like a ratty green towel that heaven had used to wipe off its feet. There were great, black blotches of ruined trees all over the landscape, but a few swipes of green still streaked the horizon, signifying the fact that Seven Pines was not completely dead yet.

There was a renewed commitment by those who had prayed and stayed with Candle, to do what ever it would take to reproduce the magic that their city had possessed while all seven trees had stood tall.

Let's be honest, the bliss that Seven Pines had known before was not achieved without cost. The happy town had felt such pressure to be quaint and postcard-worthy that it had severed its ties with reality and the fact that real happiness often comes by noticing the imperfections.

So with this renewed commitment came the understanding that what was great about Seven Pines hadn't been George, Peter, Ralph, Edward, Bruce, Joseph, or Mary. It had been every Tom, Dick, and Harry who had put down his roots and called this place home.

It's worth pointing out, however, that the new attitude that now permeated the air would not have come about had the constant prayers of the town not softened and enlightened so many hearts. Or if the only daughter of Wilton Wood had not had the courtesy to become ill at the same moment the tree bearing her name had fallen.

Sally sat across from Deni and smiled. The afternoon was perfect. The beauty of the late August day seemed almost surreal. Sally couldn't believe that this was the same place she had sneaked away from two weeks ago. Sally had come back to the hospital a couple of days before to have the tests done that she had originally run from. The tests had been performed, and every person in the hospital now knew that Sally was destined for greatness. She had beaten far too many odds not to be. Deni looked at her hard, trying to act stern.

"Am I supposed to be sad?" Sally asked, having just heard the great news herself.

"You're perfect," Deni said suspiciously.

"I told you I wasn't sick," Sally insisted.

Deni stood up and looked closely at Sally. "It's more than that," Deni said slowly. "I can't tell what, but somethin' is different," she observed.

"I'm Mormon," Sally said bluntly.

Deni gasped. "They didn't."

"That's true, but I did."

Sally couldn't believe her life. She sat staring at Deni, feeling nothing but happiness and hope. It was far cry from what she had felt in this building such a short time before. She had gone to Seven Pines to find security, and she had walked away with a peace that she could have never comprehended. She thought about the small town that had helped her find her life. She thought back to the tree-lined streets and the many fine restaurants. She remembered walking with Ryan on the crooked footpath behind the courthouse and him telling her all about a boy named Joseph Smith. She thought about the feelings of warmth and of how happy she had been there. She thought about her baptism and the marvelous blessing Bishop Skablund had given her.

It was a funny thing. If a person had been able to climb inside Sally's head and relive all the experiences she had gone through in Seven Pines, they might have walked away with a far different story than you have just read. In Sally's mind, Seven Pines was cool and peaceful and filled with touch points and people who had been set in certain spots simply to change the course of her life. She remembered the blue skies and the tall trees, the smell of summer, and the feel of dirt that had not all been covered up by structures or pavement. She remembered Candle and Aza and Bishop Skablund and that good-looking boy.

She had gone to Seven Pines wanting honestly to find something more than what she had. That honesty had paid off. Now as she sat with Deni, telling her about the cute shops and nice people she had met, she had to stop herself from falling to her knees and thanking her Heavenly Father.

"So you *wanted* to be a Mormon?" Deni asked in confusion.

"More than anything."

"I bet it had to do with one of those boys in a tie," Deni said, disgusted. "I can't believe God saved you from a parachute fall and illness jus' so that you could start worshippin' with the Mormons."

"So can I tell you about them?" Sally asked.

"If it helps you t' talk," Deni said, grudgingly.

An extremely tall nurse, wearing red tights under her white uniform, came in and handed Deni a piece of paper. Deni looked at it quizzically.

"What's that?" Sally asked, still a bit anxious about being back at the hospital.

"When you ran out on us like that a couple of weeks ago, we got a little worried," Deni scolded. "We had people everywhere lookin' for you. I remembered where you said you were born. So I did the math and called, lookin' for information on a Sally that might have been born in 1978. They found you, and sent me a copy of your birth certificate. You never tol' me that Sally was a nickname."

"I didn't think it was," Sally said honestly, having never seen her birth certificate herself.

"Well, right above where your father signed, it says, 'Salvation' not 'Sally.'"

Sally took the paper and stared at it. There in black and white was her full name, along with the names of her birth parents and the signature of a father she had never known.

"I've never seen this," Sally said in awe. "I had no idea."

"And to think you've gone Mormon, with a name like that," Deni tisked. "It's almost blasphemous."

Sally smiled as she looked at her birth certificate. She studied the names and the dates and the signatures. She imagined her father signing his name, knowing that he had just lost his wife. She couldn't understand why he had named her Salvation when he had felt the way he had toward her. Sally didn't care. She would have walked a path four times as hard if it had meant that she would end up where she was today. She thought about her adoptive parents and her stepbrothers and stepsisters that she had run away from so many years before. She now could think of so many good things and so many people that she needed to see again. She thought about the parachuting accident and Mark and Ryan.

"I did meet a boy," Sally said, happily.

"Those Mormons are so sneaky," Deni complained.

Sally smiled. It was a secure, self-assured smile.

"So tell me 'bout him," Deni added, reluctantly.

Sally was all too happy to oblige.

CHAPTER TWENTY-SIX

THE EIGHTH TREE

With Mary's (Candle's) departure, her father, Wilton, had nobody. His children had all gone, his wife had passed away, and he was growing old and feeble. It became hard for him to climb the hill that Peter sat on, and it was a chore to push through the woods where Bruce stood. In spite of his infirmities, he managed to plant one final tree.

It was a tree for Maria.

Wilton knew that he had never been a real husband. He had done nothing to make her life beautiful. So Wilton planted a plum tree, because its annual blossoms were as beautiful as Maria had been when he had first met her. He planted the tree in secret, not wanting the town to gossip every time he sat beneath it or looked at it lovingly. In fact, in order to avoid an audience of onlookers, he bought an unwanted piece of land that sat at the edge of the town's cemetery. There he had planted Maria. It was beneath that tree that Wilton eventually died, his heart broken over what he had not done right in life, and his spirit nervous over what Maria was going to say to him when he got to the other side.

🌲　🌲　🌲

Ryan sat across from Todd and smiled. Just a couple of days before, his friend had opened his eyes for the first time since the accident. The hospital staff had been stunned. They had, in fact, given up hope that he would ever come to and had debated how long to wait before telling his family the grim news.

Upon regaining consciousness, Todd said that while he was asleep, a kindly old lady with tall hair and a joyful, weeping older couple had come to him and coaxed him out of his coma. Todd's mother was busy searching through their family genealogy, trying to discover just who the people might have been, working magic for their family on the other side.

The first thing Todd said when he saw Ryan was, "I told you to slow down."

"I never did listen to you," Ryan said, taking a seat next to Todd's bed and holding his friend's hand. "Of course, I always should have."

"It's about time you saw the light," Todd joked. "Being near death doesn't seem like such a waste if its finally made that clear to you."

Ryan was so happy. He thought back on the darkness he had experienced for so many weeks. He remembered vividly the hole in his soul as he arrived in Seven Pines, wondering why on earth God would point him to that part of His earth. He thought about the boulder-lined lakes and majestic mountains. He could see the sun coming over Trudge Ridge and wondered how heaven had ever thought to smear light like that. He saw the quaint homes and happy faces of people as they went about living in such a magical place. He could see Candle and Aza and Ezra and Bishop Skablund. He could see Jane, and that guy with the thick hair.

In fact, if you were to climb into Ryan's head and see what he saw, you might be quite surprised by how different his memories were than the story you've just read. Ryan had gone to Seven Pines because he had honestly thought that God was pointing him there. He had arrived, wanting nothing more than to be straight with Heaven again. In Sally he had found a reason to hope and wonder once more. He had discovered in the ring of trees a part of him that could not die, a part that no tragedy or triumph or setback could ever completely squelch.

His Heavenly Father knew him.

"So I met this girl," Ryan said to Todd.

"Unbelievable," Todd laughed. "I get thrown into a coma, and you meet girls. So, who is she?"

"A convert," Ryan smiled.

"Nothing better," Todd smiled back.

"Of course, she'll have to pass the shelf-life test," Ryan pointed out, alluding to the fact that both Ryan and Todd had been told last night by their stake president that missions were still a definite possibility for both of them. Todd would need additional time to heal, but Ryan's condition was such that it wouldn't be long before he would be out in the field. Ryan had always known that he would be able to go, but it had been Seven Pines that had helped him forgive himself and realize that his Heavenly Father still loved him.

"Do me a favor," Todd said. "Don't take me on any trips before we go."

Ryan smiled again like his old self.

"So tell me about this girl," Todd added.

"There aren't enough long words to describe her," Ryan said in a daze.

"Then start with the short ones," Todd suggested.

Ryan was happy to oblige.

CHAPTER TWENTY-SEVEN

BEFORE AND AFTER

When Candle left her home all those years before as Mary, it was with the understanding that she would never return. She had moved two states over and had changed her name to Candle because she liked the sound of it much more than Mary. Of course, if she were to be completely honest, she would have admitted that it also made her feel better about her father. She went to school for some years and graduated top in her class and landed a nice job at a local paper in the town she was in. The paper was run by a man by the name of Aza Hick.

Aza was a confirmed bachelor who cared nothing for women or the traps they set. He liked to get up when he wanted, leave his clothes where they fell, and eat as he pleased. However, two weeks after hiring Candle, he proposed to her. She said no. He tried harder. She still said no. He tried gifts. She said maybe. He tried losing twenty pounds, shaving off his mustache, and buying new clothes. She said perhaps. He tried all that last bit plus the gifts again. She said yes.

Shortly after the two of them married, the paper experienced some financial difficulties in the form of seven libel lawsuits. The Hicks had found out, the expensive way, that you just can't lie about somebody's good name for the sake of filling your pages.

Aza and Candle were broke.

It was about that time that Candle began to long for the town she had grown up in. She would have dreams and experience reminders that seemed to pull all her waking thoughts toward Seven Pines. Having never told her husband about her real past, she approached him about starting a new life in a small town, in say, "Seven Pines, Montana."

Aza had wrinkled his eyebrow at first, but he soon began to catch the fever that Candle had for getting out. So they packed up their things and moved to Seven Pines. Candle had figured that she would tell her husband the truth about her growing up there the moment they got into town. But when they arrived, not a single soul recognized her. She was considerably taller, and she styled her hair so high that her face seemed twice as long as it had been when she left. Even people who had known her parents or had baby-sat her or had taught her piano had no idea that she was Mary.

Candle was fine with that. She kept her secret a secret, letting the town grow on her husband at a more natural pace. After a few months Candle worked up the nerve to begin asking around about her father's final days. She was surprised at how few people knew anything about him or his death. Those who did profess to know all, had conflicting stories. One person remembered him dying from illness. Another person remembered him leaving town and not dying there at all. Still another person remembered that he died exactly in the middle of the ring of trees while standing out in a windstorm calling out his children's names.

Candle liked that account best.

Regardless, she didn't buy it. She stopped asking questions and figured she would never find out. Then fate put her on Elm Street late one August night. She had been walking home from church when she heard her name being called from the front porch of one of the older homes. What caught her attention most was that the voice was yelling, "Mary! Mary Wood? You come up here from off that street and tell me where you've been."

Candle had quickly stepped up onto the porch of the old woman, wanting nothing more than for her to be quiet.

"My name's Candle," she had tried.

"Poop," the old woman spat. "I'd know that forehead from a mile away. You're Maria's girl."

The old woman was Linda Fold. She had lived in town as long as she had been alive, and *that* was one impressive span of time.

"Listen," Linda said with a toothless mouth. "I've been sitting on this porch, waiting, for twenty-five years. I've got something to tell you."

"You've been waiting for me?" Candle had asked, confused. "For twenty-five years?"

"I go in to use the bathroom and eat and watch my TV shows, and Beth picks me up for church on Thursday nights and Sunday mornings. Other than that, I'm here, naming squirrels and waiting for you."

"Why would you be waiting for me?" Candle asked, her insides in a knot.

"Sit down," Linda demanded. "Listen, your father came to see me."

"As a ghost?" Candle had asked honestly.

Linda looked at her queerly. "No. He came to me shortly before he died. He was in bad shape—older than Moses and empty as my bins after Wednesday morning trash collection. Anyhow, he knew how I was good with faces and how I spent an unhealthy amount of time out on my front porch. Those two things seemed to suit his needs. He told me that one day his daughter would come driving, or walking, or flying . . . he loved that science fiction," she explained. "Anyhow, he said you'd come down this street and asked if I could please tell you something. He knew you'd come back. He didn't put much faith in those boys of his, but he had a feeling that his girl couldn't stay away forever."

"What did he want you to tell me?" Candle almost demanded.

"Twenty-five years is a long time. I honestly can't remember. I should have written it down," Linda said.

"Can you remember any of it?" Candle asked frantically.

"Bits and pieces. There's an eighth tree—for your mother. Yes, that's what it was, a tree for your mother."

"And? . . ."

"Oh, things are coming back to me." Linda slapped her forehead with her hand. "I remember now where I left my glasses, in the flour bin."

Linda got up and tottered into the house, leaving Candle there alone on the porch, wondering about the eighth tree. She didn't wonder long. Linda soon came back out, wearing white powdered glasses.

"You're still here?" she asked.

"I want to know more."

Linda rubbed her head, pretending to think and playing Candle along. She shifted and "hmmmed" and scratched. "Oh, yes, he had money."

"Money?"

"He said he had money. All the money he had socked away. All the inheritance that he wanted to leave to his children but couldn't. Said he'd leave it with Maria."

"My mother was dead."

"Then I don't know how he pulled that one off."

Candle tried for hours to get more out of Linda, but nothing ever came from it. She had since spent many days wondering where the tree was that memorialized her mother and if her father had really buried some kind of treasure beneath its limbs.

Later on in life, Candle often told the story to her young son, Ezra, of the father who lost his children and had buried his wealth beneath a tree.

🌲 🌲 🌲

August sat across from Bishop Skablund and sighed. The bishop had stepped out to answer a telephone call in the clerk's office. August looked around. Bishop Skablund's office looked considerably different than the first time he had sat in there. For one thing, the place was plastered with pictures of him and his wife. There was one of Sister Skablund gardening, one of her sitting on a couch, one of her standing in front of a big bell. In all the pictures she was smiling.

Bishop Skablund came in and apologized for keeping him waiting.

"How are you, August?" he asked.

"Fine," August answered honestly.

"A lot's happened since we last talked," Bishop Skablund pointed out needlessly. "I mean, it's like Seven Pines is putting itself back together anonymously."

"Yeah," August agreed. "Interesting."

"I'm still amazed that someone was able to plant seven new trees without anyone noticing. And such nice new trees, they must have cost an arm and a leg."

"Odd," August agreed.

"It's also odd that all those businesses that were burned down and the farms that were in trouble received those huge, mysterious gifts of money."

"Weird," August concurred.

"And those new animals for the petting zoo just showing up on their doorstep."

"Strange, strange times."

"I'll say. Now, what was it that you and I talked about last time we met?" the bishop wondered aloud.

"I wanted to know what it would take for me to be a Mormon."

"Oh, yes," Bishop Skablund said. "But, there was something specific you were curious about."

"Restitution," August reminded him.

"That's right. You were worried about fixing some of the things you'd done in your past. How's that coming along?"

"Pretty good."

"Only 'pretty good'?"

August had done his best. By now you know that the coffin he pulled up from beneath the plum tree in the Memorial Gardens was filled with nothing but cash, stocks, and jewelry. It had been Wilton Wood's entire fortune—the fortune he had hoped to give to one of his kids someday. Of course, August had not known it was supposed to go anywhere but to himself. He had figured that he had simply found the mother lode and that heaven was giving him a chance to live lavishly.

After he had pulled the coffin full of money from the ground and hidden it in the caretaker's shed, he had pocketed a few piles of cash and gone to make sure that Justin wouldn't get out of jail and find it before August was able to buy a truck to cart the coffin off. Of course, as you also know, those plans didn't completely work. In fact, with Candle falling into a coma and the town praying for her, August had stayed away from the money, thinking he needed a clearer head before he did anything. He was forced to do something, however, when he saw Justin walk out of the jailhouse a couple of days after the fire.

"What happened to the town?" Justin had asked as he looked around at the burnt buildings and trees.

"There was a fire," August answered. "Didn't they move you out?"

"Fire? I never heard there was a fire," Justin said. "There was a day or two when nobody but me was in the building, and it seemed hotter than usual."

August left it at that. He had then congratulated Justin on getting released and run to the shed and pulled the coffin into the woods. There he covered it with branches until he could figure out what to do.

But as much as he thought about it, he still couldn't decide what the right thing to do would be.

Then one afternoon, while proofreading one of Ezra's short stories, August was surprised to hear Ezra mention that his mother used to tell him a story about the seven children who had spawned the trees and the father who had planted them. August had heard the story at least a dozen times, but Ezra's version had a little extra ending. The way his mother, Candle, had always told the tale was that before the unhappy father died, he buried his entire fortune, which he had accumulated by never spending anything on his wife or children, in the ground next to an eighth tree.

"Did your mother make that up?" August asked Ezra.

"My mother has no imagination," he said glumly.

It had only taken August a little over an afternoon to begin putting some pieces together. Candle's age, her unknown past, her collapsing when Mary had fallen . . . it all pointed to one thing. August had then made his way over to the material center and asked Candle if she preferred to be called Candle . . . or Mary.

"I knew you were smart," she smiled. "I never thought that it would be an outsider who figured it out."

August went on to ask Candle a hypothetical question. What would she do if someone discovered that money her father had supposedly buried? Candle's hand flew to her mouth, and she began to cry. So did August, but for a different reason. He assumed she was overjoyed to learn he had found the money and that she was now going to be rich. August would have to give up his find. It turned out, however, that it wasn't the money she was crying about.

"You found the tree?" she cried.

"And the money," August answered.

"I don't care about the money," Candle said. "I've only wanted to know where my father planted my mother's tree."

"I can show you."

Candle gladly locked up the material center and accompanied August to the Memorial Gardens, where she stood under the plum tree for three straight hours, smiling. She probably would have stayed there longer, but the Smith family showed up and asked her to please get off their grandmother's grave.

August had gently begged Candle to take the money, but she had insisted that she wanted no part of it and that August could just have it. There was no way that her dad was going to make things right by buying her off. She had learned to forgive and love him years before. Having that money would only complicate things.

August had not fought her on this point, wondering if perhaps her brothers, if they were still alive, might be interested in it. Candle had persuaded August that not a single one of her siblings would touch a cent. August thought it was very noble of her and her siblings to have such an attitude.

He also thought he would be thrilled to call the money his. But the moment he knew the money belonged to him, he began to remember all the things he had inflicted on Seven Pines and think of all the ways he could use that wealth to make things right.

He needed to be honest.

It was at that point that August began meeting with Bishop Skablund. He felt compelled to change his ways—live a life of honesty and purpose. He wanted to look like Ryan as he shook Aza's hand. He wanted to smile openly, like Sally had as she told him of her baptism. He wanted to someday walk into his hometown of Buttercrest, knowing that his life was in line with what his Heavenly Father wanted him to be.

"Only 'pretty good'?" Bishop Skablund asked, bringing August back to reality.

"*Really* good," August corrected, looking him directly in the eyes. "There's just one more thing I need to do."

"Then do it."

"I'd have to leave Seven Pines," August pointed out.

"There are lots of places outside of these borders."

August stood. He could feel the sense of invincibility growing inside him again. It was completely different than before. This feeling was stronger, more scary, and honest.

"Thanks so much," August said.

The bishop stood and extended his hand. "Thank you, August. Don't be a stranger."

"Good-bye, Bishop."

"Good-bye, August."

August left the church and headed down Main Street and toward the hotel, where he told Clancy good-bye. After that he stopped by to see the Hicks and was saddened to hear that Candle was away for the afternoon and wouldn't be back until late. Ezra begged August to stay and wait for her, but August knew that he needed to be on his way. Ezra offered to give August his good travel cloak, but August passed.

"So Candle's not at the material center?" August asked, knowing that ever since the fire Candle had spent much less time there and more time with her husband and son.

"No," Aza said, "she had something personal to attend to."

August said his good-byes and then stepped away from the Hicks's home. He looked down Elm Street, and in the far distance he could see the tiny pine that now stood in Mary's old place.

He smiled, thinking about his sister, Rachel, and Sally and Ryan, and his own future. He was, at last, happy about all the things in his life that had brought him to this point. He had always looked upon his upbringing as a curse. Now he saw that the troubles he had survived had blessed him with an incredible present tense.

He went by the café, but Jane was out. So he left her a note and a promise that he would be back someday to check and see if everything was still clean. He then headed out of Seven Pines.

When August got to the edge of town, he cut across the church lawn and the wide prairie that led to the cemetery and provided the most direct route to the freeway. As he entered the cemetery he turned and looked back at the town that had done him so much good. The afternoon was cool and pleasant, and if he squinted, he could almost pretend that most of the scene wasn't charred and black.

August was making his way through the cemetery but stopped when he noticed a group of people off in the distance. They were standing near the spot where August had dug up the money. He stayed behind the trees and worked himself a little closer. One of the people was Candle, and she and six elderly men were holding hands, forming a circle around the tree that Wilton Wood had planted for his wife, Maria. August studied the men. There was a tall one, a heavy one, a short one, a frail one, a mean-looking one, and a smiling one. Candle was saying what sounded like a prayer, and then they all started hugging each other and crying.

August suddenly missed his family. It was fitting, seeing how that was where he was headed. It was the last thing he needed to take care of before he could feel completely honest with himself. It wasn't going to be easy, but for the first time in his life he felt up to it.

August watched Candle and her brothers move away from the cemetery, all of them reaching to touch the tree that was planted for their mother. He wanted to step out and tell Candle good-bye, but he knew that he would be interrupting something very important.

As soon as they were gone, August walked out into the open and took one last look back toward Seven Pines. In the distance he could see someone coming his way. That someone waved, and August waved back, still not certain who he was waving to. A couple of steps closer August could see that it was Jane, and she was carrying a large paper sack. He headed toward her so as to save her some distance. They met above the headstone of a Gerald Gelm. His epitaph read: "One less thing for you to worry about, Ethel."

"What are you doing here?" August asked Jane.

"I saw the note you left me and thought you might need something to eat on the road," Jane said, trying to sound casual and hiding the fact that she had raced to throw something together and had then run through town hoping to catch up with August. "I took a chance that you came this way," she said, out of breath.

"You didn't have to do that," August said, sort of feeling out of breath himself.

"No big deal," she continued. Jane handed August the bag. He opened it and looked inside. He had never seen such an organized sack lunch. There were compartments and color-coded, neatly covered Saran-wrapped items.

"You didn't have to," August smiled, wondering if Jane could possibly be any prettier.

"If we only did what we have to, then life would be pretty awful," Jane smiled back, her incredible eyes shining. "Good luck, wherever you're going," she said.

"I've got some family things to take care of," August explained. "I'll be back. I just—"

If Jane had been a snake, August would have been dead, or in need of someone to suck poison out of his lips. Jane sprang forward and kissed him on the mouth. Then as quickly as she had struck, she stepped back, smiling at him.

"So I'll see you when you return?"

"For sure," August said in a daze.

"Good-bye, August," Jane said, turning.

"Good-bye," August managed to say.

August watched Jane until she was a speck on the horizon. He then turned and became a speck in the opposite direction.

ABOUT THE AUTHOR

Robert Farrell Smith was born in Murray, Utah, one of seven children—two daughters and five sons—born to Farrell and Sandra Smith. He attended Ricks College and the University of Utah and now lives in Albuquerque, New Mexico, where he manages a Deseret Book bookstore. He and his wife, Krista (whom he describes as "amazing"), have four children: Kindred Anne, Phoebe Hope, Naomi Rose, and Bennett.

Smith's writing has been praised as inspirational, enlightening, and highly entertaining. His ability to identify and write about the small, often unnoticed things around us is at the heart of his off-beat, often humorous point of view. Appreciative readers have responded enthusiastically to his novels, helping him earn a spot among the top LDS fiction writers.